COOKIN' THE BOOKS

A Selection of Titles by Amy Patricia Meade

A Marjorie McClelland Mystery

MILLION DOLLAR BABY
GHOST OF A CHANCE
SHADOW WALTZ
BLACK MOONLIGHT

The Tish Tarragon Series

COOKIN' THE BOOKS *

The Vermont Mystery Series

WELL-OFFED IN VERMONT
SHORT-CIRCUITED IN CHARLOTTE

* *available from Severn House*

COOKIN' THE BOOKS

BOOKS

Amy Patricia Meade

Severn House Large Print
London & New York

This first large print edition published 2019
in Great Britain and the USA by
SEVERN HOUSE PUBLISHERS LTD of
Eardley House, 4 Uxbridge Street, London W8 7SY.
First world regular print edition published 2018 by
Severn House Publishers Ltd.

British Library Cataloguing in Publication Data
A CIP catalogue record for this title is available from the British Library.

ISBN-13: 9780727829955

Severn House Publishers support the Forest Stewardship Council™
[FSC™], the leading international forest certification organisation. All
our titles that are printed on FSC certified paper carry the FSC logo.

Typeset by Palimpsest Book Production Ltd.,
Falkirk, Stirlingshire, Scotland.
Printed and bound in Great Britain by
T J International, Padstow, Cornwall.

One

'But everyone loves the way the "blood" gushes out when you bite into them,' Julian Jefferson Davis argued. Tall, trim, and sporting an immaculately coiffed and gelled head of chestnut hair, he leaned against the display cases that separated the public part of the shop from the kitchen and pleaded his case.

'I know they do, Jules. And I truly enjoy the squeals when people bite into them, but it takes some time and effort to pipe the center of each Tell-Tale Heart cupcake with raspberry preserves. Right now I can't afford to hire staff, so I need to use my time wisely.' Letitia 'Tish' Tarragon, dressed in slim, dark-wash cropped jeans, a black short-sleeve T-shirt, and a pair of leopard-print canvas sneakers, balanced herself on the top step of her vintage red kitchen step-ladder and went about mounting the last of eight whitewashed shelves upon the sage-colored walls of her new restaurant and catering business, Cookin' the Books Café.

'Honey, I live right down the road. I can help you. Mary Jo is just the next town over. I'm sure she'd help too.'

'Hmm, maybe for Halloween? That'll give me two months to settle in.'

'Halloween would be perfect. The whole business district shuts down and parents bring their

1

little ones for trick or treating. You'd make a killing! Er, no pun intended.'

'I got it.' Tish laughed.

'You truly couldn't pick a better spot for your business. It's kismet.'

Located on a quaint main road halfway between Richmond and Fredericksburg and with access to the interstate, the early twentieth-century white clapboard building once served as the first general store for the town of Hobson Glen, Virginia. In time, the general store closed and the building was repurposed as a delicatessen, then a butcher's shop and, in its most recent incarnation, a specialty bake store. Indeed, a sign reading *Cynthia's Baked Goods of Distinction* still hung over the front porch.

'From your mouth to God's ears,' Tish answered hopefully.

'No need for prayers. Once people get a taste of your food, they'll be lined up outside the door. What you got planned for opening day?'

'A Hogwarts-inspired back-to-school menu: Dobby's pasties, cheese broomsticks, Butterbeer cakes, Sorting Hat pita bread and hummus, and miniature steak-and-kidney pies. I'll also have my usual range of salads and sandwiches.'

'Sounds delicious. Kids and parents should love it.' Jules fanned himself. 'Just one little word of advice? Air conditioning. Switch it on. The only thing keeping me from fainting on the spot is the cool relief I feel by having my butt planted up against these refrigerated cases.'

'Thanks for the visual, Jules,' she muttered as she hammered a second bracket into a section of wall to the left of the store's front picture window. 'Better not let the health inspector catch you. He'll fine me.'

'Fine you? It's ninety-five degrees in the shade. He'd probably pay me to trade spots.' Jules watched as Tish balanced the shelf upon its brackets. 'So, what are we doing with those?'

'These are my global displays,' Tish explained as she stepped down from the ladder and ran a hand through her wavy, bobbed blonde hair. 'Each one represents a different culture, its literature, and cuisine. There's one for France, England, Italy, India, Spain, China, Africa, and, of course, America. Eventually, I'll add one for Japan – once I master sushi and tempura, that is. And then there's Greece, the Caribbean . . .'

'Whoa, slow down. Don't outgrow the wall space before you've actually opened for business.'

'Sorry, just excited,' Tish chuckled. 'I also have to leave room for the bookcase out on the porch. That'll be my lending library. If someone wishes to read while they eat, they can borrow something. If they wish to take it home and continue reading, they need to—'

'Buy the book?' Jules guessed correctly.

'Or bring another book in to replace it.'

'Hmm, so what are we putting on the shelves you just hung?'

'Cookbooks, books, and cooking paraphernalia. So for France, we'd have cookbooks by Julia Child and Jacques Pepin—'

'Natch,' Jules remarked.

'Literary works by Proust and Flaubert, and, in the middle, a vintage madeleine pan.'

'And England would be Jamie Oliver, Nigella Lawson, and your blue Staffordshire tea pot?'

'Indeed.' Tish nodded. 'As well as some Dickens and Christie.'

'Clever. And where would I find these goodies?'

'In the big box behind the counter. You want some help?'

'Nope, I'll be fine.' Jules rolled up the sleeves of his neatly pressed white linen shirt and retrieved the box in question. 'You have tons to do. If I get stuck, I'll ask for help.'

As Tish set about threading a home-stitched valance made from vintage tea towels on to a brass curtain rod, a curvy brunette in her early forties entered the café bearing an oversized thermos jug.

'Sorry I'm late,' she panted. 'I had to drop Kayla off for her shift at Chick-fil-A, Gregory forgot to tell me football practice started this morning, and then Glen called – he forgot his lunch so I had to drop it off at his office.'

'We're fine,' Tish replied. 'I'm just sorry you had such a tough morning.'

Jules, however, took a tougher line. 'Mary Jo Okensholt, are you telling me that your husband made you drive all the way to Fredericksburg to deliver his lunch? Why didn't he just *buy* lunch today? Or better yet, why didn't he drive home and pick it up himself.'

'Well, he was busy.'

'So were you. You were out driving your children – *his* children – to their activities.' He shook his head and went about steadying a Martin Yan cookbook against a bamboo steamer basket. 'I hope that family of yours knows how lucky they are to have you.'

'I hope you know how lucky you are too.' Mary Jo held the insulated canteen aloft. 'A double batch of Arnold Palmers with extra ice.'

'MJ, you're my favorite woman. I love you!' he exclaimed as he hastily placed a copy of Amy Tan's *The Joy Luck Club* alongside the steamer and charged toward the thermos. 'Tish, do you have a funnel?'

Mary Jo dropped the canteen on to the counter and folded her arms across her chest. 'We're not in college anymore, Julian. I am not letting you make an iced-tea/lemonade bong from my tailgate cooler. We're—'

The appearance of a tall, handsome man in the doorway of the café brought an abrupt end to Mary Jo's ultimatums.

'Schuyler,' Tish greeted her new landlord, curtain rod still in hand. She had first met Schuyler Thompson two weeks earlier when he showed her the property after his evening jog. For that meeting, Thompson had been wearing baggy athletic shorts, a sweat-stained T-shirt, baseball cap, and a pair of runners. Today, he was immaculately dressed in a dark-blue suit that brought out the intense azure of his eyes, a red Italian silk tie, well-polished dress shoes, and a mane of neatly styled blond hair. The wardrobe change was not displeasing.

'Hey, Tish.' He smiled. 'I just stopped by to see how things were progressing.'

'Slow, but sure,' she declared before going on to introduce her helpers.

'Pleased to meet you both,' Schuyler announced after an exchange of handshakes. 'Just two little things I wanted to tell you. First, Celestine, the caretaker, is going to swing by today and give you all the details about the hot-water heater, the air conditioning, the plumbing – all that stuff. She knows this place better than I ever could.'

'Air conditioning. Thank you, Lord,' Jules exclaimed.

'The second piece of news is that Binnie Broderick, the executive director of our local library, is one of my clients. She was in my office yesterday and asked me what I was doing with my mother's old place. I told her I had rented it to a literary caterer. The library is holding a fundraiser and Binnie's caterer backed out at the last minute, so I suggested she speak with you.'

'That's terrific news. Thank you!'

'Well, don't thank me just yet. The event takes place in three weeks.'

Tish swallowed hard. 'Three weeks?'

'Actually, two weeks from this coming Friday. Also, even under the best of circumstances, Binnie can be . . . difficult.'

'No worries. We'll be right by her side.' Mary Jo stepped forward and placed an arm around Tish's shoulder. 'It will be the best fundraiser the library's ever seen.'

'I'm sure it will. I have the utmost confidence in Tish's abilities. And if I can be of any help, please let me know.'

'Thanks, but I—' Tish started.

6

'Oh, she'll definitely let you know,' Jules interrupted.

'Great. See y'all later.' Schuyler took off through the door and hopped into the driver's seat of the black 2016 BMW 3 Series sedan parked outside the store.

'What was I saying about kismet?' Jules asked. 'Not only do you have a business in a prime location, but now you have a prime gig, and, I might add, a very fine, very prime man checking in on you.'

'That very fine, very prime man happens to be my landlord,' Tish pointed out.

'He also happens to be a small-town Southern lawyer. Hello, *GQ* meets Atticus Finch! Does it get any dreamier?'

'I'm not sure I'm ready for that, Jules.'

'It's been over a year since the divorce,' Mary Jo cajoled. 'Don't you think it's time to get out there again?'

'Yeah, even if it's only to flirt or have a fling,' Jules rejoined.

'I'm not a "fling" sort of gal. You both know that. I'm also not into all those fads, like online dating or speed dating or Tinder—'

'Oh, no. You definitely don't want to go on Tinder.'

'What's Tinder?' Mary Jo asked.

'I'll show you when you're older,' Jules teased.

'I don't want to go on anything,' Tish continued. 'I would love to meet someone eventually, but right now I'm focused on starting my business.'

'That's great, but you just can't work here and

7

then go upstairs and binge-watch Netflix every night,' Mary Jo argued.

'She's right, you know. It's not like fate's going to drop Mr Right on your doorstep.' Jules brought a hand to his face in mock surprise. 'Oh, snap! It just did!'

As Tish dismissed Jules's silliness with a wave of her hand, a white Mercedes E-Class with tinted windows rolled in and parked in front of the porch. The trio watched as a stout woman in her early to mid-sixties emerged from the driver's side. She was dressed in a gauzy floral sheath dress, pearls, white sandals, and a wide-brim white hat that would have fit in better at Ascot than in a small Virginia town on a Monday morning.

'Good morning,' she greeted in a well-bred Virginian accent as she stepped through the screen door. 'I'm Lavinia Broderick, Executive Director of the Hobson Glen Library. You must be Miss Tarragon.'

'I am, but, please, call me Tish.' The caterer extended a welcoming hand.

Without accepting the greeting, Binnie Broderick pushed past Tish and went into the shop. 'Mr Thompson told me that you are something of a caterer.'

Tish retracted her hand and pulled a face. 'Yes, a literary caterer.'

'Hobson Glen Library holds their annual fund-raising dinner in less than three weeks and our previous caterer has cancelled on us. Do you think you could do the job, Miss Tarragon?'

'Possibly. Why don't we discuss the details first?'

8

Binnie drew a heavy sigh and removed her hat, revealing a head full of hot-rollered and teased hair that proved that the Southern adage of 'the higher the hair the closer to God' was still alive and well. 'The library benefit, along with our Strawberry Social and decorated holiday homes tour, is one of the highlights of Hobson Glen's social season. Approximately three hundred people from Hobson Glen and neighboring towns – including some of Richmond's finest families – attend the event for a three-course dinner and dancing.'

'Guests travel from the city for this?' Tish was slightly incredulous.

'Of course. Hobson Glen Library is one of the oldest libraries in the Commonwealth.'

'That's quite an accomplishment for a state so rife with history,' Tish praised.

'We are quite proud.'

'With good reason. So, given that this is a county-wide affair, I assume that I need to create a relatively high-end yet budget-friendly three-course menu for three hundred guests?' Tish surmised.

'That's right, and a signature cocktail or two.'

'Cocktails?'

'Yes, we sell them in souvenir glasses. Some years, those drinks raised more money than the admission tickets themselves.' Binnie gave a loud guffaw.

'Hmm.' Tish hadn't anticipated the need to create original cocktails. She flashed a panicked glance in Jules's direction; his mixology skills were legendary.

'Cocktails won't be a problem, ma'am,' he assured.

'I should hope not. Schuyler assured me that you could handle all my needs.'

'And he was correct,' Tish agreed. 'So what sort of theme did you have in mind?'

'Theme? Well, books of course,' she scoffed, as if Tish were completely daft.

'Yes, I understand that books are the focus, but which works would you like to highlight? I offer themed specialized menus for events like these. I don't have anything printed right now, but I can, for instance, do a Hemingway-inspired menu based upon the food described in his books, a Midsummer Night's Dream lawn party, a recreation of Babette's Feast, a Great Gatsby gala, an Alice in Wonderland tea party, a Christie-inspired murder mystery dinner—'

'Good heavens, no! We don't want any of that nonsense. This is a gathering of business people, not readers. These folks are too busy *doing* things to sit around with their nose in a book. The fundraiser is about wearing your prettiest, sparkliest clothes, drinking cocktails, posing for photos, and going home feeling that you did something good for your community.'

'So you don't want a literary theme?'

'Of course I do. It's a library, for heaven's sake. Make the food about books. Book titles, authors – make it cute, though. Nothing too deep. The most we want our guests thinking about is how many zeroes to write in their checkbooks.' She grinned.

'That isn't really what I do—'

'Maybe not, but it is now, isn't it? Otherwise, I'll take my business elsewhere.'

Tish had never before experienced such strong dislike for someone she had just met. 'Cute theme,' she noted as she typed into her phone. 'What about menu options?'

For the first time during her visit, Binnie Broderick was nonplussed. 'Menu options? What do you mean, "menu options"?'

'Fish and chicken for those whose diets don't include beef, meat-free dishes for the vegetarians and vegans. Then there's the whole gluten-free issue—'

'Gluten-free? Oh, we do *not* have any of those. I don't know where you were raised but this is the South, darlin'. Most everyone I know eats meat, pickles, and fried food. It's also been my experience that these benefits always run more smoothly and people are always far more generous if a steak dinner is offered. However, I suppose we do have a *few* of those "new-agey" sorts. Mostly the younger generation.'

'New-agey?' Mary Jo asked.

'You know . . . the folks who do yoga, wear hemp clothing, get henna tattoos, and won't eat anything that has a face.'

Jules rolled his eyes and wandered behind the counter to pour himself a glass of Arnold Palmer.

'Sounds like I need to add some vegan options,' Tish stated.

'Yes, I guess you should.' Binnie sighed.

Tish typed more some notes into her cell phone. 'What's the venue for the event?'

'Our local Masonic Lodge has donated the

11

space, the tables, the chairs, even the dinner- and serve-ware. All you have to do is show up, cook, and serve.'

'That certainly makes things easier. And what's your budget for this event?'

'Thirty dollars a head,' Mrs Broderick stated emphatically.

'I'm very sorry, Mrs Broderick, but I can't do a three-course plated dinner, steak included and with vegetarian and vegan options, for that price. Not when I need to hire a wait staff as well.'

'Really? Why, don't you have nerve! This is your first job.'

'And I appreciate the opportunity to make it the first of many, but I simply can't make it work for that little,' Tish replied. 'I can do it for sixty, but that's as low as I can go.'

'Sixty? Why—'

'You can call Richmond's finest caterers and they'll quote you three times that, I'm sure. I'm not trying to make a profit off a library fundraiser, Mrs Broderick, but I do need to be able to cover expenses.'

'Yes, well, I suppose we can make it work. I just expected you to be cheaper. Disappointing to find otherwise.'

'I *am* cheaper,' Tish stated in as polite a tone as she could muster. She desperately wanted the job, but she also knew that lowballing the price of her first job would set a dangerous precedent. 'I also promise to be more reliable than the caterer who cancelled.'

'Do you?' Binnie challenged as she pinned her hat back on to her head.

'Yes, I do,' Tish promised.

'I suppose you do have a selling point there,' Mrs Broderick finally relented. 'And it's far too late to go to anyone else. All right, sixty dollars a head it is.'

'Thank you, Mrs Broderick,' Tish replied and extended her hand once again. This time, Binnie Broderick extended hers as well.

'Thank you, Miss Tarragon. I'm sure you'll come up with something to "wow" me because, you do realize, I need to be wowed in order to give you a reference. Ta-ta!'

Tish watched as Binnie pranced out of the front door and back into her Mercedes. 'Grrrrrrr,' she snarled as soon as the woman was safely inside her vehicle.

'That was quite possibly the single most horrible woman I've ever encountered in my entire life,' Mary Jo opined.

'Woman?' Jules challenged. 'That was no woman. If there were a mirror in here, I bet twenty dollars we wouldn't have seen her reflection.'

After a hearty belly laugh, Tish mimicked, *Remember, I need to be wowed to give you a reference.*

'Wowed? She's so uptight, I doubt she's ever been wowed. Or wooed.'

May Jo and Tish burst out in laughter.

'I see ya'll been "Binnied,"' a voice noted from outside the screen door.

They whirled around to see a heavyset woman in her late fifties dressed in a pair of denim Bermuda shorts, flip-flops, and a wide-strapped

Hawaiian-printed tank top. Her short hair was dyed a bright, unnatural shade of red, and a hot-pink-framed pair of reading glasses hung around her neck. The woman gave a deep, throaty smoker's laugh. 'Sorry to scare y'all. I'm Celestine. I've been lookin' after the place since Miss Cynthia left us.'

'Celestine? Oh, yes! Schuyler Thompson told me you'd be stopping by today.' Tish swung open the door to allow the woman admittance. 'How nice to meet you.'

'Nice to meet you too, Miss Tarragon.'

'Oh, please, call me Tish. And this is Jules and Mary Jo.'

'Pleased to meet y'all.' Celestine nodded her greeting. 'Expectin' some young, waif-like French girl, weren't you?'

'What? No. Not at—'

Celestine didn't give Tish time to finish. 'Don't bother to tell me no. Everyone hears my name and expects to see some angelic creature. Even my mama hoped I'd be some tiny sweet thing like her. She was French-Canadian, beautiful face and figure. Very religious. Was studying to be a nun until my daddy charmed the pants off her. Wound up married and with three daughters: Celestine, Evangeline, and Yvette. Not sure where Mama got the name Yvette from, but that's OK, my youngest sister's always been a strange 'un. Anyways, Mama thought I'd turn out like her, but I wound up like my daddy's side – snaggle-toothed and bow-legged. Didn't wind up being a nun neither. Instead, I met Mr Rufus and came into the family way. Got married under

14

the gun and been making it work for forty years now. So, Binnie Broderick hired you to cater for the library soiree, did she?'

Tish, unaccustomed to Celestine's stream-of-consciousness conversational style, took a few moments before realizing she had been asked a question. 'Hmm? Oh, yes. Yes, she did. How did you know?'

'It's a small town, darlin'. News around here travels faster than a toupee in a hurricane,' she chuckled. 'Besides, when I saw Binnie's car parked here, I figured she came over to strong-arm you into giving her a cheap catering deal. Please, tell me you held firm.'

'I gave her a bit of a discount, but overall, yes, I held firm.'

'Good girl. The woman's like a barracuda, except her teeth are implants. The mayor and half the town council are trying to run her out of a job, yet here she is trying to wheedle you out of a few bucks.'

'Wait. What's all this about Binnie Broderick being fired?' Jules asked.

'Oh, there's a big hullaballoo about the library missing books. Apparently, Binnie Broderick is responsible.'

'Could Binnie be fired before the fundraiser? I mean, what if Tish starts working on the catering job only to get stiffed because the board didn't hire her?'

'Jules makes a good point,' Tish stated. 'I've already invested a lot of money in this business. I can't afford not to be paid for this event.'

'Don't you worry. I've known the president

15

of the board, Augusta May Wilson, for years. She wouldn't do that. Besides, this whole thing has been dragging on for months. Binnie's not going away that quick. At least not without a fight.'

'So, the missing books – what happened to them?' Tish asked.

'Destroyed. Sold. No one knows, except Binnie Broderick.'

'I can't believe she wasn't fired on the spot.'

'Good ol' Binnie claims it was a part of the library's "weeding" process.'

'Well, it's a well-known fact that libraries do cull books when they've become soiled or damaged,' Mary Jo noted. 'Or, in the case of non-fiction books, when the information they provide is outdated and no longer accurate.'

'That was Binnie's excuse. Problem is the list of "weeded" books Binnie provided the council listed two hundred titles on it. There's nearly five hundred books missing.'

'More than double the number?' Tish was incredulous. 'But surely there was an explanation. Binnie is a librarian, isn't she?'

'Librarian? Heck, no. The only book I've ever known Binnie to read is the Bible. And for that I even think she uses the CliffsNotes.' Celestine shook her head. 'Nope. Binnie graduated from some fancy girl's school with a business degree.'

'So that explains her unenthusiastic attitude toward Tish's literary menus,' Mary Jo commented.

'How did a businesswoman get to be executive director of the library? Not that I wish to engage

16

in gossip. I'm just curious because . . . well . . .'
Tish stammered.

'Because Binnie's about as likeable as a four
a.m. car alarm,' Celestine answered. 'Connections,
hon. When Binnie was appointed, the library
was in dire need of repairs. It's the oldest one
in Virginia, as I'm sure she told you. With her
endless supply of wealthy friends and her
husband's business contacts, Binnie was able to
raise the money needed to repair the library with
just one cocktail party.'

'And hence the annual library fundraiser was
born,' Jules assumed.

'Yep. And the library board, needing an
executive director and seeing a valuable ally with
experience in the business world, hired her.'

'What do they think of her now?' Tish
asked.

'They're standing by their decision. Well, the
board is, at least. The president is none too happy,
though.'

'Five hundred books pulled by one woman?
That's quite the coup. Sounds like I should bring
her with me to Dillard's next Black Friday,' Mary
Jo remarked.

'She's not that fast. She's had four years to
pull it off.'

'But why?' Tish questioned. 'What possible
reason could she have for pulling all those
books?'

'Beats me. All I know is that our tax dollars
were spent purchasing those books she pulled.
She should, at the very least, be forced to tell
us what she did with them, if not repay the

17

town for all the money she flushed down the drain.'

'And what about the information in those books?' Tish added. 'What if a kid needed one of those for a school paper? I mean, I know kids have the internet these days, but still . . .'

'I hear ya. It's a sad state of affairs, to be sure,' Celestine commiserated. 'So, how about I take you down to the cellar and I'll show you the new oil burner I installed.'

'*You* installed? Schuyler said you were the caretaker of this place. He didn't tell me you were in the plumbing and heating business.'

'That's because I'm not. Mr Rufus is. He was supposed to do the job but he was too busy, so I did it myself. Figured I'd seen him do it a thousand times and that I might as well give it a go. I figured right. Went in with no problem whatsoever.'

'So, you're a caretaker, a plumber, and you're up on local gossip. Do you have any other hidden talents I should know about?'

'Baking,' Celestine answered matter-of-factly. 'That's how I got to be the caretaker here. Cynthia Thompson and I were great friends. She did the bread and fancy pastries. I did the pies and cakes, and helped serve and clean up when needed. Wedding cakes are my specialty. The bakery's been closed eleven months now, but I still get calls for my cakes.'

'Really? Do you have a portfolio?'

'As it so happens, I've got some photos on my phone.' Celestine grinned.

Tish scrolled through a gallery of cakes that celebrated everything from marriage to a child's

18

first birthday. Each design was more impressive than the one that preceded it.

'Wow,' Mary Jo exclaimed. 'I'm going to have to keep you in mind for my son's graduation next year.'

'These are exquisite,' Jules noted.

'Thanks. What's more important is that they taste good. I offer a dozen different flavors of cake. All of them are moist, yet light – not your typical bakery stuff. I also offer a bunch of different fillings: raspberry, strawberry, lemon, blueberry, chocolate mousse, chocolate ganache, chocolate chipotle cream . . . the sky's the limit.'

'Wow,' Tish muttered as she scrolled through the remaining album to see a cake shaped like car and another with a Disney *Frozen* theme.

'And, my cakes are far less expensive than those you'll find in those exclusive Richmond bakeries.'

'OK, you have me sold,' Tish declared. 'What are you doing two weeks from this coming Friday?'

'Making dessert for the library benefit and helping you serve,' Celestine gleamed.

'Deal.' Tish reached out and shook Celestine's hand. 'By the way, I'm not sure if Schuyler told you, but I'm a literary caterer, so all the events I handle are literary-themed.'

'Literary-themed? You mean my desserts have to be book inspired?'

'For this event, book or author inspired, yes.'

'Hmm, I did a *Fifty Shades of Grey* cake for a bachelorette party last month, complete with handcuffs. Think that would make the cut with Binnie?' Celestine joked.

'Only if you're OK with me being run out of town before I've even moved in.' She frowned.

Two

The morning of the library fundraiser loomed dark, potentially stormy, and unbearably humid. Perched upon a foot-tall portable stool in the kitchen of the Hobson Glen Masonic Lodge, Tish stood over a forty-quart stock pot and systematically placed seeded and stemmed sweet red bell peppers into the gently boiling water, waited for them to blanch, and then promptly removed them with a sizeable wire spider strainer and placed them on brown paper bags to dry.

With the wild rice, quinoa, and black bean filling and the tomato sauce having been cooked the day before, the blanching process was the final preparatory step before Tish's For Whom the Vegan Stuffed Bell Pepper Tolls were stuffed, doused with sauce, sprinkled with vegan cheese and baked in the oven for a satisfying main course without either dairy or meat.

Ah, yes, the meat, she recalled as she gazed out of the kitchen window at the ominous clouds forming just beyond the horizon. Silently, she prayed that the imminent meteorological disturbance did not interrupt the town's power supply, for she had filled the Masonic

Lodge's stainless-steel industrial-sized refrigerator with one hundred and fifty pounds of standing rib roast and fifty pounds of English Stilton for The Prime Rib of Miss Jean Brodie (the port and shallots required for the gravy sat happily in crates upon the counter); fifty pounds of southern Virginia-caught rockfish to be served with sautéed spinach, mushrooms, capers, lemon, and artichoke hearts for The Old Man and the Sea Bream; a ten-pound boiled country ham and twenty pounds of Cheddar cheese for the Who's Afraid of Virginia Baked Ham on Cheesy Edgar Allan Poe-lenta appetizer; a vat of E.B. White Bean Hummus – also prepared the night before – to be served over freshly grilled crostini for a vegan starter; locally grown, brightly colored squashes, heirloom tomatoes, garlic, eggplant, basil, and onions that would be sautéed together as the perfect seasonal side to both main courses, and an abundance of individually wrapped butter pats, vegan butter spread, sour cream, chives, lemons, limes, oranges, and assortment of condiments and garnishes.

Then, finally, there needed to be space for Celestine's fabulous dessert.

Tish extracted the last of the bell peppers from the simmering water and swallowed hard as perspiration dripped from her neck and down her back. What on earth had she been thinking taking a three-hundred banquet as her first gig? The biggest party she had ever thrown had been for fifty people, and even that had been exhausting.

Before she could reflect upon her previous life

and career, Tish spotted an elderly woman wandering outside the kitchen window. She was about eighty years of age and quite frail and withered-looking. Her silver hair was pinned neatly into a bun high upon her head and she was dressed in a floral-printed periwinkle house-coat, dark-green Wellington boots, and, despite the August heat and humidity, a chunky-knit camel-colored cardigan sweater.

But the most remarkable feature of all was the small green parrot perched upon the woman's shoulder.

Tish stepped down from the stool and continued to watch through the kitchen window as the elderly woman, the skirt of her dress whipped against her legs by the gusting winds, wandered around to the front of the building, her eyes scanning the area in search of something or someone.

Setting off through the kitchen door, Tish strode through the freshly mowed green grass, the damp clippings of which adhered to the rubber soles of her bright-red canvas sneakers. As she drew up on the woman, a familiar silver mini-van crunched its way into the lodge's gravel-lined parking lot. 'May I help you?' Tish inquired of the elderly woman.

'Is this where Binnie Broderick is holding the library fundraiser?'

'It is,' Tish acknowledged as she spied Celestine stepping out of the driver's side door of the mini-van.

'You go tell Binnie that Enid is here to speak with her.'

'I'm afraid Mrs Broderick isn't here at the moment.'

'When do you expect her?'

'I have no idea. Not until this evening, most likely.'

'Tish, Enid,' Celestine greeted as she approached the two women. 'What's going on?'

'She's looking for Binnie Broderick,' Tish explained.

'I need to give her a piece of my mind,' Enid nearly shouted.

'She still lives down the road from you, doesn't she? Why not check there?' Celestine suggested.

'I did. She's not at home.'

'Did you try the library?'

'The library is the problem. I'm not allowed admittance there. At least not with Langhorne on my shoulder.'

'The sign on the door says *No Pets Allowed*, Enid.'

'That's precisely what the librarian told me yesterday. But Langhorne is not a pet. He's my companion. He's also better groomed than most of the residents in this town.' Enid addressed Tish, aside, 'He gets a shampoo and blow dry twice a week.'

'Really? Well, they um . . . they seem to be working wonders. He's quite a beautiful bird.' Tish raised a hand to Langhorne as an invitation to visit, but the parrot, instead, delivered a firm nip with his beak.

'Ow!' Tish pulled her hand back.

'Langhorne is also better educated than most folks round here. He can say "hello" in ten languages. Can you do that?' Enid challenged Celestine.

Meanwhile, Langhorne began reciting, on cue, '*Bonjour . . . Ciao . . . Kon'nichiwa . . .*'

'Will you get to the point, Enid.' Celestine sighed.

'*Hola . . . Marhaba . . .*'

Enid pulled a crumpled piece of paper from the pocket of her cardigan and thrust it at Celestine. 'The point is this. After not allowing Langhorne entry yesterday, this morning I went back to find this taped to the door.'

'*Guten Tag . . . Salaam . . . Namaste . . . Ni hao . . . Zdravstvuyte.*'

As Langhorne completed his demonstration, Tish leaned over Celestine's shoulder and watched as she smoothed the paper to reveal a photo of a bird identical to Langhorne and the words *Companion Birds/Parrots Not Permitted*.

'Can you believe it? First, there's that atrocious photo. If they think the wretched creature in that picture looks anything like my Langhorne, they are either utterly blind or completely ignorant. And then there's the use of the words "bird" and "parrot." Langhorne is a green conure; to compare him to a parrot or your garden-variety sparrow is the height of insolence.'

'Perhaps they weren't aware that Langhorne is a conure,' Tish suggested. 'Not everyone is up on their ornithology.'

'Is the library not an educational facility?'

'Well, um, yes—'

'Then they should know better.'

'Maybe you should go to the town hall and

24

apply for a companion animal license for Langhorne?' Celestine offered. 'I don't know if they give them to parrots but—'

'Conures!' Enid corrected. 'You had better be sure I'll go to the town hall and talk to anyone who will listen. Binnie Broderick has gone too far this time. Too far! And she will pay.'

The eccentric old woman marched off toward the main road, mumbling to herself as Langhorne flapped his wings and struggled to remain perched upon her shoulder in the blustery weather.

'She didn't even take the time to introduce herself, did she?' Celestine asked when the woman was out of view.

'Nope.'

'Enid Kemper. Comes from a brilliant family, but they've always been one pimento cheese sandwich short of a picnic.'

'What did Enid's family do?'

'Lip balm. You know that stuff you buy at the drugstore for two bucks a tube? Enid's father bought the rights up in Lynchburg and then produced it in Richmond back in the eighteen hundreds.'

'Wow. So her grandfather—'

'Was the father of soft lips.' Celestine paused. 'And, after that, laxatives.'

'So, the father of soft lips and soft . . .'

'Yup. And, on that note, let's empty out the van, shall we?'

Tish followed Celestine to the silver Honda Odyssey and opened the back hatch. The rear seats had been flattened to the down position and tray upon tray of white-iced cupcakes filled the storage area. The smell that filled the vehicle was heavenly.

'Are these what I think they are?' Tish asked.

'Finnegan's Cake. Three hundred and twenty of them in miniature. Soon to be three hundred and nineteen.' Celestine grabbed a cupcake from the nearest tray and passed it to Tish.

Tish peeled back the paper liner and eagerly sunk her teeth into the gold-glittered confection. The cake was moist, light, and filled with spicy chocolate flavor. The icing was rich and creamy with a slightly boozy finish that balanced the sweetness of the cake perfectly. 'Oh. My. Goodness. What's in these?'

'The cake is cocoa powder, Irish stout, sour cream and the usual cake suspects. The frosting is your classic buttercream mixed with a couple of shots of Irish cream liqueur. And the gold on top represents what the leprechaun might be hiding. I made a vegan version of the recipe too.'

'Good Lord, woman. These are so good they should be illegal.'

'Thanks. I figure between the whiskey, the stout, and the cocktails Jules's whipping up, the party should be plenty happy. Maybe we should throw some extras Binnie's way – might improve her personality.'

The two women giggled for several seconds.

'Binnie's the least of my worries. If this storm knocks the power out, I don't know what I'll do. The meat, your cupcakes . . . it would mean a whole lot of spoiled food.'

'Now don't you worry about that. Good ol'

Celestine's got you covered.' She gestured Tish to the front passenger side door, which she swung open wide to reveal what appeared, at first glance, to be a red-and-black gas can, replete with handle.

'It's a generator,' Celestine stated upon seeing the confusion on Tish's face. 'Mr Rufus bought it years ago. He's since upgraded to a bigger, better one, so this one was sitting idle. Figured we might as well commandeer it for the business.'

'Celestine, you are a lifesaver.'

'Nah, this just ain't my first rodeo. When you're raising four kids, you dread the prospect of losing television, hair dryers, stereos and anything else electronic that might prevent them from killing each other.'

Tish chuckled. 'Well, whatever the reason for having the generator, I'm glad you had the presence of mind to bring it along with you today.'

'Ain't nothing. By the way, my granddaughter, Melissa, and her friends from her mixed martial arts class will be by around noon to help set up the tables and get their instructions for tonight. They're all over the age of eighteen, so they're legal to serve drinks. I got their paperwork in my pocketbook.'

'Wonderful. Mary Jo will be in charge of the servers. She's bringing her kids, Kayla and Gregory, to help out as well.'

'That's not all she's bringing,' Celestine grinned as a black SUV parked alongside them.

Mary Jo, her two teenaged children and Jules emerged from the car's dark interior.

'Jules?' Tish cried in surprise. 'I thought you had to work this morning.'

'What? And let you handle this without me? This is your first *real* gig. I'm going to be here every step of the way.'

Tish hugged him. 'Are you sure you won't be in trouble? I don't want you to lose your job over me.'

'We're totally fine. Actually, my station manager has been very understanding since I got buried by that snowplow on-air outside the Poe Museum in January.'

Mary Jo giggled.

'I could have died, MJ,' Jules chastised.

'Yes, I know. I was in panic while watching it, but still . . .' Mary Jo's voice broke into stifled laughter.

'*That's* who you are!' Celestine exclaimed. 'I thought I knew you from somewhere.'

'Yes, I'm the Channel Ten weatherman,' Jules stated drily.

'I *love* you because you're so—'

'Hilarious? Yes, I know,' Jules interjected. 'That's how half of America describes me too. The video of the snowplow incident went viral. Our station's ratings surged. Unfortunately, I'm now the default man in the field.'

'Are you kidding?' Celestine challenged. 'Whether we're in for one-hundred-degree heat, heavy winds, or a monsoon, you're the guy out on the street corner telling folks to stay safe. I admire that.'

'You do? Well, thank you. I admit, it does give me a unique bargaining tool for raises and paid time off. Still, I didn't go to journalism school to be some Weather Channel wannabe.'

'You'll get there, Jules,' Tish said supportively.

'Give it time,' Mary Jo urged.

'You're very talented,' Celestine chimed in.

'Thanks, guys. That means a lot to me.'

'Sure thing,' Celestine smiled sweetly. 'Now, let's get you in the kitchen. There's fish that needs skinning.'

'Wait a minute. I'm going to be skinning fish?' Jules asked.

'You don't have to, if you don't want to. We also have over two hundred potatoes that need scrubbing, oiling, and wrapping,' Tish offered.

'Oh, hell! And to think I complained about that snowplow.'

Three

Despite heavy thunderstorms, the electricity continued to flow in the lodge kitchen and the Hobson Glen Library fundraiser got off to a successful start. In a last-minute stroke of brilliance, Tish requisitioned Mary Jo's camping tarps and, with Celestine's assistance, erected a series of tent shelters to protect partygoers from the elements as they walked along the cement path that led from the parking lot to the Masonic Lodge. Once inside the lodge, revelers were welcomed by a plush red carpet (a ruby-colored rug that once served as a hall runner in Tish's

Richmond bungalow) which effectively dried damp and muddy feet while adding a touch of Hollywood glamour.

If anyone was still in an ill-mood upon arriving in the reception hall, Mary Jo, Melissa, and the mixed martial arts wait staff were on hand to take drink orders and submit them to Jules who, dressed in his best red tuxedo jacket, stood at the bar like a gunman awaiting a duel. He had skewered candied ginger and maraschino cherries on to hundreds of decorative toothpicks and mixed a veritable vat of ginger beer and hard English cider, in equal parts, to create his Ginger Tristram Shandy. He'd also prepared several cocktail shakers with tequila, watermelon-basil puree, and agave syrup in anticipation of serving up multitudes of Tequila Mockingbird cocktails.

Back in the kitchen, Kayla and Gregory – at ages fifteen and seventeen, respectively, too young to be serving – had been recruited to work the plating station. Kayla had been assigned to dish out ramekin after ramekin of cheesy polenta topped with slices of syrup-glazed country ham before placing them under the warming lamp until serving time. Gregory was in charge of smearing a seemingly endless supply of crostini with a scoopful of white bean hummus, placing the bread on a bed of micro-greens, and then drizzling the dish with an herb-infused oil vinaigrette.

As the starter plates were assembled, Celestine extracted the standing rib roasts from the oven and covered them with aluminum foil to rest. She then raised the oven temperature and set about roasting the tomato, eggplant, onion, and summer squash for the evening's ratatouille-inspired side dish. Tish, meanwhile, got to searing the sea bream or, in this case Virginia rockfish, on a wide cast-iron griddle. Within minutes, she found herself slapping the fillets on the grill, flipping them over, and removing them in time with the ragtime music the Dixieland band was playing in the reception room.

The selection of music gave Tish pause. Outside of New Orleans, the only place she had ever seen a Dixieland band perform was on Main Street in Walt Disney World. The genre was, she thought, a curious soundtrack to what Binnie described as Hobson Glen's upscale event of the year.

Still, it was difficult for Tish to deny that the syncopated rhythms lent a positive, happy air to what was, otherwise, a repetitive culinary task. Placing the fish on to the oiled griddle, listening to the sputter and hiss of the oil and juices, turning the fish to the other side, letting it brown, and then removing it to a waiting platter had developed its own rhythmic pattern. *Slap . . . sizzle . . . flip . . . sizzle . . . flop.*

Tish repeated the words as she cooked the remaining fillets. *Slap . . . sizzle . . . flip . . . sizzle . . . flop. Slap . . . sizzle . . . flip . . . sizzle . . . flop.*

'Looking good. Can I be of any help?' A familiar man's voice rang through the kitchen door, snapping Tish from her reverie. She turned to see a dashingly tuxedoed Schuyler Thompson standing near the plating station, admiring the children's handiwork.

31

She felt the color rise in her cheeks. 'Oh, hello, Schuyler. What brings you back here?'

'Just wanted to check in and see how things are going.'

'They're . . . well, they're going.' She removed the last rockfish fillet from the griddle and placed on the tray. *Flop.*

'I can see. By the way, erecting tents over the walkway was a great idea. Everyone's talking about it. In a good way, of course,' he quickly added.

'I'm glad it's working. I can't imagine having to wade through this monsoon in a gown and stilettos.' Tish eyed Schuyler as she covered the platter of fish. 'Or in a tuxedo and freshly polished shoes.'

Schuyler bowed humbly. 'This old thing?' he teased. 'So what can I do to help out? I'm not a cook, but I can plate with the best of them.'

'Thanks, but I couldn't possibly accept your help,' Tish declined. 'You're a guest. You paid for your ticket.'

'There will be plenty of time for me to mingle later this evening. Right now, let me help you. Please?'

Before Tish could open her mouth to decline the offer once again, Celestine stepped forth with an apron and a spoon. 'She'll tell you no. *I* say we need all the hands we can get.'

Tish laughed. 'OK . . . Celestine might be right. Another set of hands would really help ensure we get the first course out on time. Thanks for asking.'

'Not a problem,' Schuyler replied. 'So what will I be doing?'

'You'll be helping Kayla dish out the Who's Afraid of Virginia Baked Ham and Cheesy Edgar Allen Poe-lenta. Not because Kayla isn't doing an excellent job,' Tish reassured her friend's daughter, 'but because the ham orders outnumber the veggie orders nearly two-to-one.'

'Yep, the prime rib orders too,' Celestine concurred. 'I swear every steer and pig in the county must shudder in fear the second Binnie starts hanging flyers.'

'Well, Binnie warned us there had better be meat on the menu. Now we know why.'

'Guilty carnivore here.' Schuyler raised his hand sheepishly. 'Although I admit to being tempted by The Old Man and the Sea Bream. Local rockfish is a favorite of mine, especially when cooked properly.'

At Schuyler's remark, Tish placed the mushrooms, artichoke hearts, and asparagus spears on the same griddle she used to cook the fish. 'You mean with fresh veg, lemon, wine, butter, dill, and capers?'

'Is that what's in the fish dish?' Schuyler asked as he hung the apron on the back of a nearby chair and started spooning polenta and ham into ramekins.

'Uh-huh,' she smirked.

'Is it too late to change my order?'

'Uh-huh.'

'Will you still let me buy you a drink later?'

'How about I buy *you* a drink to thank you for your help? Besides, I'm friends with the barman,' Tish countered with a wink.

* * *

33

Tish and crew had been working in focused silence for nearly twenty minutes when the sounds of the Dixieland band suddenly ceased, replaced by the high-frequency hum of a microphone being adjusted. As the shrill voice of Binnie Broderick filled the lodge, Mary Jo and her staff of servers flooded the kitchen doorway.

'When Binnie finishes her speech, it's go time. We need to get the first course on the table,' Mary Jo announced.

'Good thing we finished,' Schuyler replied, giving his fellow plating-station mates a high five. 'Is there anything else I can do, Tish?'

'No, you've done plenty, thanks,' Tish answered. 'You'd better get out there before Binnie notices you're missing.'

'Sure. See you later?'

Tish nodded.

Mary Jo addressed Schuyler on his way out. 'I hope those weren't billable hours, counselor.'

'Strictly pro bono,' he smiled and stepped into the reception area.

Mary Jo slid a sly glance in Tish's direction – to which Tish smiled and shrugged before jumping into action. Following detailed order sheets, she loaded trays with the appropriate items, stopping to clean any messes on the edges of the plates, and dispatched her wait staff to their designated tables, starting with the Binnie Broderick's table. 'Melissa, you take this to table number one,' she ordered, passing Celestine's granddaughter her tray. She then loaded up another tray and dispatched it to table number two, then another to table three, and so forth.

As Mary Jo emptied the plating station, Tish stacked it with plates featuring a beautifully sculpted pile of vegetables and rockfish, and Celestine, busy at the carving board, loaded it up with medium-rare slices of prime rib. To these dishes, Kayla and Gregory added perfectly baked potatoes slathered with butter. The bell pepper entrées and the remainder of the sauces, sides, and various garnishes would be added just prior to serving.

Mary Jo loaded a tray for table number seven with the intention of passing it to Melissa, who had returned from serving the Brodericks' table. However, the girl looked somewhat dismayed. 'Mrs Broderick won't eat her ham and polenta without hot sauce,' she reported.

'What?' Celestine cried in disbelief.

'Did she even taste it?' Mary Jo asked.

'No, she flat out refused,' Melissa answered. 'I'm sorry.'

'No need to be sorry,' Tish spoke up and made her way to the refrigerator. 'There's always one in every crowd and we all knew she might be it.'

'I say she's putting it on,' Celestine opined. 'Probably a test just to see if we have it.'

'Whether she is or isn't putting it on, we still need to give her what she's asked for.' Tish extracted a bottle of sriracha from the door of the fridge and handed it to Melissa.

'I'll take it to her, if you don't mind.' Celestine snatched the bottle from Tish's hand. 'Melissa, go bring the first course to the next table.'

'I don't mind bringing in the hot sauce, Gran,' Melissa insisted.

35

'Nope. I don't want Binnie to think she can give my girl a hard time. I'd also like to know what she's playing at. If that's OK with you, Tish.'

'Totally fine with me. Just remember she still owes us a check,' Tish reminded with a friendly yet cautious smile.

'Oh, honey, believe me, I remember about getting paid. I ain't about to jeopardize that. I just need to let Binnie know she's on notice. Woman to woman.'

Tish, trusting outwardly that Celestine would do her best not to aggravate the maker of the feast, yet questioning inwardly the potential course of their dialogue, turned her attention back to the plating yet to be done. After dishing up the rest of the rockfish and vegetables, she checked in on her port-and-Stilton gravy – made with the pan juices from the roasts – and picked up the long twin-tined fork and butcher's knife Celestine had been using to continue to slice the standing ribs into individual servings.

As she leaned in to carve another helping, Tish noticed the figure of Enid Kemper standing in the parking lot. She had returned to the lodge sans Langhorne, and stood just outside the tented walkway, staring at the front door as heavy rain poured down upon what appeared to be a threadbare raincoat.

Tish was torn between rushing outdoors to offer the woman shelter and charging outdoors to shoo the woman away, but a flash of lightning followed by a momentary power outage ended any such deliberation. When the lights came back on in the kitchen, Enid had vanished.

The standing rib roast and the three hundred people in the reception hall, however, had not.

'You OK?' Mary Jo quizzed, genuine concern in her voice.

'Yeah. Yeah, I'm fine,' Tish assured. 'I just need to get the main course plated.'

'Is that why you were staring out the window?' Mary Jo teased, as she loaded up another tray for delivery. Kayla and Greg, in the meantime, both snickered and rolled their eyes at their mother's sarcasm.

The familial scene immediately brought Tish back to earth. There was no fooling her old friend. 'Sorry, things are just a little weird tonight,' she explained as she went back to carving and the ragtime band resumed playing.

'Um, like three hundred people to feed and water, a dragon lady librarian nipping at your heels, and Jules doing his Tom-Cruise-in-*Cocktail*-impersonation weird? Yeah, I feel you.'

Tish laughed out loud. 'Oh no, Jules hasn't started juggling the cocktail shakers yet, has he?'

'Not with this crowd. They're keeping him way too busy mixing drinks. He's had just enough time to twirl a few bottles and toss a couple of garnishes.'

'Whew.'

'Oh, the night's still young. There's plenty of time for him to juggle the cocktail shakers, do a dance on the bar, or accidently pelt a society matron with a wayward maraschino cherry.'

'Awesome.' Tish sighed.

'Well, Binnie's not playing at anything,' Celestine announced upon her return to the kitchen, 'at least not as far as I can tell. She took the hot sauce, doused her ham with it, and dug in.'

'That's that, then.'

'Oh, she also said she would like to see you when you get a moment.'

'Sure. I'll go out as soon as we're finished plating the entrée.'

True to her word, upon plating the last of the garnishes and sides, Tish washed her hands, removed her apron, donned a pristine white chef's jacket (which she had purchased for just such an occasion) and excused herself from the kitchen just as Kayla and Gregory had finished loading the empty first-course dishes into the high-capacity dishwasher, and shortly after Mary Jo sent Melissa out to begin serving the main course.

As the Dixieland band replaced their jubilant jazz with a slow, soft swing standard, Tish wended her way to table number one. There, she waited for Melissa to complete the dinner service and watched while Binnie took a bite of her prime rib, frowned, and then doused the entire plate with sriracha.

Tish felt a hole develop in the pit of her stomach. Yet she stepped forward to accept her fate. 'Mrs Broderick, I hope you're finding everything to your liking.'

Binnie pulled a face. 'It's satisfactory. The tents outdoors were a bit too rustic for my taste, but my guests appreciated not being rained upon. I've also received some compliments on the food thus far, although I find it rather bland myself.'

'Well, I for one disagree. This prime rib is one of the best I've ever put in my mouth,' the fortyish peroxide blonde to Binnie's left contended.

'You always have been easy . . . to please.' Binnie eyed the blonde and the ruddy-faced man seated beside her. 'Ms Tarragon, allow me to introduce you. The woman you see wearing the inappropriately low-cut dress and scarfing down on prime rib is my daughter, Cordelia. The inebriated man alongside her is my son-in-law and Cordelia's husband, John Ballantyne. As you can see, John is a fan of your bartender friend.'

'Nice to meet you.' Tish extended an awkward hand to the couple. 'I'm glad you're enjoying the event.'

'Yes, it's lovely.' Cordelia shook Tish's hand. 'One of the best in years.'

'The company on the other hand,' John added with a devilish glance at his mother-in-law.

'We're also finding everything quite delicious,' a black woman in an elegant, one-shouldered red evening gown announced from her side of the table. 'I've never had rockfish that was so moist and flavorful. I'd ask you for the recipe, but I know chefs need to preserve their secrets.'

'Thank you very much,' Tish said with a bow.

'No, thank you.' The woman rose from her seat and extended a long slender arm. 'Augusta May Wilson, President of the Hobson Glen Library Board.'

'Pleased to meet you. Tish Tarragon, new owner of Cookin' the Books Café and Catering.'

'Welcome to the neighborhood,' a tuxedoed gentleman hailed, introducing himself as Augusta's husband, Edwin.

Out of the corner of her eye, Tish noticed Binnie take another bite of beef, chew it, and cringe.

As if in response to Binnie's reaction, Augusta continued the praise. 'If your café menu is as good as the food you've cooked up tonight, I look forward to visiting you for lunch.'

'There's a terrible a shortage of eateries in Hobson Glen,' Cordelia added. 'Your place will be a long-awaited addition.'

'Will you feature a wine list or a bar?' John inquired.

'Not straight away, no,' was Tish's honest reply. 'I'm going to focus on breakfast pastries and lunch first.'

'I was joking. Just looking to get a rise,' John added, hiking a thumb toward his mother-in-law.

As if on cue, Binnie clutched at her throat and made a gagging sound.

'John was only kidding, Mother.' Cordelia sighed in exasperation.

Binnie, however, was not. Her eyes wide with terror, she gasped for air and clutched at her abdomen with one hand, while banging on the table with the other, as if to drive home the direness of her situation.

'Oh my God, Mother!' Cordelia exclaimed as she rose to her feet, overturning her chair in the process.

40

'Doctor! We need a doctor! Is Doctor Livermore here?' John shouted as he stood and placed a consoling hand on his wife's shoulder.

The remaining two occupants of the table – a tall, slender woman with short-cropped black hair and equine features, and a small-framed man with graying hair, glasses, and a non-descript countenance – leapt from their seats and covered their mouths.

'I know the Heimlich maneuver,' Edwin suggested before racing to the other side of the table.

He was intercepted by a silver-haired man in a white dinner jacket. 'I'm Doctor Livermore,' he hastily introduced himself to Tish. 'What's the problem?'

'Oh, Doctor Livermore,' Cordelia cried. 'Thank God you're here! My mother's choking. Help her!'

Before any such anti-choking treatments could be attempted, Binnie Broderick stood up, gurgled, gasped, and fell face forward into her plate of Prime Rib of Miss Jean Brodie, splattering Stilton gravy all over the white table cloth, the white floral centerpiece, and the garments of those who surrounded her.

Cordelia released a blood-curdling shriek that resonated from the floorboards to the rafters.

At the sound of the scream, the kitchen staff surged into the reception room, a member of Tish's wait staff dropped her tray, sending plates of food crashing to the dance floor, and the light dinner music came, instantly and abruptly, to a halt.

'Everybody stay calm. No one panic,' Tish commanded. 'Someone call nine-one-one.'

'Already dialing.' Jules rushed forth from the crowd.

'That won't be necessary,' a dark-haired, mustached man in a red-and-white striped jacket, white pants, shirt, and tie declared as he moved through the crowd, a highly polished brass instrument still encircling his body.

'I appreciate you wanting to help, sir,' Tish responded, 'but as the caterer in charge, I don't think a tuba player is precisely what's needed right now.'

'Sousaphone,' the man corrected while pulling a wallet out of his back pocket.

'Sousaphone? This woman is fighting for her life and you—'

The man coolly displayed his sheriff's badge and ID. 'I've already radioed.'

Tish's mouth drew into a tiny 'o.' 'Oops.'

'That's not all you were wrong about,' Doctor Livermore pronounced as he felt Binnie Broderick's neck for a pulse. 'Mrs Broderick isn't fighting for her life. She's already dead.'

Four

After the body of Binnie Broderick had been wheeled out of the Hobson Glen Masonic Lodge on a gurney, Tish and company, along with the three hundred guests in attendance, provided

42

their contact information to the police and were allowed to go home.

Sheriff Clemson Reade (whose name she learned shortly after their extremely awkward first meeting) left strict orders that apart from leftovers, which could be wrapped and refrigerated, nothing in the lodge – food served, dirty dishes – should be touched or removed from the premises until further notice.

That notice arrived at noon the next day, when Sheriff Reade called Tish to inform her that the lodge was cleared for cleaning and to request that she stop by the precinct at three o'clock that afternoon.

'Oh, by the way,' the sheriff added before hanging up, 'we got the coroner's preliminary report. Binnie Broderick was poisoned.'

With the sheriff's go-ahead, and her stomach in knots about Binnie's death and what it might mean for her business, Tish called Celestine, Mary Jo, and Jules to share the news. The quartet, along with Mary Jo's children, met at the Masonic Lodge shortly afterward to commence with the scrubbing, washing, and drying.

Not even an hour into their work, Jules took a break to microwave himself a serving of prime rib, gravy, vegetables, and a baked potato. He stood, hunched over the counter, devouring it with gusto.

'How can you eat at a time like this?' Tish scowled as she emptied the first of many loads of dishes from the dishwasher.

'What? I finished clearing all the tables. I'll disassemble the tables and chairs and get to the mopping when I'm done.'

'No, I mean, how can you eat with everything that's happened?'

'Better question is how can I not? Not only haven't I eaten breakfast, but I am a major stress-eater. I always have been. I just can't help it.'

'He's telling the truth,' Mary Jo substantiated. 'Remember how he'd plump up right around mid-terms and finals?'

'Oh, that's right. We thought we'd have to expand his graduation gown,' Tish recollected.

'I was never *plump*,' Jules maintained. 'And I'd like to remind you, Mary Jo, that your children are in this kitchen. What kind of example are you setting for them? How about young Kayla here? She doesn't need to hear her mother fat-shame another human being. Do you, honey?'

Kayla grinned as she dried a pot lid her mother washed and rinsed. 'I saw the yearbook photos, Uncle Jules. To be fair, you were just a wee bit on the plump side.'

Jules reared back. 'That's it. You're out of my will.'

'But you were still fabulous,' Kayla swiftly added.

'Aw, honey. You're so sweet,' Jules gushed. 'MJ, you're doing such a fine job with your children.'

Tish cleared her throat. 'Child rearing, plumpness, and other issues aside, you do realize that eating the same meal the dead woman ate might not be the best idea.'

'Humph?' Jules questioned, his eyes wide and his mouth full of potato.

44

'Sheriff Reade said she was poisoned.'

'This was in the refrigerator. Never served, never plated. It couldn't possibly have harmed anyone.'

'Not unless the poisoning Sheriff Reade referred to was food poisoning,' Tish posed. 'Food-borne botulism can cause both difficulty swallowing and trouble breathing.'

Mary Jo and Celestine stared at Tish, their faces a question. 'What? I learned it in a food safety class,' she explained.

At the word 'botulism', Jules had looked up from his prime rib. 'Wait. You really think Binnie could have died of food poisoning?'

Tish nodded. 'Possible. That might be why the police want to see me later today.'

Jules stared hard at his plate. 'It tastes just fine to me. In fact, it's absolutely delicious.'

'That's the thing about food poisoning. Food doesn't have to taste "spoiled" to carry bacteria.'

'Oh, come on, Tish,' Mary Jo reasoned. 'You're a perfectionist. You wouldn't have put any of this food at risk of contamination.'

'Not normally, no. But I've never cooked for a crowd this size before. I could have goofed somewhere along the line.'

Jules stared a few more moments at his plate. 'How much did Binnie eat?'

'Two bites.'

Tish's answer appeared to make Jules shrug off his concerns. 'Well, I've already eaten seven times that amount and I seem to be doing OK.'

'Seven? More like ten,' Mary Jo remarked.

'Hey, I'm not going to let the best cut of beef

I've ever eaten go to waste. I may even have another when I'm done with this one.'

'Two pieces of prime rib that *might* have food poisoning. Your stress eating has just reached a whole new level.'

'Y'all just stop with the food-poisoning talk already,' Celestine requested. 'I was in this kitchen all day with Tish, helping her prepare. We all were. There's nothing wrong with that food. I'm willing to swear to it.'

'Thanks, Celestine,' Tish said in a near whisper.

'No need to thank me, I'm just saying it as it is. I'm sorry to have seen Binnie go the way she did, but truth is, she was a miserable woman. That sort of misery has a way of catching up with a person.'

'You're so right,' Jules agreed. 'I don't know of anyone who really liked the woman. Not only was Mrs Broderick mean, but she obviously had absolutely no taste whatsoever. To say what she said about your food, Tish? Why, had she said that to me, I would have dragged her into the parking lot and shot her. Oh. I mean . . .'

It was Jules's turn to be the subject of questioning stares.

'Sorry. Wrong phrase.' He self-consciously put a forkful of vegetables in his mouth.

'Well, food poisoning or not, my reputation as a caterer is shot,' Tish sighed.

'That's not true, honey,' Celestine soothed. 'As soon as the police prove it wasn't food poisoning, you're in the clear.'

'Legally, perhaps, but not in the minds of the locals. Whatever the cause of her death, the last

46

thing Binnie did was take a bite of my food. Everyone at that table saw it. Everyone in the reception room knows it. None of them will ever eat at my café or hire me to cater their event. Not after this.'

'You know, when I worked in marketing and PR, we had a saying, "There's no such thing as bad publicity,"' Mary Jo shared. 'At least people are talking about you and your food.'

'Great. But how do I make them talk about it in a positive light?'

'Well, when my clients would get a bit of bad press, I'd first make them apologize for the action and make amends—'

'Not applicable here.'

'Then I'd send them out on a goodwill project. A visit to a hospital, a donation to a charitable foundation, that sort of thing.'

As Mary Jo provided her professional advice, Jules had finished his prime rib lunch and extracted a Finnegan's Cake from the refrigerator.

'What are you eating now, Uncle Jules?' a bemused Gregory asked.

'Just a little something sweet to complete my lunch.' He plopped the cake on to a dessert plate and dug in with the same fork he had used on the prime rib. It had, naturally, been licked clean before slicing into the chocolate confection.

'Are you here to clean dishes or create more?' Tish teased.

'The word "poison" mean anything to you, honey?' Celestine asked, shaking her head in both bewilderment and amusement.

'These are totally safe. They were never served to anyone. Not even Binnie Broderick.' He licked his lips and took a bite.

'He does have a point.' Mary Jo salivated as Jules licked the creamy frosting from his lips. 'Celestine, these are pure genius.'

'Why, thank you,' the baker blushed.

'No, I mean it. Rich and yet light as a feather.'

'They are awfully good,' Tish stated. 'Maybe it's time we all take a break?'

Tish didn't have to ask the question twice, for Mary Jo and her kids were at the refrigerator door within moments.

Tish grabbed dessert plates and forks for everyone and then dug into her own cake. 'Mmm . . . this is heavenly!'

'Outrageous,' Mary Jo agreed. Gregory and Kayla, meanwhile, plowed through their cakes as if they had been denied such sweet treats all their lives.

'May I have another one?' Gregory asked.

'How much booze is in the icing?'

'Oh, just a couple shots for the whole batch,' Celestine replied.

'OK . . . it's fine with me, but you need to ask Tish and Celestine.'

'It's fine with me too, honey. I don't need them' – Celestine placed a hand on a well-rounded rounded hip – 'and Mr Rufus doesn't much like sweets.'

'Totally good with me too,' Tish concurred. 'I mean, we only have nearly three hundred of them to get rid of or freeze or . . .'

Like lightning, a thought flashed into Tish's

mind. She immediately rushed to the refrigerator and opened the door to admire the stacks of pristine miniature cakes lining the appliance's shelves. 'Three hundred of them,' Tish repeated. 'Celestine, do you happen to have a smaller carrier for these? Say, something to transport about a dozen cupcakes at once?'

'Yeah, got a few in my car, why?'

'Because I'm going to go out this afternoon and spread a little Cookin'-the-Books goodwill.'

Five

Before any will – good, bad, or otherwise – could actually be spread, Tish needed to keep her appointment with Sheriff Clemson Reade.

With the clean-up at the Masonic Lodge nearly complete, Tish excused herself and zipped home. After transferring the leftover Finnegan's Cakes to the café refrigerator, she headed to the bathroom for a quick shower. Leaving her hair to dry naturally, she applied a bit of gel and some make-up and then slipped into a cool, sleeveless floral summer dress and a pair of deep-pink gladiator sandals and jumped back into her bright-red 2015 Toyota Matrix. With the car windows down, she then drove to the outskirts of town to the Hanover County Police outpost that served both Hobson Glen and the neighboring town of Piper's Ridge.

There, after giving the uniformed police officer

at the front desk her name, Tish was waved into Sheriff Reade's office.

'Ms Tarragon,' Clemson Reade greeted as he rose halfway from his chair. Having traded in last night's straw boater, striped blazer, and fake handlebar mustache for a mane of spiky, dark hair, a light-blue T-shirt, and a face of heavy stubble, Reade was more apt to be mistaken for the bass player in a grunge band than a member of small-town law enforcement.

'Sheriff,' Tish replied and took the seat opposite his desk.

'Thanks for coming in this afternoon.'

'No problem.' Tish flashed a brilliant smile with the hope that it might help compensate for any perceived impoliteness on her part the previous evening. After all, if Tish had any chance of salvaging her business, she needed to be on the good side of the local constabulary. 'I appreciate you letting me and my staff into the lodge so quickly.'

'Just happened to work out that way,' Reade shrugged. 'Some cases, the forensics team works faster than others.'

Tish frowned. Ingratiating herself with the taciturn law official was not going to be easy. 'Well, I appreciate being able to get in there and clean just the same.'

The sheriff made no comment.

Strike one. 'I also wanted to let you know how much I enjoyed your band and its music.'

'Really?' Reade arched a dark, quizzical eyebrow.

'Yes, I've not listened to a lot of Dixieland

music, but I found myself really getting into your performance last night. It was the perfect soundtrack for my cooking.'

'Are you trying to tell me we had you dancing in the kitchen?' Reade smirked.

'Not dancing, no, but flipping fish,' she said with a broad smile.

The sheriff's smirk quickly turned into a frown. 'Flipping fish?'

Tish soon regretted her hasty reply. 'Yes, in time with the, um, the beat of the music. It was . . . energizing.'

'Awesome. If we ever put out an album, I'll make sure we work fish flipping into the title,' Reade quipped and went back to reviewing the contents of the folder before him.

Strike two. 'Er, well, one thing's for sure, your sousaphone playing is fantastic. I thought for sure someone had a bass guitar out there.'

'That's very kind of you.' Reade stared at her through narrowed, deep-set gray eyes. 'And incredibly astute considering last night you couldn't tell that sousaphone from a tuba.'

Tish cringed as she flushed a bright crimson. *Strike three.* 'Um, actually, I studied music theory and played some tunes by ear on my recorder in elementary school and joined the choir in high—'

'And probably still can't tell the difference.' Reade brushed Tish's commentary aside before adding, 'By the way, before you cause yourself an aneurism trying to flatter me, I didn't call you in because I suspect you of murder.'

'Thank goodness.' Tish sighed. 'I mean, I

always keep a clean kitchen and I passed my food safety classes with flying colors, but I confess that I've never catered an event this large before. So if I somehow managed to give Binnie Broderick food poisoning, it certainly wasn't intentional.'

'Although I appreciate your honesty, Ms Tarragon, unless arsenic has suddenly been classified as a food-borne pathogen, I'm pretty sure your cooking is in the clear.'

'Arsenic?' Tish repeated before drawing a deep breath and leaning back in her chair.

'Relieved it wasn't food poisoning?' Reade flashed an ironic smile.

'Up to a point. I simply can't believe someone killed Mrs Broderick. I mean, she was a difficult woman, to be certain, but murder?' Tish shook her head in disbelief. 'You don't think someone poisoned her food or drink last night, do you?'

'We're not yet sure how the arsenic was administered. We're still waiting for the lab results, but it's a distinct possibility, yes.'

'But why? Why would someone do such a thing?'

'That's what we're going to find out,' Reade announced. 'Am I correct in assuming that you met with Binnie Broderick a few times prior to the event?'

'Yes,' Tish replied, 'we met about a week and a half ago for a food tasting and then late last week to review the schedule for the party.'

'Did you meet yesterday at all?'

'No. Mrs Broderick arrived at the lodge just before the fundraiser was about to get off the ground. She popped into the kitchen to see that everything was under control and then went out into the reception room. It was less of a meeting than a check-in.'

'During this check-in, as you call it, or any of your previous meetings, did Mrs Broderick mention any personal troubles she may have had? Maybe a guest at the party she didn't look forward to seeing? Was there anything about the party that might have been worrying her?'

'Personal troubles? No, my interactions with Mrs Broderick were always of a professional nature. Conversation always focused on the business at hand. Mrs Broderick had a clear vision of what she wanted for the fundraiser and that's all we ever discussed. She wanted the event to be a success and the only thing she ever expressed any concern about was my ability to meet her expectations.'

'You said your meetings with Mrs Broderick were professional. Would you use that term to describe Mrs Broderick's behavior as well?'

'What a leading question, Sheriff.' Tish smiled. 'I think you already know the answer to that question – otherwise you wouldn't have asked it.'

Reade returned the smile. 'Humor me.'

'No, Mrs Broderick was not what I would describe as professional; she was what I would describe as difficult.'

'So difficult that you might wish her out of the way?'

It was Tish's turn to raise an eyebrow. 'I thought you didn't suspect me.'

'I don't, but seeing as I'm not always correct

in my assumptions, I thought it best to cover my bases.'

'Then, to answer your question, I worked in banking for twenty years before giving it up to become a caterer. In both professions, killing difficult clients would hardly be considered a viable career plan.'

'Did you ever witness Mrs Broderick being "difficult" with other people?'

'Not until last night. Mind you, I'd heard stories from townsfolk. But it wasn't until I stepped out of the kitchen to check in on Mrs Broderick and the other guests that I actually got to see her "in action," so to speak.'

'What happened?'

'Well, after disparaging my food by calling it bland, Mrs Broderick went on to criticize her daughter's evening gown as too low-cut and then comment upon her son-in-law's drinking. Oh, she also passed some snide remark about her daughter being "easy to please."'

'How did her daughter and son-in-law react to her comments?'

'They didn't have a chance to react. Much to everyone's relief, Mrs Wilson, the president of the library board, quickly changed the topic of conversation. Binnie Broderick began choking only a minute or so afterward.'

'And the incident with Mr and Mrs Ballantyne – you're sure that was the only time you witnessed Binnie Broderick being "antagonistic" toward someone?'

'Yes. As I said earlier, I've heard stories and have one or two of my own, but I never actually saw Mrs Broderick behave that way toward anyone else until last night.'

Reade nodded and typed some notes on to a small computerized tablet device. 'Did you notice anything else last night? Anything out of the ordinary?'

'Out of the ordinary?' Tish snickered. 'I'm sorry, Sheriff Reade, but I've been in town just under a month and I've already learned of a library scandal and witnessed a murder, so forgive me if I'm not quite sure what passes as "ordinary" here in Hobson Glen.'

Tish expected Reade to explain why Hobson Glen was a wonderful place to put down roots, but instead he leaned back in his chair and pulled a face. 'It's been a strange few months, for sure. I've been sheriff for ten years and during that time the bulk of my job has entailed traffic accidents and infringements, acting as referee during the occasional domestic or alcohol-fueled dispute, and assisting the State Police when necessary. But this . . .' Reade straightened in his chair. 'The last suspicious death we had in Hobson Glen occurred back in 1948. And that was eventually ruled a suicide.'

'I'm sorry,' Tish expressed. 'Having lived in Richmond for so long, I've sadly grown somewhat immune to daily reports of shootings and robberies, but for you and the other residents of Hobson Glen, this must be quite a shock.'

'Yeah, well, given the world we live in, I should probably be thankful we've been tragedy-free for so long,' Reade replied wistfully. 'So, going back to my previous question: did you notice anything or anyone unusual last night?'

'Come to think of it, yes.' Tish described how she saw Enid Kemper outside the kitchen window.

'And to the best of your knowledge, Miss Kemper wasn't a guest.'

'I doubt it. Not only wasn't she dressed for the event, but if she had a ticket, she would have come right into the lodge rather than lurking outside. Also, Enid had stopped by earlier in the day to try to track down Mrs Broderick.'

'Did she say why?'

'Yes. Enid was quite angry to learn that she wasn't allowed to bring her pet parrot into the library.'

'Conure,' Reade corrected.

'What?' The reply caught Tish off guard.

'Langhorne, Enid's pet bird, isn't a parrot. He's a conure.'

Tish's eyes grew wide. Good heavens, the people of Hobson Glen were awfully particular about terminology. 'Oh, yes, that's right. Sorry . . .'

Reade burst out laughing. 'I'm joking. After the sousaphone thing, I couldn't resist.'

'Funny,' Tish remarked with a frosty smile. Inwardly, however, she acknowledged that the sheriff had earned the right to have a laugh at her expense. 'I don't think Enid Kemper would be laughing, though. She seems to be exceptionally devoted to that bird of hers.'

Reade's demeanor grew somber. 'Langhorne is the only companion Enid Kemper has in the world. She never married or had children, and

56

her family's all gone now. That bird is a beloved pet, best friend, and a longed-for child all rolled into one.'

'No wonder she was so livid about Mrs Broderick banning him from the library.'

'Well, she and Binnie never did get on well,' Reade explained.

'This was more than two people not getting along. Enid Kemper was downright furious. She vowed to make Binnie Broderick pay.'

'Those were the exact words she used? That she'd make Mrs Broderick pay?'

'Yes. Celestine Rufus was there with me. We both heard it.'

'And you weren't overly concerned by those words?' Reade prodded.

'No,' Tish stated flatly. 'There's a world of difference between wishing to make someone pay and actually doing so. Also, Celestine made it clear that Enid was something of the town eccentric, so it seems even more unlikely that she'd actually do anything.'

Reade typed some notes into his tablet. 'Did you notice anything else unusual last night? Anyone apart from Enid who shouldn't have been at the lodge but was?'

'No.' Tish shook her head. 'Not that I can recall, but then again I was in the kitchen all evening.'

'Yes, about your kitchen staff,' Reade segued into the next question. 'Did I get the names of everyone who helped out last night?'

'I believe you did, yes.'

'So no one left early or stopped in during

57

the day to act as a pinch hitter or anything like that?'

Tish was reluctant to reply, but she knew if she didn't tell the sheriff about Schuyler Thompson's presence in the kitchen, someone else would. 'Actually, yes. Schuyler Thompson came in to help us plate the first course.'

Reade grunted and poked at his tablet keypad. 'Was this prearranged between the two of you?'

'Prearranged? No. Schuyler simply stopped into the kitchen to see if we needed help.'

'And you did?'

'Well, we were dragging a bit with plating; there were several components to each dish, and it took some time and care to guard against spills, splashes, and overall sloppiness. We probably would have finished in time, but Schuyler's help bought us a bit of breathing room. Because of him, we were able to start plating the main course while the first was still being served.'

'And did Thompson assist with the plating of that as well?'

'No, he went back to his table to enjoy his first course and to listen to Binnie Broderick's speech.'

'Did you find Mr Thompson's offer of help at all suspicious?'

'Suspicious? No. Not only is Schuyler Thompson my landlord, but he was the person who referred my services to Mrs Broderick. It seemed only natural for him to want to ensure a successful evening. Oh, and he also wanted me to join him for a drink once the serving had been done.'

'However, Mr Thompson did, in fact, have access to all the food served that evening,' Reade persisted.

'Not all the food, no. Only the first course; the cakes were in the refrigerator and he never went near the back of the kitchen where the entrée was being prepared,' Tish explained.

'Mmm,' Reade murmured as he typed more notes into his tablet.

'Besides, Schuyler Thompson had no idea which plate would be served to Binnie Broderick. Poisoning anything in that kitchen would have been absolutely pointless,' Tish blurted out as the temperature in the room seemed to rise considerably. Why she should feel the need to defend a man she had only met a few weeks ago was beyond comprehension.

Reade stopped typing.

'I mean, unless Mr Thompson was simply out to murder some random individual,' Tish amended, feeling more than a bit self-conscious.

'You have a very valid point there, Ms Tarragon,' Reade allowed. 'Could you describe the serving process for me?'

'Sure. After being plated, the first course and entrée were placed on a table with a heat lamp or, for the cold appetizer, on a rolling rack which was then placed into the walk-in refrigerator. When we were ready to serve, Mary Jo Okensholt, my friend and volunteer for the evening, loaded the trays using a detailed seating chart. Our wait staff then took the trays out into the reception hall where they commenced with serving.'

'Did your wait staff ever leave the trays unattended?'

'Um, I don't know. They might have left them on a tray stand while they served, but I still don't see how it matters. The murderer still wouldn't have known which plate was going to be served to Binnie Broderick.'

'So her plate was no different from anyone else's?'

'It shouldn't have been, no. Unless she ordered her prime rib exceptionally well done or exceptionally rare, but I don't recall that being the case when I filled out the chart for Mary Jo.'

'And no double potato, extra butter, or an additional garnish?'

'No. I was quite pleasantly surprised to find not a single write-in request included among the three hundred plus menu cards returned.'

Reade sighed. 'The bottom line being that Binnie Broderick didn't eat anything outside what was on the menu that evening.'

Tish nodded in agreement and then recalled otherwise. 'Wait a minute. I almost forgot the hot sauce.'

'Hmm?'

'Shortly after being served her main course, Mrs Broderick asked for hot sauce.'

Reade leaned forward in his seat. 'Whom did she ask?'

'Her server, Melissa Rufus, Celestine's granddaughter.'

'And Melissa brought Mrs Broderick's plate to the kitchen for the hot sauce?'

'No, no, we brought out the whole bottle.'

60

'Melissa Rufus . . .' Reade dictated as he typed into his tablet.

'Melissa Rufus didn't bring the hot sauce to Mrs Broderick,' Tish hastened to mention.

'Oh, who did? Another server?' Reade asked, still focused on his note-taking.

'No,' she replied. 'Melissa's grandmother, Celestine.'

Six

Tish pulled into the Cookin' the Books parking lot to find Jules and Mary Jo drinking lemonade on the front porch. 'Hey,' she greeted as she stepped out of the car.

'Hey,' Mary Jo called from her spot on the swing. 'How'd it go?'

Tish shook her head. 'Where are the kids?' she asked, reluctant to discuss details of the investigation in front of them.

'Glen came by and took them home. Jules and I stuck around in case you needed anything else.'

'I do need something else.' Tish sighed. 'I need to save my café.'

'What happened?' Jules asked from his seat on the steps, as he poured her a glass of lemonade from a nearby glass pitcher.

'Thanks,' she muttered absently, taking the glass in her right hand and flinging her purse on to the swing beside Mary Jo with her left. 'Binnie

Broderick was definitely murdered. Arsenic poisoning.'

'Yeah, we know,' Jules thrust his phone in front of Tish's nose. 'It's all over town.'

Once her eyes acclimated to the shade offered by the porch ceiling, Tish's focus zoomed in on the main headline on the home page of the *Richmond Times Dispatch*: LIBRARY DIRECTOR FATALLY POISONED AT ANNUAL FUNDRAISER. 'Oh no,' she moaned.

'Don't worry,' Jules assured. 'The *Dispatch* doesn't mention your name or who did the catering.'

'Thank goodness for small favors,' she replied before taking a swig of lemonade. 'At least I have some time to spread those cakes around, talk to the townspeople, and find out what really happened.'

Mary Jo cleared her throat and motioned to Jules.

Their exchange wasn't lost upon Tish. 'What? What is it? What aren't you telling me?' she demanded.

'Well, as you know, I've been a weatherman for years. So, the folks from my station are on their way into town to cover the story and I, um, I may have accidentally told them who you are,' Jules timidly confessed.

'What? Why would you do that?' Tish demanded.

'Listen, we can't undo what's been done,' Mary Jo leapt between her two best friends. 'We simply need to spin this in a positive light.'

Tish collapsed on to the cushion beside Mary

Jo. 'There's no point, MJ. Not only was a woman poisoned at an event I catered, but I may have hired the person who did it.'

'You know who killed Binnie?' Jules gasped

'Of course not.' Tish detailed her conversation with Sheriff Reade.

'You don't seriously believe Celestine poisoned Binnie with hot sauce?' Mary Jo challenged when Tish had finished.

'I don't know,' Tish admitted. 'But the very fact Celestine's a suspect in this case doesn't reflect well on me. After all, I hired her without any sort of background check. I got sucked into her cake portfolio, trusted she did a great job at the bakery, and – oh! Oh, wait! Schuyler's mother owned the bakery and she's dead too! What if Celestine murdered her as well? Good Lord, I might have hired a homicidal maniac!'

'A homicidal maniac who bakes and decorates fairy princess cakes for little girls' birthdays,' a sardonic Mary Jo noted.

'And adores the heart and humor of my man-on-the-street weather forecasts,' Jules added.

'A jury could have her institutionalized on that count alone,' Mary Jo said under her breath, eliciting a smile from Tish.

'Hey,' Jules objected, although he knew Mary Jo had only made the comment to lighten Tish's mood.

'Listen, honey' – Mary Jo placed an arm around her best friend – 'I used to work in advertising and public relations, remember? It's been a while, I know, but my previous boss maintained that all publicity is good publicity.'

'MJ's right,' Jules agreed. 'The best thing you could do is issue a statement to the press. Get to them before they get to you.'

'A statement saying what?' Tish challenged. 'I'm sorry your library director is dead, but it wasn't my fault.'

'Um, kinda. Say you're sorry Mrs Broderick died in the manner she did, extend your condolences to her family and friends, state that you have the utmost confidence that your food was not involved in the crime, and make it clear that you're cooperating with police to find the perpetrator of this dastardly deed.'

'Dastardly deed? That makes it sound as if she was tied to train tracks by some guy wearing a black hat and an elaborate handlebar mustache.'

'How about heinous crime?' Jules suggested.

'Not if I have to say it on television.'

'We'll work on something else,' he promised.

'While you and Jules work on the press statement, I'll generate some positive buzz for the café.' Mary Jo explained her part of the scheme. 'Do you think we can set a date for the grand opening?'

'Sure, so long as I'm not a suspect in the case,' Tish stipulated.

'Oh, honey, I don't see how you could be,' Mary Jo dismissed. 'Anyway, I'll plan a great party with lots of food samples, giveaways, and the like, and I'll promote the heck out of it in all the papers. In the meantime, you'll do your own personal PR work.'

'Well, I was going to distribute the rest of the

Finnegan's Cakes to the townsfolk. Get their view of things . . .'

'That's an excellent start, but I think we should also deliver a tray of sandwiches to the police – you know, a goodwill gesture for their hard work.'

'We can get some press for that, too.' Jules smiled.

Tish was hesitant. 'Um, not to be a Debbie Downer here, but mightn't my bringing food to the sheriff's office be construed as a bribe? Especially since either the food or the hot sauce I provided the victim is probably the murder weapon?'

Jules and Mary Jo groaned in unison.

'Yeah.' Tish frowned.

'OK, scratch that idea,' Mary Jo stated. 'Give me a chance to brainstorm; I know I'll come up with something terrific!'

'You mean like donating several pints of blood, adopting a pack of shelter dogs, or maybe even delivering a week's worth of meals to a convent run by elderly nuns?' Tish half joked.

'Nuns! That would be – oh, wait, no.' Mary Jo swung from excitement to dismissiveness. 'The nearest convent is over an hour and a half away. That would do you no good here in Hobson Glen.'

Tish rolled her eyes and drank back the remainder of her lemonade. 'On that note, I'm going out.'

'Out?' Jules asked. 'You only just got here.'

'Public relations stuff,' she answered and then got up from the swing with a broad stretch. 'I have cakes to distribute, people to schmooze, babies to kiss. Oh, and a visit to a certain cake decorator who may owe her new employer an explanation.'

Seven

The Rufus residence consisted of a white-shingled, single-story ranch home nestled at the end of a shady, tree-lined dirt road. Tish pulled into a dusty driveway littered with tricycles, bicycles, sporting balls, a hard-sided kiddie pool, and a little red Radio Flyer wagon. At the top of the drive stood a white-shingled double-car garage, complete with a basketball hoop over the door. It was clear from the scene that Grandma's house was a favorite gathering place.

Tish swung open the driver's door, only to be greeted by Celestine herself. 'Hey, girl! How you holdin' up?' the older woman asked with a welcoming embrace.

Tish returned the hug. 'A lot better than Binnie Broderick.'

'Crazy. Just plain crazy. Though I suppose when you go through life being mean, it catches up to you eventually. Still, it's not proper someone should go that way.' She clicked her tongue. 'So you said on the phone you needed to talk to me?'

'Yes, if you're not too busy.'

'Nah, just baking a cake for my son-in-law.

He passed his head mechanic test over at the town garage. He'll be making three dollars more an hour than he was before. Maybe now my daughter can lay off the night shifts and spend more time with the kids. They spend their afternoons with me most days until my son-in-law can pick 'em up in the evening.' Taking a break from her storytelling, Celestine swung open the white aluminum storm door that led into the kitchen, and allowed Tish to step inside before following behind her.

Tish glanced around the kitchen in wonder; it was as if she had been transported back to the 1980s. Oak cabinets with raised arched panels and large brass handles fronted the wall and base cupboards, square white tiles with contrasting grout lined the countertops and backsplash, and white, brick-patterned linoleum covered the floors. Despite its outdated style, Celestine's kitchen was as warm and welcoming as the woman herself. African violets bloomed on the ledge of the over-sink window and were framed by a pair of lacy tier curtains, the aging refrigerator was covered with photos, thank-you cards from satisfied customers, and children's drawings, and atop the bank of wall cabinets rested a collection of vintage cookie jars.

It decidedly was not, Tish determined, the kitchen of a murderess. At least, not unless Binnie Broderick had committed some terrible crime against a member of Celestine's family or cadre of close acquaintances. If Binnie had, then, as the saying goes, all bets would have been off.

'So, you said you needed to talk to me. I can

only imagine it's about this Binnie Broderick business,' Celestine surmised as she pulled a lidded plastic pitcher from the refrigerator. 'No other reason for you to drive all the way up here on a hot day like today. Unless it was just to see my pretty face.'

'I'm actually glad to see you,' Tish said honestly. 'And your home. It's lovely – very warm and welcoming. But, yes, I did come to talk about Binnie. I saw Sheriff Reade not too long ago.'

Celestine poured the contents of the pitcher into two tall glasses. 'Lemon for your tea?'

'Sounds great,' Tish accepted. 'Thanks.'

'Yeah, Clem called here a few minutes ago.' Celestine called the sheriff by his more familiar nickname. 'I'm scheduled to see him first thing tomorrow morning.'

'I'm afraid I may have had something to do with that,' Tish confessed with a grimace. 'When he asked me who served Binnie last night, I told him about Melissa. Then I remembered that it was you who had delivered the hot sauce. I'm sorry for pulling you into this.'

Celestine handed Tish her glass of tea and invited her to sit at the round oak dining table. 'Oh, don't you worry, honey. All you did is tell the truth. No need to apologize for that.'

'No, I suppose not.' Tish settled into a carved oak Windsor kitchen chair and took a sip of tea.

Celestine took her spot at the table. 'Now then, you didn't come all this way just to apologize, did you?'

'No, I didn't,' Tish confessed. 'I, um . . . well, as we know Binnie Broderick was

68

poisoned, and it was most likely something she ate that contained the arsenic, I was . . . well . . . I was . . .'

Celestine's voice held the gentle yet perceptive tone of a mother who knew her child was hiding something. 'You were wondering what happened when I brought the hot sauce out to Lavinia,' she said, completing Tish's sentence and calmly taking a sip of her iced tea.

'Yes, I was. Although now I'm sorry I even thought it—'

'Oh, don't be, honey,' Celestine shooed. 'You invested your life savings in this business of yours, and even though you hired me to bake cakes for your parties, you really don't know me from Adam. If the shoe were on the other foot, I'd be sitting right where you are just about now.'

'Thanks, I appreciate your understanding.'

'No problem. Last night, I brought the hot sauce to the table and slammed it down in front of Lavinia. Not polite, I admit, but she needed to know that I wasn't gonna put up with her guff.'

'What did she say to you?'

'Not much. She was too busy watching the mayor, who had stopped by the table to say hello to everyone. He's always campaignin'. He was talking to Roberta Dutton, that strange woman who runs the library circulation desk. Lavinia took the hot sauce without even looking at me, soaked her ham and polenta, and started eating. In between bites she mentioned that you were to come out of the kitchen to see her. That was it.'

'Did Roberta Dutton appear angry when speaking with the mayor?'

69

'Angry? No, more like amused. Augusta May Wilson, on the other hand . . .' Celestine whistled. 'If looks could kill. She wasn't talking to the mayor but her eyes were. I wouldn't have been surprised to find that knife of hers in his back.'

'Hmm, wonder what that's about?' Tish mused.

'Couldn't say.'

'Well, thanks for your honesty, Celestine. And, again, for your understanding. Although I still don't feel very good about questioning you in your own kitchen.'

'Nonsense. The whole town knows how I felt about Mizz Lavinia Broderick. Only a matter of time until you found out that I hated her.'

Tish felt a hole suddenly develop in the pit of her stomach. 'Hated her?'

'Hate is a strong word, I know. And I try never to use it. I've lived my life giving people the benefit of the doubt.' Celestine added with a half-smile, 'Until Binnie. With that woman it was all doubt and no benefit.'

'What did she do?'

'Well, aside from being a self-righteous, stubborn, stuck-up cow of a woman, Lavinia Broderick killed my best friend.'

Tish stared at her glass of tea, her soul in turmoil. What the hell was she doing here, invading this woman's privacy? Saving one's business was one thing, but Cookin' the Books was not a business. It was simply a dream – nothing more. If she'd been smart, she'd have sold her Richmond home, moved to the coast, kept her bank job, and retired in twenty years. But no, she had to come to Hobson Glen . . .

Before Tish had further time to reflect, questions tumbled from her subconscious to her mouth. 'What? Who? How?'

'Cynthia Thompson, the previous owner of your café there. I told you how she ran a bakery. Cynthia wasn't just my boss; she was the best friend a gal could ever have. I was already working the counter and register and cleaning up at closing when Mr Rufus's arthritis flared up, causing him to take a month off work. Knowing I had some money woes and seeing how I loved to bake – always have; thought about doing it as a career back in the day – she – I mean, Cynthia – sent me to formal baking and decorating courses. Two years in total, entirely on her own dime. As I learned more about baking, my job evolved and so did my paycheck. It was a future I'd never dreamed I'd have. An actual career instead of just a job.'

'Cynthia sounds like a wonderful human being. Why would Binnie Broderick wish to kill her?'

'Because Cynthia was a *bon vivant*. She grieved for her husband, Schuyler's father, to be sure, but she loved living too much to spend her life in mourning. She baked, danced, enjoyed making other people happy through her food and her work. And, like any warm-blooded, straight woman under the age of ninety, she enjoyed the company of men. Oh, I don't mean a revolving-door situation; Cynthia was too classy and far too invested in her son's well-being to expose him to that kind of life. However, if Schuyler

71

was at a friend's house or away at Boy Scout camp, she'd go out for dinner with a gentleman, maybe dancing and a few drinks. Sometimes she'd come right back home after. Other times, I'd get the message that she'd be late the next morning and would I mind opening. I never minded. There's more to life than work and raising kids. Woman's gotta feel like a woman sometimes too.'

'But if it didn't bother you, why should it bother Binnie?' Tish asked and drank her tea, all her previous concerns having dissipated.

'Why should it, indeed?' Celestine asked and stared at a spot on the floorboard, seemingly lost in the past. 'Except for the fact that Lavinia Broderick was a judgmental bitch.'

Tish watched as Celestine drew a deep breath and, with a look of fury, gulped down the rest of her tea. When she had finished, she set her glass on the oak table and went to the refrigerator to retrieve the pitcher.

'One of Lavinia's board members owned a coffee shop down the road from Cynthia's. It's long gone now and has since become the local restaurant and watering hole. Business at the coffee shop was already bad for Lavinia's friend when Cynthia set up shop. I mean, if you can't fix a decent pot of coffee, you have no business using the word on your sign.' Celestine chuckled as she poured herself another glass of sweet tea. 'But that didn't matter to Lavinia. She was determined to ruin Cynthia's business before it even started.'

'But still . . . why?' Tish asked as Celestine

offered her another glass of tea, which she readily accepted. 'I know Binnie was tight with her library donors, but to run someone to the ground for no other reason than to save a donor's failing business seems awfully extreme. Even for her.'

'Because, to Lavinia, Cynthia was an immoral, self-serving woman taking business away from a hard-working, God-fearing family man.' Celestine refilled both glasses with tea and returned to her chair. 'That, and Lavinia's own brother was one of Cynthia's gentleman callers for a time. He was widowed, Cynthia was widowed, and they provided each other with a measure of companionship, but neither of them was ready for a full-on committed relationship, so they parted ways. That didn't sit well with ol' Binnie, who was quite clearly from the "once you taste the milk, you'd better buy the cow" school of thinking.'

'Wow!' Tish shook her head. 'What year is it again?'

'I often wonder,' Celestine commiserated.

'So how exactly did Binnie kill Cynthia Thompson? And if she did kill Cynthia, why wasn't she in prison?'

'It wasn't a direct kill with a gun or poison. This was rendered quietly. Steadily. Wearing Cynthia down bit by bit until the cancer in her body multiplied and consumed her. You see, Mizz Lavinia was always of an argumentative nature. Whether it was because she believed someone was ripping her off, or she disliked the way someone dressed, or disagreed with a person's lifestyle choice, Lavinia was always looking for a fight. She felt it her duty to call people out on their, um, "misdeeds."' Celestine drew a pair of quotation marks in the air. 'When she waged war against Cynthia Thompson, it was just another in a long string of skirmishes for Lavinia, but for Cynthia, who only sought the good in people, it was a terrible battle. Cynthia never could wrap her head around Lavinia's cruelty – it was in such contrast to the way she lived her own life.'

'And you? From the toys outside and the crayon drawings on the refrigerator, I can see that you're a woman who adores, and is adored by, her friends and family. Would you kill to avenge the murder of someone you loved?'

'I considered it,' Celestine admitted. 'There were moments during Cynthia's last few days when I'd watch Schuyler blink back the tears as he held his mama's hand. Times when her pain was so unbearable that the nurses had to hook her up to yet another morphine drip, only to be unable to find a usable vein cause they'd all been tapped into. Those nights, I'd drive home from the hospital and stop in front of the Broderick house, my foot hovering over the gas pedal as I wondered if I shouldn't just drive Mr Rufus's big ol' Dodge pickup right through Lavinia's bedroom and end it for both of us.'

'Why didn't you?' Tish posed.

'Because of my kids, my grandkids – I'd never be able to hold them again and tell them I love them. Because I'd promised Cynthia that I'd always watch over Schuyler, even though he's a grown man and has more sense than I do at times. And because, well, I'll be quite frank, I don't think Mr Rufus would be able even to find his socks without me.' She emitted a soft chuckle as she wiped away a wayward tear from her cheek with the back of a hand bearing a rather prominent mother's ring. 'But, more than that, I actually am a Christian. I wasn't about to take Lavinia away from her family. She may not have been the nicest woman, and perhaps not even the greatest of mothers, but Lavinia's daughter loved her. To put Cordelia and her daughter through that . . . well, if I had done that, I'd have been no better than Lavinia.'

Tish leaned back in her chair, relieved that her new dessert master had exonerated herself.

'Then again, if I knew Binnie Broderick was about to do to another human being what she did to Cynthia,' Celestine added, causing Tish's uneasiness to return, 'I'd have been sorely tempted to say to hell with Cordelia and drive that truck on through.'

Eight

Tish arrived at the Hobson Glen Public Library to find a familiar sign posted on the glass front door. Only this time, someone had drawn, in red ink, an arrow to the photo of the green bird and scribbled a note on its margins: *This is a Parrot, NOT a Conure. If you mean to defile the name of Langhorne Kemper by categorizing him as a pet, at least use the appropriate photo!*

Pushing the door open with one hand and balancing a container of Finnegan's Cakes with the other, she stepped out of the Virginia heat and sun and into the cool, fluorescent-lit space. Once her eyes had adjusted to the light, she was greeted by the same unnamed, dark-haired, equine-faced woman who had occupied Binnie Broderick's table the night prior.

'May I help you?' the woman asked from behind the dark-paneled circulation desk.

'Yes, I'm Tish Tarragon from Cookin' the Books,' she introduced herself. 'I came by to deliver some cakes and offer my condolences to you and the staff.'

'Cakes?' The woman stared down her long, pointed nose. She made no mention of Tish's offer of sympathy.

Her tablemate from the fundraiser emerged from the back office carrying a stack of books. 'She's the caterer, Roberta,' he announced as he gazed at Tish over the top of his half-framed glasses.

'Yes, that's right. Since we didn't get to the dessert course last night, I figured I'd stop by and see what the library wants to do with them. I brought about a dozen with me for you and the staff to enjoy, but there's roughly two hundred and fifty' – recalling that Jules and Mary Jo were still at the café 'brainstorming,' Tish adjusted her estimate – 'er, um, two hundred cakes left in my refrigerator. I'd be happy to distribute them however you wish, since the library did pay for them.'

'Ah, yes,' the woman named Roberta answered

76

knowingly. 'Mrs Broderick didn't pay you, did she? Well, we don't handle that here. If you haven't already, you need to send an invoice to Augusta Wilson, the head of the library board.'

'Um, thanks, but that's not really why I'm here.'

In the meantime, Roberta's coworker had set his stack of books on the desk and relieved Tish of her Tupperware container. 'Daryl Dufour,' the diminutive, bespectacled man introduced himself with an almost elfin-like smile. 'Unlike Roberta, I'm not one to look a gift cake in the mouth. Come, we'll bring these to the break room.'

Daryl called to a silver-haired female volunteer dressed in a resplendent aqua caftan with magenta-and-green floral embroidery. 'Veronica, dear? Would you place those books back into circulation, please? Thank you.'

As Veronica struggled to extricate herself from her chair at the inquiry desk, Tish followed Daryl to the break room. It was, as expected, a utilitarian space comprised of white-wash cinder block and fluorescent lighting, and furnished with a small table, two chairs, a microwave, miniature refrigerator and a sink.

'Now then,' Daryl declared as he opened the Tupperware container, grabbed a cake, peeled back the liner with his fingers, and sank his teeth into the delectable confection.

'Pretty good, huh?' Tish asked with proud grin.

'Good? Magnificent. Miss Celestine has certainly outdone herself this time.' He licked dollops of the unctuous Irish cream frosting from his fingers with a lip-smacking fervor typically displayed only by young children and the starving. 'I'm glad she's found a new home for her baking at your café. She was in a terrible state after Cynthia Thompson died. Simply terrible.'

'Yes, Celestine told me that she and Cynthia were quite close.'

'Like sisters. When Cynthia passed, Celestine completely lost her spark. She gave up baking altogether. Schuyler offered to keep the bakery running with Celestine in charge, but she just couldn't bring herself to accept the offer. She didn't go out much, started to put on weight – I'm not telling you that as a criticism, by the way, just an illustration of how distraught poor Celestine was at the time. God knows, we could all afford to lose a few.' Daryl Dufour patted his slightly rounded belly. 'Only recently did Celestine start re-offering her specialty cakes for local functions. That's why it's a good thing you came along when you did. Now we can all enjoy Celestine's baked goods again, and Celestine can try to pick up where she left off.'

The portrait of Celestine Rufus drawn by Daryl Dufour was at odds with the hearty, good-natured image Celestine herself projected. Which version of Celestine was the 'real' one? And how, and from whom, did Dufour gain his information?

'You and Celestine must be good friends,' Tish ventured.

Daryl Dufour swallowed a bite of cake and frowned. 'Um, yes, well, not anymore. We go way back, though. Grew up together. Attended the same school. We drifted apart after I graduated from high school. I went off to college; she married Lloyd Rufus and started a family. But we still talk from time to time. She brings her grandchildren to the children's functions here at the library. She's a fine lady. Extremely fine.'

'Yes, I haven't known her very long, but I already hold Celestine in high regard. I'm very happy to have her on board at the café. I just hope my business survives the fallout of Binnie Broderick's death long enough to help her get her baking career back on track.'

'Don't worry. Your business will be fine,' Dufour assured. 'Not only do these situations draw the curiosity seekers out in droves, but, in my estimation, whoever fed Binnie that arsenic should receive a medal and a letter of commendation from the Governor of Virginia. Hell, for all we know, the governor might have killed her himself just to guarantee re-election.'

'I know Mrs Broderick wasn't liked by some folks, but was she really as unpopular as that?' Tish gasped.

'You haven't been in town very long, have you, Miss Tarragon?' Dufour observed before popping the last morsel of cake into his mouth and tossing the cake liner in a nearby trash can.

'A little less than a month.'

'Hmph,' Dufour grunted. 'Then you have no idea the ordeal Binnie Broderick has put this library – nay, this entire town – through these past several months.'

'I did hear something about a book-purging controversy,' Tish acknowledged. 'However, given the turnout at last night's event, I assumed that overall Mrs Broderick was quite well revered.'

'Revered? More like feared. Binnie Broderick was born a Darlington – one of Virginia's oldest and wealthiest families. They fought in the Revolution in favor of independence and again in the War Between the States in favor of slavery. When Binnie married Ashton Broderick, her financial assets nearly tripled. She had wealth, power, and influence and wielded them over everyone in order to get what she wanted.'

'If she had all that, then why become a library director?' Tish challenged. 'What could Mrs Broderick possibly have gained from such a position, other than the satisfaction of performing a vital public service to the community?'

'Public service? Ha,' Dufour scoffed. 'I assure you, whether it was to exert more influence over the community, to censor the reading habits of her neighbors, or just to swan about at the annual library fundraiser, Binnie Broderick took the directorial position for less than benevolent reasons. Why, her very first act as director was to roll back Roberta's and my responsibilities. Binnie took over acquisitions, circulations, and children's programming, which she cut down to the bone, even eliminating our extremely popular summer story hour.'

'Didn't the board object?'

Dufour shook his head. 'Knowing her board members were focused on the bottom line as much as she was, Binnie described her actions as austerity measures.'

'What about you and Roberta? Did you file a grievance with the board?'

'We did. But, of course, our complaints were put down to sour grapes since we had both been relegated, by Binnie, to the position of clerks. However, the president of the board, Augusta May Wilson, listened to our case and sided with us. She was uneasy about Binnie having so much control over library resources and warned the board about the dangers of allowing a director to rule unchecked. When the whole "Bookgate" scandal broke, Augusta May essentially went to the press and said, "I told them this would happen."'

'What did the board do?'

'Ah, that's the nice thing about being a member of not one but two influential Virginia families. The majority of the library board members owed their livelihoods or reputations to either the Darlingtons or the Brodericks, or both. None of them were going to compromise decades of prosperity and goodwill over a few missing books, even if those few missing books totaled in the hundreds. They'd simply cut a bigger check at this year's benefit and hope that all would soon be forgotten.'

'Seeing as Mrs Broderick is now dead – murdered – I think it's safe to assume that the board members were overly optimistic,' Tish noted. 'This isn't about to fade away. At least not any time soon.'

'Well, I know Augusta May wasn't willing to

forget or forgive. She wanted Binnie gone from the library and charges brought against her. But I honestly don't see Augusta murdering anyone. She's far too principled for that sort of thing. The mayor, however, is an interesting character. I saw him having a very heated discussion with Binnie just before dinner was served.'

'And you?' Tish stared blankly at Daryl Dufour. 'How about you? Were you more forgiving than Augusta? Or did you, perhaps like the mayor and other people in town, hold a grudge against Mrs Broderick?'

'Forgive a woman who destroyed a library? Never. Do you know she even got rid of works by our local authors? Marjorie Morningstar, the romance writer – have you ever heard of her?'

'I think so. They've made some of her books into movies for that women's channel, haven't they?'

'That's the lady,' Dufour confirmed. 'Ms Morningstar was raised here in Hobson Glen. Owns a little cottage just outside town. Well, Binnie Broderick purged each and every Marjorie Morningstar book from our shelves. You can just imagine the outcry. Our readers were horrified and Ms Morningstar was none too pleased, either. Her agent called immediately and threatened our library with a lawsuit if we didn't make those books available again. Oh, the embarrassment! Oh, the shame!'

'What reason did Mrs Broderick give for removing Ms Morningstar's books in the first place?' Tish asked.

'That they were far too salacious to be

considered culturally relevant to the town.' Dufour clicked his tongue. 'As if she had any credentials whatsoever to judge creative content. Oh, how I despised that woman.' Dufour must have realized how his comment might sound to Tish, for he immediately qualified the statement. 'Not that I disliked Binnie enough to kill her, of course.'

'The thought never occurred to me.' Tish feigned nonchalance. 'Although you *were* seated at Mrs Broderick's table. It would have been easy for you to lean across the table to make conversation and secretly add the arsenic to her food.'

'Yes,' Dufour chuckled, 'that would have been clever. But I assure you it didn't happen. No, no, no . . . whoever poisoned Binnie Broderick was sly, cunning, and calculating. Someone with a true axe to grind. Someone like Roberta Dutton.'

'Roberta? You mean the woman out there at the front desk?'

Dufour nodded. 'Don't let her icy demeanor fool you. As my mother used to say, still waters run deep. Roberta used underhand tactics to become the senior librarian on staff here. She was in the running for the director's position until Binnie Broderick snatched the job. Roberta hated Binnie, a non-librarian, for taking over the directorship and then proceeding to treat us like office staff. Also, and you didn't hear it from me' – Dufour's voice lowered – 'I saw John Ballantyne, Binnie's son-in-law, slip something into Roberta's hand the night of the fundraiser.

A love note, maybe? A hotel room key? An arsenic tablet to put in Binnie's drink? Oh! What if, by killing Binnie Broderick, Roberta not only got the director's job, but ensured her boyfriend gained a sizeable inheritance? Wouldn't that be deliciously convenient?'

'It would, but once again, why? From what I hear, Augusta May Wilson got the mayor involved in the book-purging situation, meaning that Binnie was probably on her way out of the director's chair and Roberta might have been on the way in. Why would Roberta do anything to jeopardize that?'

'Apparently, you didn't hear,' Dufour surmised.

'Hear what?'

'It was all over the news yesterday.'

'I was at the lodge cooking all day yesterday so I didn't see the news. What did I miss? Tell me,' Tish urged.

'Well, it appears that Mayor Whitley did get involved in our little book controversy. He initiated a so-called fact-finding commission to investigate the case.'

'And?'

'Well, that's the hot topic of conversation, isn't it? After receiving the commission's report, our illustrious mayor absolved Binnie Broderick of any and all wrongdoing.' Dufour sneered. 'So it would seem that our dear Roberta's motive just got stronger, didn't it?'

Nine

Her conversation with Daryl Dufour having produced more questions than answers, Tish bid the librarian adieu and prepared to leave the library and drive to Augusta May Wilson's home under the pretense of delivering more Finnegan's Cakes.

No sooner had the break-room door shut behind her than she ran headlong into Roberta Dutton.

'On your way out, Miss Tarragon? I presume Mr Dufour was helpful to you,' Roberta inquired.

'Yes, quite helpful. He put the cakes in the refrigerator for you and the staff to enjoy and I'm going to stop by Mrs Wilson's to see what she wants to do with the remainder.'

Roberta Dutton was, quite clearly, not at all concerned about the longevity of Celestine's cakes. 'I'm sure Mr Dufour also gave you an earful of lies.'

The comment caught Tish completely off guard. 'I beg your pardon?'

'Lies. About the relationship between me and, now that she's been murdered, Binnie Broderick.'

'No, I don't recall him mentioning you at all,' Tish feigned ignorance.

Roberta's brown eyes seared a hole through Tish. 'I find that hard to believe, knowing—' She glanced over her shoulder and, seeing

Veronica, the caftan-wearing volunteer, watching, pushed Tish back into the break room and shut the door behind them.

'Knowing how much Daryl Dufour despises me,' Roberta completed the thought.

'I don't understand. Why should Mr Dufour despise you?'

'Because I don't play along with his games. Daryl thinks himself quite the charmer. You heard him out there with Veronica. Always with the "dear" and "honey." That never flew with me and I let him know it.'

Tish shrugged. 'So, you let him know you were uncomfortable with that sort of talk. That's no cause to hate someone.'

'Well, I didn't exactly tell him. I had only just started working here and wasn't sure how he would react, so I went to our previous library director and complained to him. Daryl was officially reprimanded. Though, as you can see, it didn't do much good.'

Tish recalled Daryl having described Roberta as sly, cold, and calculating. Was this why? 'Pardon me for asking, but if you started working here after Daryl Dufour did, how did you wind up being senior librarian?'

'Experience. I worked in the Charlottesville library system for twenty years before moving to Hobson Glen. Daryl Dufour may have ten years on me, but he hasn't put in the miles I have. The Charlottesville library collection is far more extensive and its audience more broad and diverse than Hobson Glen's, thereby providing me with a far greater depth and breadth of experience than Daryl could ever have achieved during his lengthy tenure here. Of course, if you ask Daryl, he'll say my sexual harassment complaint harmed his chances of advancement.'

'Did it?' Tish asked. 'I mean, it's not something the library director or the board should, or could, casually dismiss.'

'How should I know? You'd have to ask Augusta Wilson. All I know is that I was, and still am, eminently more qualified for the position of senior librarian than Daryl Dufour.' She smirked and meandered to the refrigerator. 'Now, where are those cakes? I shouldn't indulge, really, but I'll do some extra cardio this evening to compensate.'

Tish wondered if Roberta's additional cardio routine included John Ballantyne, but she decided to stick to the topic at hand. 'What about Binnie Broderick? Were you more qualified for her position as well?'

'Did you take any English literature classes during college?'

'Yes, quite a few actually.' Tish resisted the temptation to explain that her café was literary-based because she had double-majored in English Literature and Business.

'Then I dare say *you're* more qualified for the director's position than Binnie Broderick was,' Roberta quipped as she sunk her teeth into a Finnegan's Cake. 'Oh my God!'

'Are you OK?'

Roberta nodded as she gobbled two more bites of cake and then tossed it in the trash can with an upturned nose. 'Ick. That's far too sweet! I can't see how anyone can view Celestine as anything other than a purveyor of sugar, butter, and fat. Only Binnie Broderick with her ridiculously bitter tongue could have viewed *that* as palatable.'

'You seem to be in the minority. Those cakes have actually gone down quite well with everyone else who has tasted them,' Tish replied with a pasted-on smile.

'Well, I guess if sweets are your sort of thing,' she dismissed with a wave of a hand. 'I'm sure Daryl raved about it. If only because it was made by Celestine Rufus.'

'What do you mean?'

'Oh, he's sweet on her. Pun fully intended. Has been since they were kids. Honestly, I'm surprised it wasn't old Lloyd Rufus who was bumped off. Rumor has it Daryl's been waiting for the playing field to be clear for years.'

Tish filed away the information about Daryl; their conversation had suggested that his feelings for Celestine were more than just neighborly. 'How about you? Were you surprised by Binnie Broderick's death?'

'Surprised, yes. But not shocked.'

'I don't quite understand.'

'Well, I was surprised to see her die, especially the way she did. Poisoned at our table. It was horrifying, really.' Roberta's dry tone belied her words. 'But I'm not shocked that it happened. Why, just hours before the fundraiser, she had provoked Enid Kemper and got into a heated argument with Augusta Wilson and her husband.'

'Yes, I heard about Enid's bird being banned from the library,' Tish conceded. 'Why did Binnie have it in for her?'

'No idea.' Roberta shrugged. 'Seemed to be an ongoing feud between them. Personally, I couldn't have cared less if Langhorne was in the library. So long as he didn't bother other patrons or poop on the circulation desk, he was more than welcome. Daryl felt the same way. It was one of the few things on which he and I agreed.'

Tish was tempted to remark upon how the maintenance of poop-free circulation desks was a cause probably every librarian could get behind, but given Roberta's distinct lack of humor, she thought better of it. 'And the Wilsons? You said they engaged in an argument with Binnie. Do you know what it was about?'

'Oh, the usual, most likely. Augusta May had been demanding Binnie's resignation for weeks. This was the first time Augusta's husband, Edwin, had accompanied her to such a meeting, though. I'm not sure why he did. Augusta is entirely capable of handling these things on her own. However, I did notice that she didn't look at all well that morning.'

'Perhaps she heard about the mayor's decision to back Binnie?' Tish suggested.

'I haven't a clue. I'm not the sort of woman to listen at keyholes, you know,' Roberta said with a smirk that implied she might, however, be the sort to engage in other equally dubious behavior. 'All I can say with any certainty is that the conversation ended in a shouting match. Binnie declared – at the very top of her lungs, so that the entire library could hear it, no less – that she was going nowhere and that perhaps Augusta May Wilson should be the one to resign. Edwin volleyed by announcing he'd see Binnie in hell first.'

'Wow. What did Augusta say?'

'Nothing. She followed her husband as he stormed out of Binnie's office. She looked even more tired than she had when she first entered the library, although I wouldn't have thought it possible.' Noticing Tish's frown, Roberta added, 'That wasn't a catty remark, by the way, and Lord knows I'm capable of them. That was simply an observation. Typically, Augusta May Wilson is the epitome of confidence and grace.'

'Yes, I noticed that at the fundraiser,' Tish said. 'She was quite elegant.'

'Yes, well, Augusta was back to her usual self at the fundraiser. She was far from it that morning.'

'Tell me, did you take Edwin Wilson's words as a threat?'

'Well, of course I did. Men will do crazy things for the women they love. Not that I would know, of course.' Roberta stared into the distance. After several seconds had passed, she asked, 'Have you ever been married?'

'Yes, but I'm divorced now. And you?'

'I've never been married. Never even came close.'

Tish used the conversation as a springboard to dive into the subject of John Ballantyne. 'And no significant others?'

'None to speak of, no.'

'None *to* speak of or none you *can* speak of?' Tish asked with a sly grin.

'My, you are observant for a caterer, aren't you?' Roberta cleared her throat and awkwardly shifted her weight from one foot to another.

'Not inordinately. I'm simply reacting to what I've heard in town these past two weeks.'

'And what might that be?' the librarian demanded.

'That you and John Ballantyne are . . . close.'

'Me and—? Why, that's preposterous! He's a married man.'

'Married or not, it's rumored that he slipped a message into your hand at the fundraiser last night.'

'And I can guess who started that rumor. Daryl Dufour!'

'Um, well—'

'Tell me no all you like. I know what that weasel is capable of both saying and doing. From online role-playing and gaming to his love of sci-fi and werewolves to his obsession with Celestine Rufus, Mr Dufour leads a very rich fantasy life. A very rich fantasy life, indeed.'

'Um, actually—' Tish attempted to argue, but Roberta shut her down without hesitation.

'Now, if we're finished, I have a valuable, non-catering job to which I need to attend.' With that, Roberta Dutton slammed the door to the break room and headed back to the circulation desk.

Ten

Having created more turmoil than she had wished for, Tish exited the Hobson Glen Library as discreetly as she could – despite Veronica's fervent waves, mouthed goodbyes, and silent 'thank yous' for the cupcakes – and climbed behind the steering wheel of the Matrix. Once there, she locked both the windows and the doors, turned on both the ignition and air conditioning, and leaned back against the headrest, her brain and body both appreciating the silent, familiar comfort of controllable surroundings.

She was cut out to be a cook, a baker, a creator of food, a nurturer of people, and, perhaps, in her past life, a banker, and maybe even a writer, had she been given the opportunity. But being a detective, the person who listened to everyone's tales of woe and then sifted through their words to separate the truth from the lies, was tiring in the extreme.

Tish was drawn from her reverie by the ring of her cell phone. 'Hello?' she asked upon pressing the green 'answer' button and drawing the phone to her ear.

The phone's Bluetooth activated and Jules's voice came booming through the Matrix's stereo speakers. 'Tish? Thank God you answered.'

Startled and inundated by sound, Tish flung her head against the headrest before lowering the car radio volume and replying. 'Jules, are you OK?'

'Oh, I'm fine. Positively peachy. But I desperately need your recipe for cornmeal rosemary madeleines.'

'Sure, I'll write it down for you when I get back.' Tish smiled as she once again relaxed and leaned back against the headrest.

'No, no, no. You don't understand. I need it now.'

The sense of urgency in Jules's voice caused Tish alarm. 'Why do you need it now?'

'Because we're nearly out of cupcakes,' came Julian Jefferson Davis's breathless reply.

Tish leaned in toward the radio, as if questioning Jules face to face. 'Out of cupcakes? I left you with just under two hundred of them. I know you're a stress-eater, Jules, but seriously—'

'I didn't eat them,' Jules practically shrieked. 'At least not *all* of them. We simply need a savory alternative to all that sugar.'

'How about I make us a nice salad for supper when I get back?' Tish suggested. 'It's far healthier than all that buttery pastry.'

'Good Lord,' an exasperated Jules sighed. 'All I asked for was the madeleine recipe. Could you just tell me where I might find it? I've searched the French shelf at the café and couldn't locate it anywhere.'

'That's because it's in my head,' a confused Tish answered. 'I rarely ever write down recipes.'

'Well, a hell of a lot of good that does me right now. I guess I'm just going to have to wing it,' Jules exclaimed before hanging up the phone.

Tish exhaled and leaned back against the headrest again. She trusted Jules's and Mary Jo's judgment implicitly, yet part of her felt slightly uneasy about what might be happening back at her café.

Deeming it prudent to move on to the next visit so that she could return home as swiftly as possible, Tish sat upright, positioned her seat for driving, and, after checking in the visor mirror to ensure that her brownish black mascara hadn't smudged during her brief respite, shifted the Matrix into drive.

Upon arriving at the Wilsons' house, Tish felt foolish for even moving the car out of the library parking lot, for the three-story, gingerbread-trimmed Victorian was located high upon a hill in the center of town, just a few blocks' walk away from the library. Shrugging off her stupidity, Tish pulled the Matrix into a curbside parking spot, fed three quarters into the adjacent meter, and hiked up the flight of concrete steps that led to the cluster of late-nineteenth-century homes known locally as Hobson Glen's 'Grand Dames.'

Number seventy-two, the Wilsons' home, was a yellow clapboard edifice with dark green shutters, and gingerbead trim. Tish approached the house to find Edwin and Augusta May reposed upon the sprawling wraparound porch. Edwin, looking fresh from the golf course in a navy-blue polo shirt and plaid Bermuda shorts, swayed to and fro on a chain-suspended porch swing, his brown legs stretched out before him. Augusta, her face scrubbed clean and her shoulder-length curly hair pulled back with a white headband, reclined upon a whitewashed wicker chaise lounge, a floral-printed cushion tucked behind her head, and, despite the late-summer heat and humidity, a crocheted cotton throw draped over her legs.

At the sight of the caterer, Augusta waved an arm in welcome. 'Good afternoon, Ms Tarragon,' the library board president greeted when Tish had drawn closer. Edwin, meanwhile, left his spot on the porch swing to drag a straight-backed wicker chair from a hidden section of the wraparound porch and place it beside Augusta's chaise.

'Good afternoon,' Tish replied.

Dressed in a plain white cotton T-shirt and khaki-colored Capri pants, Augusta's appearance was far less glamorous than it had been on the previous evening. But there was more to Augusta's altered appearance than simply a pared-down wardrobe. There was, in the lines on her face and in her mannerisms, a sense of battle fatigue. 'Edwin,' she ordered her husband, 'go get my handbag from the foyer table. Ms Tarragon's check is in there.'

'Oh, there's no rush for that. I just came by to drop off some cakes.' Tish held the plastic container of confections aloft. 'To be quite frank, I'd completely forgotten that I hadn't been paid.'

'Well, I don't want you to think that we didn't appreciate your services.' Augusta asked Edwin to take the cakes to someone named Brenda and then reminded him to grab her bag on the way back. 'I assure you, I had every intention of paying you at the end of the event, Ms Tarragon, but then . . .'

'Yes, things got rather strange, rather quickly. I'm sorry about Mrs Broderick. This whole thing must have come as quite a shock.'

Edwin had returned, bearing an oversized black leather satchel which he handed to his wife. Augusta reached into the bag, extracted a windowed envelope, and passed it to Tish.

'Thank you,' Tish murmured as Augusta waved her into the seat beside her.

'It was a shock, yes. It still is in many respects, but it wasn't really a surprise.'

Tish was startled to hear Augusta May Wilson utter the same sentiment as Roberta Dutton. 'Not a surprise?'

'When a person's spent their entire life treating people the way Lavinia Broderick did, it's not surprising someone finally said enough is enough,' Edwin asserted. His sentiment echoed that of Celestine Rufus.

'Not that either of us condone murder, of course,' Augusta was quick to clarify.

'Of course not. But Lavinia could push even the sanest soul to the edge,' Edwin said with a stern glance at his wife.

'It sounds as if you both knew her for a long time,' Tish noted.

'I didn't, but Augusta did,' Edwin stated.

'Since she and I were both children,' Augusta explained.

'Oh, so you grew up together?'

'Grew up together? Oh, no. That wasn't possible back then. But I always knew who

Lavinia was. Hobson Glen was smaller than it is now, so everyone knew everyone else. But Binnie and I lived in different worlds. I went to public schools, she went to prep schools. I got my first job at age sixteen while Binnie was planning her debutante ball. I went to UVA; she went to Smith. Every now and then our paths would cross. On the playground and at local fairs when we were younger, and, in more recent years, board rooms, town hall meetings, and the occasional courtroom. Typically on opposing sides,' she added with a weak smile.

'Yes, I've heard about the great library debate,' Tish admitted.

'Oh, there's no debate about it,' Edwin said angrily. 'Or at least there shouldn't have been a debate. Lavinia Broderick made a huge mistake and she should have lost her job for it.'

'So why didn't she? Everyone I've spoken to seems to agree that she was guilty of misconduct.'

'Have you ever heard the phrase "it's not what you know, it's who you know"?' Augusta asked.

'Of course.' Tish nodded.

'If that phrase isn't scrawled in Latin across the Broderick coat of arms, then it should be etched on Binnie's tombstone. The woman had the entire board in the palm of her hand. That's how she got the position in the first place. You'd think the woman appointed as director of a library would have had, at the very least, some experience working for a non-profit, never mind running one.'

97

'I'm not sure Lavinia even understood what the term non-profit meant,' Edwin scoffed.

'What do you mean when you say Binnie had the board in her hand?' Tish felt it important to corroborate the accounts of the librarians.

'Before she became a Broderick, Binnie was a Darlington,' Augusta explained. 'Everyone who's anyone can trace their wealth and/or reputation back to the Darlingtons, a fact which Eugenia Darlington, Binnie's mother, reminded her daughter, and everyone else in town, of regularly. Eugenia raised Binnie to be lady of the manor, didn't she, Brenda?' Augusta asked the dark-skinned, apron-clad housekeeper who had emerged from the house to serve iced tea and a tray of Finnegan's Cakes. 'Brenda worked for Binnie for five years before she came to me.'

'Yes, ma'am,' Brenda agreed with a melodic Southern accent more Georgian or Carolinian in origin than Virginian. 'I'm not one to speak ill of the dead, but Mrs Broderick was a cold, cold woman. Thought she was better than everyone, even her own husband. Time and time again he asked her to move out of that old house of hers and into a new home near Washington so that Mr Broderick could be closer to work, but the answer was always no. She was a Darlington, she'd say. Darlingtons had lived at Wisteria Knolls for centuries and she wasn't going to give that up for some McMansion surrounded by heathens and Yankees.' Brenda took a break from serving to look at Tish, 'Sorry about the Yankee thing, Ms Tarragon. That was Mrs Broderick's choice of words, not mine.'

In the twenty plus years she had lived in the Commonwealth of Virginia, Tish, a native of upstate New York, had been called a 'Yankee' only once: when Jules opened the door of Tish's refrigerator to find a jar of Hellman's mayonnaise instead of the obligatory Duke's.

'That's OK.' Tish smiled and sipped her tea. 'No offense taken.'

Brenda went back to both her serving duties and her gossip. 'Mr Broderick wound up taking an apartment in Washington for during the week and driving home to Wisteria Knolls on the weekends. Of course, when he was home, there was no relaxing. Mrs Broderick scheduled the two of them to attend every party and event in the county. Drove him crazy, the schedule he was on. Sure it's what caused the heart attack that killed him, too. Why, just look what all that woman's nonsense has done to you, Mrs Wilson, and you're in far better shape than Mr Broderick was.'

Tish declined the deposit of what would have been her third Finnegan's Cake of the day on to her plate. 'Oh, I'm so sorry to have inconvenienced you, Mrs Wilson. I didn't realize you were ill.'

'I'm not ill. Brenda is overstating the matter,' Augusta maintained with a heavy sigh.

'You're not exactly well, either, honey,' Edwin argued as he removed his eyeglasses from the bridge of his nose and cleaned them with a handkerchief he had pulled from the pocket of his plaid shorts. 'It's not as if we spent the night before last at Bon Secours St Mary's emergency room because of an ingrown toenail.'

'The hospital? Oh my goodness,' Tish exclaimed. 'Are you all right?'

'I'm fine.' Augusta sighed once again.

'You're not fine,' Edwin piped up and placed the glasses back on to his head. 'I thought you were having a heart attack.'

'I wasn't. It was simply stress and anxiety.'

'And chest pains. Chest pains brought on by *that* woman.' Edwin accepted his cup of tea and immediately took a sip.

'Yes, but I'm fine now. A little tired, but much better than I was. In fact, I'm certain I'll make a full recovery.'

'Now that *she's* gone, I'm sure you will too,' Edwin chuckled.

Augusta shot her husband a warning glance. Brenda, having served the refreshments and possibly sensing that she had caused a disagreement between her employers, quietly left the porch and returned indoors.

'Well, I'm glad you're feeling better and that the prognosis for your recovery is good,' Tish stated. 'With Binnie gone, the library will need your leadership now more than ever.'

'Thank you, Ms Tarragon. That's a very kind thing for you to say,' Augusta said as she launched a fork into her cake. 'Mmm . . . delicious. However, with Roberta Dutton and Darryl Dufour at the reins, the library is probably safer now than it's been in years.'

'Sounds as if you can rest easy now.'

'Easi*er*, yes,' Augusta corrected. 'We'll need to replace what was lost, and then there's the matter of selecting Binnie's replacement, but we'll get there. In the meantime, at least we won't be losing any more books. My husband and I used to work for the county school system. I know how much the children of Hobson Glen and its neighboring communities rely upon the library to supplement their education. As an educator, I also know that allowing one person to have the power to decide what is fit to be read and what is not is just one step away from censorship.'

'With your background in education, it's no wonder this situation affected you the way it did.' Tish took a sip of tea and then shook her head in disbelief. 'It's a shame the other board members didn't back you. At least, from what I've heard, the mayor was about to step in on your behalf.'

'"Was" being the operative word,' Edwin interjected. And then, aside, 'Please tell Celestine that she has, once again, outdone herself.'

'I will,' Tish promised, distractedly. 'But, um what about the mayor? What happened?'

'Two days ago, I received a phone call from Mayor Whitley explaining that he was preparing to hold a press conference the next day,' Augusta detailed. 'During that press conference, he was to announce that an independent investigation commissioned by his office had cleared Lavinia Broderick of any wrongdoing. She was to continue her role as director without any censure whatsoever.'

'But how? I mean, even if the book purge was, indeed, an accident – and I can't see how it could have been – Binnie Broderick should have been punished in some way, be it suspension, public service, or, at the very least, monetary reparations.'

It was Augusta's turn to shake her head. 'Mayor Whitley didn't even require Binnie to apologize.'

'Wouldn't have made a difference if he had,' Edwin remarked. 'The woman was completely unrepentant.'

'All the more reason to wonder why the mayor would make such an abrupt about-face,' Tish observed.

'Well, whatever his reason, Mayor Whitley has a lot to answer for. He's gonna hear it from me too. I was going to tell him last night at the fundraiser, but then all hell broke loose.'

'Edwin,' Augusta chided.

'I don't care, Augusta. You were already tightly wound, but Whitley's announcement pushed you over the edge,' Edwin grumbled. 'As soon as you hung up the phone with the man, you went pale and started experiencing chest pains.'

'Oh, you're being dramatic. It wasn't quite that instantaneous,' Augusta dismissed.

'Close enough to lay the blame at his doorstep,' Edwin argued. 'Although we both know who was responsible for the start of your issues.'

'Did you ever tell Binnie about your health problems?' Tish asked Augusta. 'I know she wasn't what you might describe as a kindly woman, but if she knew that her behavior had put your life in jeopardy—'

'She didn't care,' Edwin interrupted. 'We went to see her at the library the morning after our trip to the hospital. The morning of the fundraiser.'

'Despite my warning against it,' Augusta inserted.

'Lavinia needed to be put on notice. She needed to understand what she had done to you and that it would not be tolerated. She needed to know that we wouldn't rest until she had resigned.'

'For all the good it did.'

'Binnie wasn't in the slightest bit sympathetic?' Tish asked, although knowing what she knew about Cynthia Thompson, she realized she should hardly be surprised by such callousness.

'On the contrary, she seemed pleased. Quite pleased,' Augusta replied.

'When we—' Edwin started.

'When *you*,' Augusta amended.

'When I told Lavinia that she should resign from her position as executive director, she actually had the audacity to suggest that it was Augusta who should resign. Can you believe that? The nerve of that woman.'

'Resign? On what grounds?' Tish challenged.

'That's what I said.' Edwin sat back in his chair and took a big bite of cake, clearly satisfied that at least one of the women on the porch had finally agreed with him.

'Did Binnie provide an answer?'

'Yeah, some nonsense about Augusta being morally compromised.'

'Compromised?'

'God only knows what was going through Binnie's head,' Augusta said as she lowered her plate and teacup on to the bamboo coffee table

103

with a clatter. 'She was obviously trying to deflect from her own misdoings.'

'Yes, of course she was, my dear.' Edwin rose from his seat and, kneeling beside his wife, stroked the back of her neck. 'There's no reason to fret. No one in their right mind could ever accuse you of wrongdoing.'

'Unless Binnie poisoned the board against me.' Augusta's voice grew shrill. 'Binnie might be gone but my board is still here. What if she stirred up trouble with them?'

'I'm sure she didn't,' Edwin assured. 'And even if she had, who cares? I'll always be here.'

Tish, wanting to give the couple privacy, rose from her seat to excuse herself. Before Tish could utter a word, Augusta brought her hand to her head as if struck by a sudden pain.

'Augusta! Are you all right?' Edwin cried.

'Yes, I–I–I just wish I shared your confidence, Edwin,' Augusta murmured, 'that everything is going to be all right.'

'It is, honey. I promise. Now that Lavinia Broderick is gone, all our troubles are over.'

As Edwin embraced his crying wife, Tish quietly took her leave, her mind awhirl with suspicion.

Eleven

Cursing her sartorial choices for the afternoon, Tish attempted to descend the concrete steps that led back to Main Street as quickly and quietly as possible – an endeavor thwarted by the confines of her long dress and the inflexibility of her strappy, hard-soled sandals. Exasperated by her slow pace, Tish hiked the hem of her dress above her knees, slipped out of her shoes and shoved them into her handbag, opting to make the final dash to her car barefoot.

Tish needn't have hurried. As she climbed behind the wheel of her car and placed her sandals back on to her feet, she saw that Main Street was a transportation nightmare. Straight ahead, in the middle of the road, the local police were tending to a traffic accident. The passenger door and front panel of the first car bore an expansive dent, while the front fender of the second car was hanging on by a thread. The drivers of each car looked to be unharmed and were providing their statements to a uniformed policeman, but the incident blocked road traffic in both directions.

Without hesitation, Tish started the engine of the Matrix, shifted the transmission into reverse, pulled away from the curb, and made a U-turn. Retracing her route, she continued past the library and on toward the west end of town, where she made a right turn. From there, Tish drove for several hundred yards before reaching the dirt-lined lane that led to Celestine's house. This time, instead of turning on to the dirt pathway, she continued along the asphalt-paved road that skirted along the northern edge of town and re-intersected Main Street diagonally across the street from Cookin' the Books.

Established centuries before the advent of

motorized vehicles, the bypass provided carriages and mail delivery riders with an express route around the congestion of Hobson Glen and its inevitable tangle of pedestrians, carts, and farm equipment. The bypass also ran through Hobson Glen's oldest and most scenic neighborhoods – the neighborhood that, not surprisingly, Lavinia Broderick called home.

As was the wont of summer afternoons in the south, the brilliant sunshine and blue skies that graced the early part of the day had been replaced by strong gusts of wind and an ominously dark cover of clouds. Forsaking the air conditioner in favor of fresh air, Tish rolled down the driver's side window to take in the cooling breeze.

Just as she perched her left elbow upon the window ledge, a flash of lightning, followed almost immediately by a violent crack of thunder, illuminated the sinister-looking sky and sent a tree of starlings scattering into the wind.

The hairs on Tish's arm stood on end, not so much because of the sudden atmospheric disturbance but because of the disturbing view through her front windshield. An elderly woman dressed in a cardigan sweater and a housecoat was sneaking out of the back door of a well-maintained and rather expansive colonial farmhouse, clutching some unidentifiable object close to her chest. As lightning flashed again, she glanced over each shoulder surreptitiously, looked up nervously at Tish's approaching car, and hastened into the woods behind the house.

Seeing no cars behind her, Tish put her foot on the brake and stopped in front of the farmhouse driveway. The sign above the gate read Wisteria Knolls.

And Tish easily recognized the woman in question as Enid Kemper.

'What? You saw Enid out wandering around in a storm again?' Mary Jo exclaimed from her spot on the café's front-porch swing. Heavy rain had begun to fall, but beneath the shelter of the porch roof she, Jules, and Tish remained cool and dry.

'Not just wandering. Lurking. I could see her quite clearly. The lightning illuminated her face and body,' Tish explained.

'Sounds like a Boris Karloff film.' Jules shuddered and leaned against one of the porch columns.

'What do you mean she was lurking?' Mary Jo asked.

'I don't know.' Tish shrugged and sat beside her. 'Just lurking. There were no cars in the driveway and, despite how dark it had gotten, there were no lights on inside Wisteria Knolls. And Enid looked suspicious. She was carrying something – God only knows what – and when she saw me, she took off into the woods.'

'By all accounts, Enid Kemper's always been a strange one,' Jules stated.

'Yeah, that's what I've been told. But why would she be in Binnie's house? There's no reason for it.'

'You'd better tell Sheriff Reade,' Mary Jo directed.

Tish nodded. 'I'll give him a call in a bit.'

'Are you going to tell him all about your snooping?' Jules smirked.

'Snooping?' Tish was indignant. 'I'm not snooping. I'm just doing the public relations stuff you and Mary Jo recommended. I can't help it if people talk to me.'

'Of course you can't.' Jules pretended to examine a perfectly manicured hand. 'Especially if they just happen to talk to you after you feed them cake. Delicious, yummy, boozy-iced cake.'

'Delicious, yummy, boozy-iced cake which, given your phone call, I can only surmise I no longer have.' Tish folded her arms across her chest.

'That's because you now have five hundred dollars. In cash.'

'Five hundred—' She leaned forward in her seat eagerly. 'What? Wait, how?'

'I took Celestine's cakes and several carafes of coffee—'

'And a large thermos of my Arnold Palmers,' Mary Jo added.

'Down to the police station where my news team was hanging out,' Jules finished. 'Turns out other reporters were there too. We sold every cake—'

'And all of my Arnold Palmers.'

'And all the coffee in less than three hours.' Jules squealed with glee. 'Everyone loved it!'

'That's . . . that's amazing!' Tish exclaimed.

'I know! Well, except that we have to do the same thing tomorrow. I was thinking something savory this time. You know, shake things up a bit.' Jules emphasized the concept with a shimmy of his shoulders.

'So that's why you wanted the madeleine

recipe,' Tish deduced. 'How many do you need? And when do you need them by?'

'Same as the cakes. Say, two hundred and fifty or so. By tomorrow morning.'

Tish nearly choked on her reply. 'Two hun— by tomorrow morning? I'm not even sure I have the ingredients, let alone the time.'

'Oh yes, you do!' Grinning like a demented Christmas elf, Jules opened the door of the café and led Tish inside. There, in front of the refrigerator case, stood a pallet bearing three fifty-pound bags of flour, two twenty-five-pound bags of cornmeal, three potted rosemary shrubs, three thirteen-pound bags each of baking soda and baking powder, one twenty-pound bag of sugar, and a five-pound bag of Kosher salt. 'There's a few dozen eggs and several pounds of butter in the fridge too. I didn't know how much to buy of everything so I just estimated. I figured you'd eventually use it all anyway.'

Tish took several moments to process the scene before her. 'Well . . . good thing we had the five hundred dollars in sales.'

'Five hundred dollars?' Jules laughed. 'Oh, no, honey, this came to *way* more than that.'

Gulp. 'Then how did you pay for it?'

'Your company credit card. I found it lying in the till and didn't want to bother you with another phone call, so I put it to good use.'

Tish tried to reply, but all she could muster was a whimper.

'Oh, don't worry, honey. Another day like today and we'll make that up in no time,' Jules reassured.

'That's right. And it's not like you're on your own – we're both sticking around to help you bake,' Mary Jo announced with the same look of unadulterated glee that Jules bore.

'Thanks. Really. But I'm not sure . . .' Tish attempted to argue.

'Sure that you'll use everything before it expires?' Mary Jo guessed.

Tish nodded.

'Don't be silly! Of course you will. Especially with all the publicity I put together for you today.'

'Publicity?'

'Yes, I have a press release ready for you to review. If I get to the news editors by the end of the day, it will appear in tomorrow's Sunday online edition.' Mary Jo handed Tish a piece of printer paper bearing three short paragraphs and retained a copy for herself. 'The first paragraph essentially states how sorry you feel about the death of Mrs Broderick, that you send condolences to her family and loved ones, and that, although you're confident that no one affiliated with Cookin' the Books had anything to do with the crime, you're cooperating with the ongoing police investigation.'

'Um, yeah, that part about being confident that no one affiliated with the café committed the crime?' Tish pulled a face. 'We may need to strike that.'

'Why?'

'Celestine's visit didn't quite go as planned.'

'Are you back on the Baking Granny murder theory again?' Jules laughed.

'No, I'm not saying Celestine's guilty, but I can't rule her out.' Tish went on to describe their

110

conversation with special emphasis on Celestine's ambiguous last statement.

'Good Lord,' Jules called out. 'What if she is a murderer? I just sold her cakes to every news reporter, photo journalist, and camera person in central Virginia.'

'How was I to know you were going to spend the afternoon pimping baked goods to your co-workers?'

'Calm down, you two,' Mary Jo urged. 'I doubt Celestine poisoned three hundred cupcakes just to murder one woman, but you're right, Tish; we'll get rid of that bit.' She took a black pen and struck the line from her own copy of the press release. 'The second paragraph announces your official grand opening in three weeks.'

'Three weeks?' Tish questioned.

'Yes. I figured that gives you enough time to plan the menu and order supplies, and gives me a chance to promote the event while not losing any momentum from the murder.'

'What do you mean, "momentum"?'

'Well, people are morbid, aren't they? I'm sure we'll have lots of people stopping by just to see who catered Binnie Broderick's last meal. We need to take advantage of that traffic.'

Tish frowned. 'I'd rather appeal to those who want to enjoy a high-quality lunch, snack, or afternoon tea.'

'If you scan down in the press release, you'll see that I've addressed that.'

'*Offering bookish breakfasts, literary-themed lunches, and killer cookies and cakes inspired by your favorite fictional characters . . .*' Tish read aloud before coming to an abrupt halt. '"Killer" cookies?'

'Oh! Oh, yes, you're right. Sorry.' Mary Jo scratched out yet another line of copy. 'How about crunchy? Chewy? Consumable?'

'Criminally good?' Jules happily offered.

Mary Jo let the joke roll off her shoulders. 'I'll come up with something. So, under the announcement of the grand opening, I've added a statement about your Grandparents Day tea party at Misty Acres. The event is open to residents of the home and their family members and runs from noon until three o'clock. You'll provide sandwiches, tea, soft drinks, and cakes.'

'What a sweet idea,' Tish said approvingly. 'I love it!'

'There's more. I've arranged for some light entertainment during the afternoon. A musician friend of mine has offered to play some old standards on the piano, the variety store here in town has donated some prizes for a raffle, and our own Julian Jefferson Davis will be on hand for tarot readings.'

'Everything sounds great, except for, um, well, perhaps, the tarot readings.'

'What's wrong with tarot readings?'

'For starters, Jules has a difficult enough time predicting the weather.'

'Helloooo,' Jules sang out. 'Irony! That's what makes it so brilliant.'

'But fortune telling? For elderly people? In a nursing home?'

Jules folded his arms across his chest. 'OK, first off, the residents and staff prefer the term "retirement facility." And, second, I plan on removing the death card from the deck before I even get there, so I don't see the problem.'

Tish drew a hand to her forehead and struggled to find her next words. Although she knew Jules and Mary Jo meant well, it was not uncommon for their enthusiasm to get in the way of common sense. Thankfully, a knock upon on the frame of the café screen door rescued her from any further discussion.

Tish wandered from behind the counter to find Edwin Wilson standing on the front porch, an umbrella in one hand and the empty Finnegan's Cake container in the other. 'You left this at the house and Augusta wasn't sure if you needed it back right away.'

Tish opened the door to allow Edwin admittance, but he refused. 'Nah, I've gotta get going. I have to pick up some things at the store before Brenda makes supper.'

'Oh, well, I appreciate you dropping this off.' She accepted the container from Edwin and placed it on an adjacent table. 'I'm sorry I left without saying goodbye, but I felt you and Augusta needed some privacy. I think I'd imposed upon you for quite long enough.'

Edwin shook his head. 'Don't be silly. It's Augusta and me who should apologize. We shouldn't have gotten into things the way we did. I thought she'd be feeling better by now, what with . . .' Edwin's voice trailed off. 'But Augusta's as stressed as ever, worrying that the board will follow through with Lavinia's final wish to fire her.'

'Lavinia's death is still fresh. Augusta, like the

113

rest of us, hasn't been able to process it yet. Give her some time. I'm sure she'll settle down.'

'I sure hope so.' Edwin bit his bottom lip and looked down at the porch floorboards. 'Augusta and I have been married over thirty years. This is the first time I've ever seen her like this. She's had some rough times at other jobs, what with teaching and then serving as an administrator, but nothing's ever brought her down the way this has.'

Tish frowned. Was there more than just book purging behind Augusta's feud with Binnie Broderick? And did Binnie have cause to accuse Augusta of being unfit for her position as board president? Or was it, as Augusta claimed, merely a case of deflection? 'Well, I do hope she recuperates soon.'

'Me, too. I'm not sure how much more of this she can take. Sheriff Reade called earlier, wanting to ask Augusta May and me some questions about last night, but I told him it's too soon. Augusta needs at least another day of rest. Besides, if there's anyone who deserves an interrogation, it's Opal Schaefer.'

'Who?' Tish's face was a question.

'Our resident romance writer. Goes by the name of Morningstar. She had a few drinks too many last night. Came to our table, glass of wine in hand, and gave Lavinia quite an earful about not restocking her books.'

'Restocking? You mean Mrs Broderick was supposed to replace the books she purged?'

'No. No, nothing like that. After Opal's books were purged from the shelves, her agent offered to restock them at no charge. Lavinia flat out refused. Called Opal's books "filth" right there in front of everyone.'

'Are her books that risqué?'

Edwin shook his head. 'Never read them. According to Augusta, they're "erotic" but nothing you wouldn't see on basic cable these days.'

'So how did Opal react?'

'Oh, she was livid. Funny, it was actually the first time I've seen her react negatively. She's an old hippie. Into yoga, organic gardening, incense, meditation, that sort of thing. But last night, there was no sign of any "Kumbaya" in her heart, let me tell you.'

'What did she do?'

'She went all Khrushchev on Lavinia.'

Tish dug through what she remembered of twentieth-century history. 'What? You mean she banged her shoe on the table?'

'Oh no,' Edwin chuckled. 'But that would have been less threatening in the long run. No, she drank back the rest of her wine and, staring Lavinia down the entire time, threatened to bury her. Those were her exact words to Lavinia; "You may be smug now, Lavinia Broderick, but mark my words, I will bury you."'

Twelve

Tish awoke the next morning to the sound of bells. With her eyes still closed, she reached an arm toward her bedside table and blindly smacked

115

at the touchscreen of her cell phone. The noise persisted.

'What in heaven's name is that?' Jules shrieked from the spare bedroom.

Tish, Jules, and Mary Jo had spent the previous night baking enough rosemary madeleines for Jules to sell to hungry journalists and Tish to distribute to suspicious neighbors. Needing to shuttle her children to church and then sporting activities the next morning, Mary Jo left for home around eleven p.m., leaving Tish and Jules to bake the last batch of madeleines and then clean up. By the time the pair climbed the narrow staircase to Tish's apartment and crawled into their respective beds, it was well after two in the morning.

Opening her eyes, Tish caught a glimpse of her cell phone display: eight a.m.

'It's the bells of St John the Baptist next door,' she called to Jules as she stretched and kicked the covers off her feet. After a relatively cool night, the morning promised to be bright, hot, and muggy. 'It's Sunday morning, remember?'

'What? They hold services this early? I mean, what time is it anyway?'

'Eight o'clock,' she yawned. 'Service is at eight thirty. This is a wake-up call.'

'Now I know why I don't go to church anymore.' Jules clicked his tongue. 'Personally, I believe in a kinder God. The God I believe in wouldn't expect us to leave the comfort of our beds so early on a Sunday morning. My God understands that after working all week, Saturday is our only day to clean the house, mow the lawn, exfoliate, and drink Cosmos with friends, leaving Sunday as the only true day to unwind. My God wants us to be fully rested before engaging in prayer. My God is a brunching God.'

Tish rose from her bed and, after adjusting the straps on her tank top and yanking the elastic waistband of her boxer shorts well over her hips, gazed through her bedroom window and down at the crowd of people gathered outside St John's in anticipation that the church doors would soon open. Amid the sea of faces, Tish was able to identify Roberta Dutton, Daryl Dufour, Augusta May and Edwin Wilson, and, surrounded by a group of elderly ladies who took turns hugging, frowning, and shaking his hand in clear expressions of sympathy, a red-faced, yet morose-looking John Ballantyne.

Feeling too much like a voyeur, Tish stepped away from the window. 'Yes, well, before you go off starting the cult of St Eggs Benedict, why don't I make us some coffee?'

'To be administered intravenously, I hope,' Jules grumbled from the other room.

'Yeah, sorry, but I let my nursing license lapse years—' Tish's sarcastic comment was interrupted by the popping of gunshots coming from the street below.

Tish ran from her bedroom and into the adjacent living room, only to be met by Jules, who immediately pulled her to the floor. 'Get down!'

When the gunfire had ceased, Tish hurried back to the bedroom. As women, children, and a small number of men huddled in the doorway of the

117

church, a crowd gathered around a man lying prone upon the concrete.

Grabbing her cell phone and dialing 911, Tish followed Jules downstairs and out of the front door of the café. The silver-haired man on the ground was dressed in a lightweight seersucker suit and a white dress shirt that was rapidly becoming stained with blood.

As Tish described the scene to the emergency responder on the other end of the line, she struggled to recall where she had previously met the victim. 'Yes, there's been a shooting outside St John the Baptist's . . . No, I don't see the shooter . . . Yes, there's a man down. I don't see anyone else who may be injured . . . The victim? He's, um, roughly sixty years of age and . . .'

Tish paused as she envisioned the wounded man standing over the body of Binnie Broderick.

'Oh my God . . . it's the doctor. It's Doctor Livermore. He's been shot in the chest. Please hurry!'

Tish and Jules watched as emergency medical technicians loaded Dr Livermore and a compendium of life-saving wires, tubes, and machinery into a waiting ambulance. Before the vehicle left, Tish took note of a tall, dark-haired man in a tailored navy suit and red tie being ushered into the back seat of a black Lincoln Continental idling just in front of the ambulance. Within seconds, both the Lincoln and the ambulance pulled away from the curb. The van carrying Dr Livermore took off for Bon Secours St Mary's Hospital, its lights and sirens providing both visual and audio warning to any vehicles that might block its path. The Continental, however, made a sudden U-turn and headed down Main Street toward the opposite end of town.

'Mayor Whitley,' Jules told Tish. 'Running in the opposite direction, as is his modus operandi.'

'I take it you didn't vote for him.'

'Nope. Too much of a holy roller for my taste.'

'I take it his God isn't a brunching God,' Tish teased.

'Honey, his God isn't even a square-dancing God.'

Exhausted from the late night, the sight of a man having been shot, and the calamity of yet another crime having been committed on her doorstep, Tish gave a yawn before declaring, 'Come on, Jules. Let's go in and get some coffee.'

'Um, Miss Tarragon,' Sheriff Reade called before they'd even taken a step toward the café. 'May I have a word?'

'Sure.'

'Are you sure now is a good time?' Reade eyed Tish from head to toe and then did the same to Jules before returning his gaze to the caterer. 'If not, I can talk to the witnesses in the church first.'

Tish, barefoot, still dressed in her pajama ensemble of tank top and boxer shorts, and her face bearing streaks from last night's eyeliner, turned to look at Jules. In all the excitement, she hadn't noticed that he was dressed in a pair of black boxer briefs accessorized by a pair of black dress socks, a wrongly buttoned lavender dress shirt, and an unruly crop of chestnut hair that

119

would not have looked out of place at an eighties New Wave concert.

'Oh, um.' Tish self-consciously wiped beneath her eyes and smoothed her hair. 'No, this is fine. We had just rolled out of bed when we heard the gunshots.'

Reade glanced between the two of them and cleared his throat. 'Eh-hem, so I, um, I take it neither of you saw anything suspicious prior to the shooting?'

Tish shook her head. 'I looked out my bedroom window, but all I saw was a sea of hats, dresses, suits, big hair, and white shoes.'

'Nothing else?'

'I did see a few familiar faces in the crowd. You know, people I met at the fundraiser, but none of them were doing anything out of the ordinary.'

'And you didn't notice anyone out of place?' Reade prompted. 'Someone who might not have belonged there?'

'No. I mean, I was a bit groggy. We had a late night,' Tish explained, spurring the color to rise in Reade's face. 'But if there was anyone out of place, I didn't notice.'

'And what happened after you looked out the window?'

'Then the gunshots rang out,' Tish replied. 'So I ran out of the bedroom, away from the window, and into the living room.'

'Where I pulled her down to the ground in case there was a stray shot,' Jules completed the thought.

'Thanks for that, by the way,' Tish acknowledged.

'Of course.' Jules shrugged.

'And then what happened?' Reade nudged the pair back to the case at hand. 'After the gunshots?'

'We got up. I looked out the bedroom window, saw someone had been injured, grabbed my phone to call nine-one-one, and then came out to see precisely what had happened. That's when I realized it was Doctor Livermore.' Tish frowned. 'Is he going to be OK?'

'Don't know. He's critically wounded and losing a lot of blood. According to the EMTs, it's touch and go.'

Tish ran her hand through her hair again, this time as more of a way to ease her mind than to flatten her humidity-curled locks.

'If his condition changes, I'll let you know,' Sheriff Reade offered. 'And if you think of anything, give me a call.' Reade handed her a card with his number, but Tish refused.

'Don't need it. I have one upstairs in my bag,' she explained.

Reade, however, did not appear to be listening. His gaze was focused on something going on behind Tish.

She turned around to see Cordelia Ballantyne rushing up the road and toward the church. 'Oh my God! I just passed the ambulance on my way here. What's happened?'

Reade stepped past Jules and Tish to greet her. 'There was a shooting, ma'am. Now just calm down and we'll—'

'Calm down? How can you expect me to calm down? First someone murders my mother and

121

now this.' She pushed Reade aside and called, 'John! Where's John? Where's my husband?'

'He's inside the church, ma'am.' Reade placed a hand on Cordelia's shoulder in an effort to prevent her from approaching the church. 'He's fine. He'll be out as soon as we take his statement.'

Cordelia remained frantic. 'Statement? Statement about what? Who's been shot?'

'Doctor Livermore, I'm afraid, ma'am. Now, he's still alive, but he's not out of the woods yet,' Reade answered as gently as possible.

It still wasn't gentle enough for Cordelia Broderick Ballantyne. 'Doctor Livermore?' she repeated, before promptly losing consciousness.

Reade, Jules, and Tish reached out to cushion the woman's fall as EMTs from a second ambulance, which had been called out to deal with possible victims of shock, rushed to the scene with a wheeled stretcher.

As Cordelia was wheeled to the ambulance, followed closely by Sheriff Reade, Jules turned to Tish. 'Why don't we go in and you can make some of that coffee you promised, huh?'

Tish gave a silent nod as Jules draped an arm around her shoulders and guided her back toward the café. 'And while you brew the coffee, I'll pack up those madeleines for you to take round town, because, girl, with a dead woman at your banquet and a man wounded literally on your doorstep, you're gonna need some serious baked goods behind you to get out of this one.'

Thirteen

'That's sweet of you, hon, but I don't do gluten,' Opal Schaefer, aka Marjorie Morningstar, took the wax paper bag bearing four rosemary corn-meal madeleines from Tish and deposited it, part and parcel, into the stainless-steel compost bin on the kitchen counter behind her.

Tish, caffeinated, coiffed, and dressed in a nautical pairing of white Capri pants, blue-and-white striped top, and red sandals, opened her mouth to protest at the disposal of perfectly edible baked goods, but the romance writer didn't give her a chance. 'Funny, I'm usually good with faces, but I don't remember seeing you at the fundraiser the other night.'

Tish was sorely tempted to point out Opal's supposed wine consumption on the evening in question, but elected to take the high road. 'That's because I was in the kitchen most of the time. I only went out into the reception room just before Binnie Broderick died.'

'Binnie. What a shock, huh?' Opal remarked as she lit an unfiltered cigarette, inhaled, and then exhaled the smoke out of the open kitchen window. Meanwhile, another cigarette still smoldered in a nearby blue ceramic ashtray. 'I always thought she was too mean to die. Sorry if that sounds heartless, but when you get to my age, you say what you please.'

Despite her slim figure and youthful attire of Lycra yoga pants, Chuck Taylor Converse high-top sneakers, and a flowing sleeveless blouse worn sans brassiere, Opal Schaeffer was seventy years old if she was a day.

'I didn't know Mrs Broderick well enough to pass judgment,' Tish maintained.

Opal laughed heartily. 'Oh, come on. I know you're new to Hobson Glen and trying to ingratiate yourself with the townsfolk, but let's call Binnie what she really was: a bitch. If my editor didn't ban me from using them, I'd even put an exclamation mark after that word to emphasize just how bitchy the bitch truly was.'

For the first time in a long while, Tish was genuinely speechless.

Opal laughed again, but this time the boisterous cackle terminated in a dry, hacking cough that shook loose the messy bun at the nape of her neck and sent tendrils of silver hair cascading down her shoulders.

'Are you OK?' Tish asked. 'Should I get you some water?'

Opal raised a hand to signify that she was in control of the situation as she rushed to the refrigerator and grabbed a kombucha. She twisted off the cap, took a swig, drew a deep breath as her coughing subsided, and then offered the bottle to Tish.

Tish had never liked the taste of the fermented beverage, but after drinking more than half a pot of coffee, the thought of taking even a small sip of kombucha from the same bottle as someone she had only just met made her feel physically ill. 'No, thanks. I'm cutting back.'

Opal took another swig before returning the bottle to the refrigerator and lighting yet another cigarette. The second cigarette lay at the bottom of the kitchen sink, the first still smoldered in the ashtray. 'By the way, I wanted to tell you that I truly enjoyed the For Whom the Vegan Stuffed Bell Pepper Tolls. Clever name and I appreciated the fact it was gluten-free.'

'Thank you.' Tish was genuinely appreciative of the praise. Perhaps her catering business would survive Hobson Glen's recent crime spree. As long as there were no more killings and shootings, that is.

'I imagine that menu item was your idea, not Binnie's.' Opal smirked and took a puff on her cigarette.

'It was,' Tish conceded. 'Not to speak ill of the dead, but Mrs Broderick didn't see the need for a vegan, vegetarian or a gluten-free option.'

'That's because she knew I was gluten-free and vegetarian. So was Roberta Dutton. There were probably more of us, but having attended many library functions together, I can vouch that Binnie Broderick knew that at least the two of us had dietary restrictions.'

'So you think she wanted to leave a gluten-free vegetarian option off the menu just to be spiteful?'

'I told you she was a bitch.'

'But why? What did she have against you?'

'You haven't heard?'

'No,' Tish, once again, pretended to be less informed than she actually was.

125

'Well, neither have I,' Opal guffawed before elaborating. 'What Binnie had against me, specifically, I couldn't tell you. However, I could take an educated guess: sex.'

Tish was caught unawares. 'Um, I beg your pardon?'

Opal's laugh became even heartier. 'The sex portrayed in my books. I'm a romance novelist. You may even have heard of me. I'm Marjorie Morningstar.'

'Ah, yes, I have heard of you. I'm afraid I'm not much of a romance reader. I'm more a fan of non-fiction and a mysteries sort of gal. Oh, and cookbooks, of course.'

'Well, my books can change that. They're not the traditional bodice-rippers. They're far more modern. My books feature strong women seizing what they want rather than waiting for Fabio – how did he ever get on the cover of so many books, anyway? – to rescue them. My women are vibrant women who enjoy life, and sex, to the fullest. They take every opportunity to enjoy themselves and their lovers.'

'Hm, they sound interesting,' Tish remarked. Inwardly, however, she still had absolutely no desire to read a romance novel. 'Do you think your strong, sex-loving women might have been an issue between you and Mrs Broderick?'

'You're quite perceptive, Ms Tarragon,' Opal chuckled. 'No, my strongly worded books didn't sit well with Binnie's puritanical sensibilities. So offended was the lady in question that she purged my books from the library.'

'Correct me if I'm wrong, but didn't Binnie

purge an exceptional number of books at once? Not just yours?'

'She did. No doubt most of them were offensive to Binnie as well.' Opal rubbed the stub of her cigarette into the ash tray and then smoked the remnants of the first cigarette before snubbing that one out too.

'Did anyone ever suggest that Binnie replace the books?'

'More than suggest. My agent and publisher both demanded that she make them available to my local readers. They even offered to donate my books to the Hobson Glen Library. Binnie flat out refused.' Opal ignited a fourth cigarette, placed it to her hot-pink lips, and took a puff. 'She was trying to silence my literary voice.'

'That must have been frustrating for you, but at least you had other venues through which you could keep your voice alive.' Tish offered a positive note. 'You are a bestselling novelist, aren't you?'

'I am, and I'm grateful to my readers for their support through the years. However, it pains me that people right here in my own community, who may have wanted to read my books but couldn't afford to purchase them, have been denied the ability to do so. It's a form of censorship. As a writer, I will never abide by censorship.'

Censorship, Tish reflected silently. It was the third time in twenty-four hours that someone had used the term in reference to Lavinia Broderick. Daryl Dufour, Augusta May Wilson, and now Opal Schaefer had all described the book purge not as a mistake but a means of suppression. Was this why Broderick had been killed? An ardent lover of both books and liberty might have killed for far less than the destruction of five hundred books. But if perceived censorship was the motive, how did Dr Livermore fit into the picture?

'The other books that were purged,' Tish started, 'were they romance novels as well?'

'Many of them were, yes, but there were other genres on the list too. Some mysteries, lots of science fiction and fantasy, some science textbooks, if you can believe it, and the usual banned-book suspects like *Catcher in the Rye*, *To Kill A Mockingbird*, and *Tropic of Cancer*.'

'Ah yes, good ol' Henry Miller.'

Opal took a puff on her cigarette and screwed her mouth up to one side. 'If it weren't for the existence of Cordelia, I'd swear Binnie Broderick never had sex in her life. But, of course, she was a slightly better person back when her husband was alive.'

'Slightly better?'

'Yeah, she . . . Well, Binnie's always been full of herself and always judgmental. But when her husband died several years ago, she really threw herself into religion.'

'Lots of people turn to God for comfort during difficult times.' Tish shrugged.

'I know, and if it helps, I say more power to them. Lord knows, I was a mess when I lost my husband.' Opal swallowed hard, as if doing so might purge the bitter taste of lost love from her mouth. 'Binnie's situation was different. Perhaps she did start going to church more often for comfort, but she wound up using it as vindication for her already bad behavior.'

'What do mean, "vindication"?'

'Well, it was one thing for Binnie to treat people poorly because she was the descendant of a notable family. It was another matter entirely when she felt that she was doing God's will. No one in town was safe from her scathing remarks.' Opal put out the cigarette she was smoking, but was too absorbed in Binnie's evil doings to pick up another. 'Binnie knew what type of books I wrote. She always had. Ever since I started writing twenty years ago. But she never made a fuss. That is, not until I made the bestseller list and brought some notoriety to Hobson Glen. That's when Binnie decided that my work was too profane. Too profane! I wrote about love. Real love. Physical love. The love that Larry and I shared, which, yes, involved different positions, and gadgets, and the outdoors, and—'

Tish, feeling the color rise to her cheeks, cleared her throat noisily.

'I'm sorry,' Opal apologized with a self-conscious grin. 'I suppose you don't really want to hear about the sex life of a nearly-eighty-year-old grandmother.'

'No.' Tish felt like a complete and utter heel. 'No, I'm not actually comfortable hearing about anyone's sex life. Maybe because I don't have one of my own at the moment, but it certainly has nothing to do with you personally.'

'I'm relieved.' Opal celebrated her elation by lighting another cigarette. 'I also want you to

129

know' – she took a long drag – 'that although I called Binnie a bitch, I didn't kill her.'

'You did visit her table, though, didn't you? I mean on the night of the fundraiser.'

'Yes, I did. How did you know? Were you there?'

The fact that Opal couldn't recall whether Tish was at the table or not gave credence to the Wilsons' story. 'No, I was in the kitchen most of the evening. I only came out shortly before Binnie died.'

Opal nodded. 'Sorry. I admit it's a bit of a blur, but, yes, I did visit Binnie's table. I'd had a bit too much wine and, while under the influence of the liquid bravado, thought I should give Binnie a piece of my mind. Well, whatever was left of my mind at that point, anyway. So, although the police have already arranged for me to meet them later today, they'd be hard-pressed to accuse a drunk woman of pulling off what appears to be a baffling poisoning. Although it's somewhat flattering to think they consider me intelligent and sly enough to be a murder suspect.'

'Make that a murder *and* attempted murder suspect,' Tish amended.

Opal narrowed her eyes. 'What? What's happened now?'

'Doctor Livermore has been shot. It happened this morning outside St John the Baptist Church.'

The writer's face registered genuine shock. 'Shot? Oh! Oh my . . . is he going to be OK?'

'Too soon to tell. He was rushed to the hospital just a few hours ago.'

130

'But who? Why?'

'No idea, but it must be related to Mrs Broderick's death, don't you think?' Tish ventured. 'Sheriff Reade told me that this is a very quiet town.'

'It is quiet,' Opal agreed. 'That's why I just can't wrap my head around Doctor Livermore. Binnie's death is shocking enough, but it's at least within the realm of possibility given all the souls she's offended through the years. Doctor Livermore dedicated his life to helping people. He wasn't my doctor, of course – my plan has a high deductible and Livermore charged over one hundred dollars for a visit – but he had a favorable reputation here in town. And he was, on a personal level, an extremely nice man. A true gent.'

'So you can't think of anyone who may have wanted Binnie Broderick and Doctor Livermore dead?'

'What, both of them?' Opal pulled a face. 'No. Then again, my mind lives in the realm of romance and love, not the ugly universe of murders. Speaking of which . . .'

Tish's blue eyes grew wide with worry as Opal snuffed out her cigarette and approached with hands in the air. 'You have just the face for my new heroine.'

'Huh?'

Opal placed a hand on Tish's chin and another on her left cheek. 'You. You should be on the cover of my work in progress. You'd make the perfect Deirdre, the lonely professional fund-raiser who decides that the recycling collection man who lectures her against the use of plastic water bottles at her functions has more to teach her than environmentalism.'

'Um, yeah, but I'm afraid not,' Tish took Opal's hands in hers, just as the writer was about to pivot her cover model's head to the left in order to examine her profile.

'Oh, but why? I'll get some hunky guy in here to pose with you, my cover artist would snap some photos, and, as they say, voilà!' Opal withdrew her hands and performed a jubilant pirouette in the middle of the kitchen.

'As lovely and fun as that sounds,' Tish fibbed, for the entire experience sounded absolutely dreadful, 'I'm afraid that's not quite the image I want to convey as a fledgling business owner.'

'No, I suppose not.' Opal frowned. 'But should you change your mind, and all that . . . You know, it might actually draw in customers.'

'Maybe, but I think I'd rather attract customers with food than the promise I might act out one of your steamy scenes on the café counter.' Tish moved toward the back door. 'And on that note, I'd best be moving along. Busy day.'

'Yes, of course.' Opal lit another cigarette and gave it a puff before opening the back kitchen door for Tish and bidding her farewell. 'Let me know when the café gets some gluten-free goodies.'

'I will,' Tish promised.

'And don't lose sight of that book cover. It could be good advertising.'

Tish nodded absently and set off through the expanse of cultivated vegetable beds that formed

Opal's back yard. As she neared the Matrix she had left parked in the rear section of the driveway, Tish took note of a rundown garden shed whose doors had rusted off their hinges. There, upon a shelf in the shabby lean-to, stood a variety of sprays and chemicals, one of which was marked boldly in red and bore an illustration of a rodent caught in the crosshairs of a rifle.

Rat poison.

Fourteen

Pulling the Matrix to a halt along the curb outside Wisteria Knolls, Tish snatched a large wax paper bag of madeleines from the passenger seat and hoped, silently, that this batch didn't end up in the waste bin.

The morning, which had – quite appropriately given the events outside the church – started off overcast, had turned into a bright, sunny, and moderately dry afternoon. Tish adjusted the sunglasses perched on the end of her nose and strode up the fieldstone-paved walk that led to the Georgian-styled home's front door.

Before Tish could press her finger to the door-bell, she heard a woman's voice shout, 'No!'

Tish reached into the back pocket of her Capri pants and extracted her phone in anticipation of dialing the police. Thankfully, the next shout eliminated such necessity.

'No, I won't move her into that horrible place,

John. If Charlotte goes anywhere, it's home. She needs to come back to Hobson Glen. Back to Wisteria Knolls.'

'Don't be ridiculous, Cordelia. Bringing Charlotte back here is apt to send her into a downward spiral. You know she had no friends here. She was miserable.'

'Yes, but things are different now. With Mother's passing, I have more time to dedicate to Charlotte's care and well-being.'

'What you mean is now that your mother's gone, you're lonely and bored, and now you're willing to put your daughter's health at risk for the sake of having someone here to hold your hand.'

'Maybe if you held it more often, I wouldn't need someone else,' Cordelia fired back, her voice cracking.

'Don't pull that guilt-trip nonsense on me, Cordelia. There was a time when I was willing to do anything for you. Anything. And where did it get us? Stuck in this godforsaken hole for the past ten years.'

'Yes, but that's all over now. We don't have to stay in this house any longer. We can move to wherever we want – just you and me – and we can take Charlotte with us.'

'Until we sell this museum and get rid of your mother's stuff, we can't go anywhere. And, as I've already told you, I'm not bringing my daughter back in this house,' John stipulated.

'She'll be safe here. This is *my* house now.'

'No. I won't allow it.'

'She's my daughter too.'

134

'Clearly,' came John's withering reply. A lengthy silence elapsed before he spoke again. 'Look, Charlotte has been doing wonderfully at the facility in Williamsburg. Better than either of us ever expected. But now it's time to move her – gradually – back into society. The center outside Baltimore is perfect for getting her reintegrated.'

'Why does she have to be all the way in Maryland? Why can't we just keep her where she is? It's not home, but at least it's only an hour away.'

'Cordelia, we've been through all this. The facility in Williamsburg is excellent, and, yes, it's nearby. However, the treatment, care, and attention they provide far exceeds Charlotte's needs at the moment. Then, of course, there's the matter of expense. Why should we pay for care she no longer needs?'

'If it's the money that concerns you, I can easily care for Charlotte here, at a fraction of the expense,' Cordelia replied, her voice a mixture of optimism and desperation.

John was having none of it. 'Stop it, Cordelia. Just stop it. First thing tomorrow, I'm making the arrangements for Charlotte's transfer to Baltimore. If you even think about interfering with the transfer, I'll call my attorney and have him draw up divorce papers.'

Cordelia answered without pause. 'Why wait? It's only a matter of time until you have them drawn up anyway.'

Once again, several seconds elapsed before John answered, 'I'm done with this. I'm going out.'

Recognizing her cue, Tish scrambled across the front lawn and to the edge of the driveway where she ducked behind a row of tall wheeled trash bins. From her hiding spot, she watched as John Ballantyne stormed out of the house, up the driveway, and into the driver's side of a black Audi sedan.

Cordelia shouted after him, 'Good. Go see your girlfriend, because the sight of you is making me sick!'

Ballantyne flung the Audi into reverse and zoomed out of the driveway and into the road, nearly backing into a passing Ford Mustang convertible. Amid a torrent of angry horn honks and threats on the part of the Mustang driver, Ballantyne then shifted the Audi into drive and, tires screeching, disappeared down the road toward the end of the bypass that connected with Main Street just outside Tish's café.

Remaining safely concealed behind the trash bins until she could be certain Ballantyne wasn't returning, Tish reached into her pocket and extracted her cell phone. Tapping at the keyboard, she issued a message to Jules: *John Ballantyne driving black Audi heading your way on bypass. Can you see where he goes?*

Within moments, Tish received a reply: *Packing madeleines. Why?*

Tish sighed. Why must Jules always need every single detail? *He's meeting girlfriend. Want to see who she is.*

Jules's next response was equally predictable: *GF???? YES! Going now!!!!*

Smirking, Tish deposited the cell phone back

into her pocket and then counted to one hundred so as to give Cordelia some additional time in which to pull herself together. At the count of one hundred and one, Tish emerged from her hiding spot, made her way to the front door of Wisteria Knolls, and pressed the doorbell.

The sound of shuffling feet and a sniffling nose preceded the appearance of someone at a nearby window. Tish smiled and raised a hand in greeting, and the person evaporated, only to re-emerge from behind the front door.

Cordelia Broderick Ballantyne, her face taut, drawn, and ruddy from crying, stared at Tish, her face a question.

'I'm so sorry to bother you, Mrs Ballantyne. I'm Tish Tarragon, the caterer of the library benefit. I feel so badly about what you've been through and I wanted to express my condolences with a small care package.' Tish presented the bag of madeleines.

Cordelia's glum expression promptly lifted. 'Oh, yes, I remember you now, Ms Tarragon. How very sweet of you to bring these by. Would you care to come in?' Cordelia opened the door wide.

'Oh, I don't wish to impose.' Tish's reluctance to enter was sincere. Business on the line or not, she had absolutely no desire to inflict more pain upon someone mourning the loss of a mother while simultaneously navigating the minefield of emotions that accompany a broken marriage.

Cordelia was insistent. 'You're not imposing. It would do me some good. I haven't had a thing to eat all morning and, well, the house is a bit too quiet for this time of day.'

With a nod of acquiescence, Tish followed Cordelia into the main foyer.

Stepping over the threshold of Wisteria Knolls was like stepping back into the eighteenth century. As was the style of the era, the entrance hall was sparsely furnished with a pair of simply carved wooden chairs and a drop-leaf maple table bearing two pewter candlesticks. The wide floorboards, covered in pale-gray paint to disguise the fact they were constructed of knotted wood from a variety of trees, boasted no rugs or other coverings. And the walls, painted in a familiar shade of Delft blue, bore just a round mirror in need of re-silvering and a set of brass wall sconces before connecting with the low exposed-beam ceiling above them.

'Wow.' Although impressive in its accuracy and detail, Tish felt as if she had entered a museum or a historical exhibit rather than a home.

'Thanks. It's usually more colorful in here, but Mother put the rugs away for the summer and I forgot to cut some flowers for the table as I usually do. Mother always puts the rugs away for summer, just as the Darlingtons have always done. She's a stickler for such things. I mean she *was* a stickler . . .' Cordelia corrected herself with a troubled expression.

'Her care and attention paid off. It's a lovely home.'

'Everything is original too. The furniture and family portraits have been in the family for years, and Mother had the walls scraped down so she could match the original paint colors. The only concessions she made were for updated electric and plumbing and a functioning kitchen.'

Functioning was a loose description, Tish discovered as she followed Cordelia into the afore-mentioned room. Located at the far back of the house, the kitchen appeared to have been added to the main residence some time shortly after the turn of the nineteenth century. Sanitary white tiles lined the floors and walls, betraying the presence of even the smallest crumb or grease splatter; a giant Hoosier cabinet with a ceramic worktop lent extra storage space to the already generous rows of white metal cabinetry; a white ceramic farm-house sink with built-in drainboard stood tall and deep enough to accommodate even the largest of cooking vessels; and a Wedgewood gas stove with elegantly curved cabriole legs and a host of burners and baking ovens promised to cook, roast, and boil all the food needed to feed a large family – which was handy since the farmhouse table in the center of the room easily seated ten.

At the time of its installation, Wisteria Knolls' kitchen must have been considered luxurious and state-of-the-art. However, it was quite likely that the first woman to cook in it had yet to have been granted the right to vote.

'Mother tried to keep this room as she found it too, but she knew she needed to yield to technology, so there's a side-by-side Viking refrigerator and a microwave in the butler pantry next door.' Cordelia turned a dial on the stove until it clicked. The front right burner roared to life. 'Tea with our madeleines?'

'Sure,' Tish accepted. 'May I help you at all?'

'No, I'm fine.' Cordelia's shaky hands belied her words. As she reached for a black ceramic mug from the Hoosier cabinet, the drinking container slipped from her fingers and shattered against the stark whiteness of the ceramic tile floor. Cordelia burst into tears.

Tish rushed to her side and guided her into one of the Windsor kitchen chairs. 'Here, you sit and I'll take care of that tea.'

'Oh no, I couldn't. I invited you in.' Cordelia struggled to stand, but Tish eased her back into her seat.

'Next visit, you can wait on me,' Tish suggested with a smile. 'This one, you're sitting out.'

'That's so very kind of you.' Cordelia blew her nose in a handkerchief she had stuffed into the pocket of her ankle-length, ecru-colored, gauzy cotton skirt. 'It may sound odd, but I don't have many friends really. My mother, my family, and the house have kept me so busy, I haven't had much time for a social life.'

'That doesn't sound odd at all,' Tish stated as she filled the copper tea kettle at the farmhouse sink. 'It's difficult to juggle life at times. A person needs to meet the demands of a job, children, and spouse, all while keeping an eye on the checkbook, the aging parents, and the mold that might be growing in the vegetable drawer of the refrigerator.'

'And all the while failing miserably at all of them,' Cordelia lamented.

Tish recollected a time not long ago when she herself was trying to make a success of her career as an investment banker and get a shaky marriage back on track, while simultaneously trying to assuage a father who wanted her to move back to New York. 'I'm sure it feels like you're failing at times, but I doubt you are. We tend to be rougher on ourselves than we are on others.'

'Do you have children, Ms Tarragon?'

'Please, call me Tish.'

'Thank you,' she replied with a weak smile. 'Do you have children, Tish?'

'No, I don't. Not that it was a conscious decision. I love children and had them in my "master plan" if that's what it's called, but I never found anyone with whom I could even entertain the possibility. I know times have changed and I might have tried it on my own, but by the time I'd divorced it felt like it was time to do the things I'd put on hold for so long.'

'Like starting a café?'

'Like starting . . . well, trying to start a café. We'll see if it takes off.'

'From the taste of your food, I'm sure it will.'

'Thanks. From your mouth to God's ears, as they say.' From their argument earlier, Tish already knew Cordelia and John had a daughter, but she saw no better way to introduce the topic into conversation. 'And how about you? Do you have children?'

'Yes.' Cordelia's wan countenance brightened as she fidgeted with her cell phone. 'A daughter, Charlotte.' With an outstretched arm, Cordelia displayed a digital photo of a smiling teenage girl with long dark hair and braces.

'She's lovely.'

'Thanks. She gets her looks from John's side of the family.' As if suddenly giving thought to her own appearance, Cordelia pulled her bleached hair out of its ponytail and fluffed it with her fingertips.

'I don't know about that. I see quite a bit of you in her too. How old is she?'

'Sixteen. Seventeen in a few weeks. I was hoping to celebrate with her.' Cordelia's glum expression returned.

'Why can't you?'

'Oh, she's been away at boarding school the past year. Normally, she'd be home for the summer, but Charlotte decided to undertake a special project. Always an overachiever.' Cordelia giggled nervously.

'You must be very proud.' Tish retrieved two mugs from the Hoosier cabinet and placed them on the table.

'I am. But I do miss her terribly.'

'Perhaps she'll fit in a visit before the new term starts. Or maybe you can manage a visit to her school? Where are the tea bags?'

'Second shelf. In there.' Cordelia nodded toward the butler pantry. 'Oh I wish that were possible. The house feels so empty and lonesome, especially now that—'

Tish retrieved a box of Earl Grey and returned to the kitchen. 'Will Charlotte be here for your mother's service?' she asked as she plopped a tea bag into each mug.

Cordelia shrugged. 'I haven't even told her yet. Charlotte can be rather sensitive at times and I don't want to distract her from her schoolwork.

I'll probably wait until her project's done and try to tell her in person.'

The kettle whistled. Tish turned off the burner and poured the boiling water into their cups. 'You're probably right. Telling Charlotte about her grandmother in person might be best. Her passing might come as a shock to her.'

'I'm sure it will. My mother was as fit as a fiddle. Some cholesterol and blood pressure concerns, but nothing unusual for a woman her age. She controlled everything with medication.'

After some direction from Cordelia, Tish retrieved a couple of spoons, plates, and a bowl of sugar from the Hoosier and then opened the bag of madeleines. 'Do you have any idea at all who may have wanted to kill your mother?'

'None whatsoever.' Cordelia took a madeleine from the bag and bit into it. 'Mmm . . . that's lovely. Really hits the spot.'

'I'm glad.' Tish sat down and stirred a small spoonful of sugar into her cup of tea. 'You really need to take care of yourself, Cordelia. You've experienced quite a shock.'

'Yes, I know. I can't believe Mother is gone. Nor can I believe that anyone would want to murder her. She may have ruffled a few feathers here and there, but my mother was a well-respected member of the community. Everyone who knew her admired her courage and honesty.'

Admiration was very different to being accepted or well liked. 'Even after the library incident? I don't wish to sound judgmental or accusatory, but it didn't seem that your mother's actions were viewed in a positive light.'

'It was an accident. I'm not sure what people expected my mother to do about it. She made mistakes, just like everyone else. This one happened to be quite costly. Quite costly . . .' Cordelia's eyes focused on some point in the distance. Whether she was contemplating the expense of her mother's book purging or some other event long ago, Tish could not determine.

'And now Doctor Livermore's been shot,' Cordelia continued with a sob. 'Why? He's been a doctor to most of the families in town for decades. Why would anyone want to hurt him?'

Tish got up to fetch some paper napkins from the Hoosier and passed them across the table to Cordelia. 'I'm sure the police are looking into it as we speak.'

'It's all too much to take in,' she cried while dabbing at her eyes. 'It's all too much.'

An unexpected electronic chime jolted Cordelia from both her seat and her sorrow. 'Oh, excuse me,' she sniffed while fishing around in her skirt pockets. As she pulled out a red smart phone and glanced at its screen, a gentle smile spread across her face.

'Well, I think I'd best be going and let you drink your tea in peace,' Tish announced. 'And maybe have a nap later? You could probably use the rest.'

'Hmm? Oh, yes – I'm sorry, it's . . . it's a text from Charlotte.' Cordelia stuffed the phone back into her pocket.

'I'm glad you heard from her.'

'Yes, I am too,' Cordelia answered absently. 'I . . . I think I will have that nap.'

144

'Good idea. I'll just let myself out through the butler pantry and you can lock up behind me,' Tish suggested, having realized that the butler pantry must have served as Enid Kemper's escape route from Wisteria Knolls on the previous afternoon. Precisely what Tish expected to see in the butler's pantry, she hadn't a clue, but the temptation to give the room a cursory scan was far too overwhelming to resist.

'Oh, we've never locked the doors at Wisteria Knolls.' Cordelia shunned the notion with a blow of her nose.

Tish reflected upon the events of the past forty-eight hours. 'This might be a good time to start.'

Cordelia was vehement. 'If I do that, then the madman who murdered my mother has won.'

Tish disagreed with Cordelia's assessment, but she was not about to argue. Indeed, she was pleased to see the woman exhibit a bit of pluck. 'That's the spirit. Now, I'd best be going. If it's OK with you, I'll just let myself out.'

Cordelia nodded. 'Oh, and thanks for the madeleines, the tea, the talk. Everything.'

'My pleasure.' Tish pulled a pen from her handbag and scribbled her cell number on to a paper napkin. 'If you need anything else – even if it's just a cup of tea and a chat – give me a call or stop by the café.'

'I will. Thanks.'

Tish pushed her way past the kitchen table and chairs and made her way through the swinging door of the butler pantry en route to the exit. Once inside, she had but a few fleeting seconds to inspect her surroundings. A narrow room, approximately six feet wide and nine feet long, the butler pantry was lined with glass-fronted cabinets that, in days of old, would have displayed the Darlington china and silver, but now held the less romantic so-called necessities of a modern kitchen: food processor, baking pans, electric mixer, and a myriad of canned, jarred, and boxed foodstuffs.

In the far right corner, a series of cupboards had been removed to make way for a stainless-steel industrial-sized refrigerator. On top of the humming appliance rested cartons and shrink-wrapped packages of supplies that had been purchased in bulk: toilet paper, paper napkins, canned tomato juice, and, perched atop a stack of disposable paper plates, a half-empty case of hot sauce.

Fifteen

'So, did you follow him?' Tish greeted the call from Jules.

'What? Not even a "hello"? You know, since you've become a detective, your manners have gone right out the window,' Jules teased. 'We may have to deport you back north. You're no longer polite enough to live side by side with Southerners.'

'Helloooo, Jules,' Tish exhaled in a tired sing-song fashion from outside the driver's door of the Matrix. Jules's call had arrived just as she was exiting the butler pantry door of Wisteria Knolls.

'That's better.' Tish could hear Jules's smirk over the phone.

'Where are you?'

'I'm in the parking lot of Short Pump Town Center Mall.'

'The mall? What are you doing there?' Tish opened the door of the Matrix and climbed in behind the steering wheel.

'Apart from trying to ignore Nordstrom's notoriously fabulous end-of-summer sale on men's shoes – remember the Italian leather wingtips I got last year? Absolutely divine. I'm staring across Route 250 at the beige stucco exterior of the Wingate Hotel into which John Ballantyne disappeared approximately three minutes ago.'

'A hotel? I knew it! Did you happen to see whom he met?'

'A woman. Brunette, great body, but with a scowl on her face like she'd just been asked to clean a gas-station toilet.'

'Roberta Dutton,' Tish excitedly named. 'She's the senior librarian.'

'You recognized her from that description? You mean she always looks like that?'

'Pretty much,' Tish replied as she started the engine of the Matrix and moved the vehicle two blocks down the road so as not to appear to be monitoring Cordelia Ballantyne. 'And she has the personality to match.'

'Charming. Between her and Binnie Broderick, I'm glad I download all my books on Kindle. So where are you right now?'

'I just left Wisteria Knolls after talking to Cordelia Ballantyne.'

'Does she know about her husband's fling with Wednesday Addams?'

Leave it to Jules to insert an appropriate pop culture reference. 'Yes, I heard them argue about it. Although Cordelia didn't mention Wednesday, erm, Roberta, by name. Say, what do you know about Cordelia and John's daughter, Charlotte?'

'Not much. Teenager. Attended a private school in Richmond until she got into some trouble last year, then she got shipped off somewhere. Why?'

'Oh, I don't know. I overheard Cordelia and John arguing over moving Charlotte to some place in Baltimore. It almost sounded like a hospital of some sort. What it may have to do with Binnie's murder, I have no idea. Doctor Livermore might be linked – doctor, hospital – but still, I have no clue how.'

'Are you sure they were talking about a hospital?' Jules questioned. 'As far as I under-stood it, Charlotte got sent to some super-strict boarding school. Bad behavior, rumor has it.'

'I suppose they might have been discussing a school,' Tish allowed. 'It's all probably nothing, but for some reason the whole conversation just struck me as odd.'

'You'll figure it out in time. Where are you headed next?'

'Not sure. Seeing John Ballantyne is out of the question,' she giggled.

'For the next little while, at least,' Jules agreed.

'And the mayor's office is closed until tomorrow,' Tish listed. 'There's only one person left to visit. My landlord.'

'You can't possibly think Schuyler Thompson could have done it, do you? He's too hot.'

'What? You don't think good-looking people commit murder?'

'No, I'm sure they do, but Schuyler's an attorney and polite and charming, and, I must say, positively perfect for you.'

Tish felt herself blush. 'I don't know about that. But I do know he owns the house I'm renting. If he goes to jail, I'd truly be sunk.'

'Don't you worry. You could stay with me and we'd continue selling baked goods from the backseat of my car,' Jules assured. 'Speaking of which, if you no longer need me to play bloodhound, I have a trunk full of madeleines and a fleet of paparazzi to feed.'

'No, I think we're good. Thanks for following Ballantyne.'

'Are you kidding? This detective thing is far more entertaining than telling Richmonders they're in for yet another ninety-degree day,' Jules said with a note of weariness. 'So, I'll meet you back at the café when I'm done?'

'Yeah, sounds good. See you then.' Tish disconnected the call and pondered her next move. She knew she needed to contact Schuyler, yet he being both single and her landlord made her not want to show up at his home unannounced.

The sudden gurgle of her empty stomach offered Tish direction. Turning the Matrix around, she returned to the café for a light lunch and then, she planned, a phone call to Schuyler.

A brief perusal of the café refrigerator, however, pointed out the error in this decision. Bearing leftover prime rib, a few red bell peppers, a handful of chives, a near-empty half-gallon jug of skim milk, a couple of eggs and the usual array of condiments, the appliance offered little to quell Tish's appetite. Upon a brief shuffle of the refrigerator's contents, she was elated to find a seasoned, grilled fillet of sea bream wrapped in a wodge of aluminum foil.

Placing the aluminum parcel on the counter, she retrieved a jar of mayonnaise from the refrigerator door and the handful of chives from the crisper, and set about making a fish salad to spread upon one of several surplus dinner rolls. Alas, she was interrupted by the vibration of her cell phone from somewhere within her handbag.

Tish stared longingly at the sea bream in quiet deliberation but, in the end, she thought it wise to take the call.

'Hello?' she asked, not recognizing the number on the display.

'Hi, Tish?'

'This is Tish.' She leaned the phone against her shoulder while she flaked the sea bream into a bowl.

'This is Schuyler. Schuyler Thompson.'

So flustered was Tish that she allowed the phone to slip from her shoulder. She fumbled to grab it and overturned the bowl in the process.

The flaked sea bream scattered across the tiled floor. Fortunately, she still had half a fillet left.

'Oh, yes, hi, Schuyler,' she endeavored to answer casually.

'Are you OK?'

'Yes, I was just fixing a sandwich and accidentally knocked the bowl off the counter.'

'No, I mean, are you OK? I was gardening all day and only just heard the news about Doctor Livermore. Someone told me he was shot right next door to your café.' Schuyler's voice was urgent.

'Yes, just outside the church this morning. It was quite a way to start the day, but I'm fine. A bit shaken at first, but fine.' *And hungry*, she nearly added as her stomach growled again.

'Do you need anything? Anything at all?'

A sandwich. Soup. Salad. A bag of chips. 'Um, no. Nothing that I can think of, but I appreciate your asking.'

'Are you sure? I could put a stronger lock on your door, if you'd like. Not to say you can't take care of yourself, of course – you're a grown woman – but, well, all the insanity of the past forty-eight hours has me concerned. For all of us.'

'That's very sweet of you, but I'm absolutely certain I'll be OK. Besides, it's not like I'm alone. Jules and Mary Jo have been here so often that I may need to report them to you as additional tenants.'

Schuyler laughed. 'Sounds as if you're in good hands. Um, but, that's not the main reason for calling. I wanted to talk to you.'

For the moment, Tish forgot about her hunger. 'Yes, I wanted to speak to you, too.'

'Really? Well, you go first,' Schuyler invited.

'Um, no. I, um, well, I wanted to speak to you in person.'

'What a coincidence. I was calling to see if you'd like to meet up and chat, seeing as we missed our chance at the fundraiser. I know you've been working hard this weekend and, most likely, feeding everyone but yourself. I was wondering if you'd like to meet me for an early dinner. The local grill has some specials this week. It doesn't quite measure up to what you served at the fundraiser, but it's good and basic.'

Tish would normally have speculated what Schuyler might have wanted to discuss before agreeing to dinner, but she was famished and the prospect of eating something other than leftover catering food was overwhelmingly attractive. 'Yes, I'd love to. What time?'

Even Schuyler seemed startled by her hasty and positive response. 'Um, I don't know. What time is it now?'

'Just going on two.'

'Um, is six o'clock OK with you? I know it's rather last minute and I don't want you to feel rushed—'

'Six o'clock is fine.' Tish didn't need much time to get ready. However, she desperately needed a sandwich.

'Shall I come and pick you up?'

Tish thought about the questions she needed to ask Schuyler. Taking the trip home together afterward might be awkward. 'No, I'll meet you there. Where is the restaurant?'

'It's just down the road from you, at the other end of town. It used to be the old coffee shop.'

'Oh, yes. Celestine told me about that place. Said they had horrible coffee.'

'That's the one. You can't miss it. Not much is open on a Sunday evening in a sleepy town like this.'

'OK. I'll meet you there at six, then.'

'Yes,' Schuyler replied with genuine excitement in his voice. 'I'm looking forward to it.'

Tish didn't reply in kind. Not only was she less than thrilled to interview her landlord about a murder and an attempted murder, but she was even less excited to hear his answers. Instead, she disconnected the call with a brief farewell and went back to making her sandwich. Six p.m., after all, was still four hours away.

Tish flaked the remaining fish into a clean bowl and was just about to chop the chives when she was interrupted by a knock on the screen door of the café. Exasperated, Tish placed her knife on the counter with a deliberate clank. If the universe was sending her a message, clearly it was that she needed to diet.

With a heavy sigh, she answered the knock by opening the main door. Augusta May Wilson stood on the other side of the screen. 'Oh, hello, Mrs Wilson. What brings you here?' Tish opened the latch to allow Augusta admittance.

'I came by to apologize for yesterday,' she explained as she swung the screen door outward and stepped into the café. 'I was so wrapped up

153

in my own little world that I didn't even say goodbye.'

'Oh, no, I should apologize. I shouldn't have left the way I did, but I thought you and Edwin could use some time alone. Speaking of Edwin, he came by yesterday afternoon to return the cake container and to apologize.'

'Edwin was here?'

'Yes. I gather you didn't know?'

Augusta frowned and shook her head. 'No, I told him to return your container, but I had no idea he'd do it so quickly. Then again, communication hasn't been our strong suit of late.'

'I'm sorry to hear that.' Tish gestured to Augusta to take a seat at one of four café tables she had purchased for future customers. 'May I get you something to drink? Some tea? Lemonade?'

'Lemonade would be lovely,' Augusta accepted. 'I hope I didn't take you away from anything important.'

Tish eyed the bowl of sea bream on the counter. There was not enough to share and nothing else to offer Augusta apart from a slab of cold beef. 'No, I just came back from Wisteria Knolls for a cold drink and bit of quiet.'

'After the shooting this morning, I'm sure you could use some peace. I think we all could.'

Tish brought two glasses of lemonade to the table. 'Especially Cordelia.'

'Yes, how is she?' a concerned Augusta inquired.

'About as well as you'd expect.' Tish sat in the chair opposite Augusta. 'It's obvious she and her mother were quite close.'

'Too close at times. It did no good for Cordelia to live with her mother all these years.'

'But Binnie wouldn't let her leave,' Tish guessed.

'I'm not sure about that. Were there times when it seemed Binnie held Cordelia on a short leash? Sure. But there were just as many times when Cordelia seemed overly protective of her mother. I can't count the number of times each of them threatened to move away or evict the other from Wisteria Knolls, only to stay put and renew their bond.'

Tish frowned at what sounded like a complicated and possibly codependent relationship. 'And you? I know you haven't been feeling well. How are you faring after this morning's events?'

'Numb. I think that's the best word to describe it.'

'There's a lot to process, isn't there?'

Augusta gave a slow, sad nod of the head. 'Ms Tarragon, may I have a word with you, woman to woman?'

Tish was uncertain what to expect from the conversation, yet she remained welcoming. 'First, call me Tish. Second, yes, of course you may.'

'I'm not sure why I'm even about to tell you all of this. It's so silly of me . . .' Augusta gave a self-deprecating laugh.

'If it's something that's been weighing on your mind, then it isn't silly. If it makes you feel better to talk to someone about it, then you should.'

'Yes, but I barely know you.'

Tish shrugged. 'People confide to bartenders

all the time. What is a caterer or restaurateur besides a bartender who serves more food than alcohol? However, if it makes you feel better, I can spike your lemonade,' she teased.

'Oh, no! After my emergency room visit, my doctor and Edwin would never forgive me if I were to drink before my next check-up,' Augusta chuckled. Then her face grew tense. 'I'm not sure if Edwin will ever forgive me as it is.'

'Why do you need his forgiveness?'

'Because I had a very good reason to want Binnie Broderick dead' – Augusta's voice grew weak – 'and it wasn't because of the library. It was because she was out to ruin my life.'

'Yes, you mentioned yesterday that you were fearful Mrs Broderick might bad-mouth you to the board. Edwin thought the idea was ridiculous, and I must say I agree with him. The board must know by now that Binnie had a vindictive streak.'

'That's because you and Edwin don't know what Binnie knew. I . . . I had a child years ago.' Tears streamed down Augusta's cheeks.

Tish rose from her chair and retrieved a stack of white paper napkins from behind the counter. If she was ever going to stay on in this town, she was going to have to invest in several boxes of facial tissues.

Augusta took a napkin from the top of the stack and dabbed her eyes as Tish returned to her seat. 'The child wasn't Edwin's. I hadn't even met him. I . . . I was an undergrad at UVA, in my sophomore year. He was a senior, on the Dean's list, the football team, from a good family, and nice-looking. Very nice-looking. He and I had met for coffee on campus before he asked me out on a date. I was excited and more than a little nervous since I hadn't dated much. Maybe a couple of boys in high school and some group-dating scenarios, but nothing one-on-one.'

Tish could already see where the story was headed. She reflected briefly upon the assault that had led to her life-changing decision to give up banking, her home, and her life in Richmond to follow her dreams in Hobson Glen. Tish had been lucky – a few bruises and cuts before her attacker ran off into the night – but she sensed Augusta's story didn't end quite as well.

'We were supposed to go to the movies. *The Last Picture Show* – remember that one with Cybil Shepherd? – was playing, only we never made it to the theater. Instead, he took the long way into town, saying he wanted to talk and get to know me. Then he parked in the middle of nowhere. I wasn't so naïve that I didn't know what was on his mind. I gave him a few kisses and then insisted that we either go to the movies as planned or he could take me back to campus.' Augusta, her hands shaking, took several sips of lemonade and wiped the tears from her eyes before continuing.

'He refused to do either. He just kept kissing me and pawing at me and unbuttoning my blouse. I begged him to stop, but he wouldn't. I screamed, but there was no one there to hear me. I tried to let myself out of the car, but he grabbed both my arms and pinned me down on the front seat. That's when . . .' Augusta's voice erupted into a squall of sobs.

Tish leaned across the table and put her hand on Augusta's in a sign of solidarity and compassion. She was tempted to excuse Augusta from sharing any more of the gory details, but she realized that, after so many years, this was a story that probably needed to be told.

'Afterwards, he left me on the side of the road. I had been discarded. I walked to the nearest town and called my roommate. She and her sister came and got me.'

'Did you report the incident?'

Augusta shook her head. 'I felt ashamed. As if it were my fault. I wondered if I had sent the wrong signals, if I didn't make my "no" clear enough, strong enough, assertive enough. I thought maybe I didn't fight back hard enough. Even if I had reported what happened, the campus officials would have done nothing. He was white, wealthy, and on the fast track to success. I was working class and one of only a handful of black students on campus.'

Augusta went on, 'A few weeks after the attack, I discovered I was pregnant. I didn't know what to do. I couldn't go to him. He looked at me with smug disdain every time I saw him, as if I had been a conquest and nothing more. I had told my roommate and she insisted that I tell my parents. They were, as you could imagine, horrified. My father wanted to hunt down the boy responsible for my "condition" and beat him to death. My mother simply cried, and prayed, and cried. Whether or not she believed I had been raped, I never knew. All I know is that she was bitterly disappointed. She was a devout Baptist, so

158

abortion wasn't an option. I was to carry the baby to full term and then give it up for adoption.'

Augusta wiped the tears from her eyes, but her voice grew stronger. 'It was March, so I went back to school and finished off the semester. I wore baggy clothing, so no one was the wiser. When the semester was done, I went to stay with an aunt outside of Memphis. Once I gave birth in November, I'd go back to Richmond to spend the holiday with the family and return to school in January for the winter semester. Only I didn't give birth in November. I went into labor in October and gave birth to a baby boy. He was beautiful. Perfect. I wanted to hold him so badly, but that wasn't permitted by the adoption agency, nor was it possible physically, for within seconds of birth he went into cardiac arrest. The pediatricians revived him, but he had suffered irreparable brain damage. He also had a congenital birth defect that not only required regular medication and monitoring, but shortened his lifespan considerably.'

Augusta paused briefly, then continued, 'As I'd mentioned earlier, my parents weren't wealthy. They couldn't afford to care for a child with his kind of needs. And I, as a student, was barely prepared to care for a healthy child on my own, let alone one requiring special care. However, we also knew that no one would ever want to adopt him. It was a heartbreaking decision, but we allowed the child to become a ward of the state. Mercifully, he didn't suffer long. He died in an institution three years later as a result of a pulmonary embolism.'

159

'I'm so sorry,' Tish expressed in a near whisper. The sound of her voice and any words she might have uttered with it felt grossly inadequate in providing comfort in the face of Augusta's revelations.

'Thank you. And thank you for listening. I . . . I hope I didn't make you feel uncomfortable, sharing that the way I did,' Augusta sniffed.

'Not at all. I'm glad you felt comfortable enough to confide in me.'

'I don't know why, but it just seemed easier to broach the subject with you, a relative stranger, than to open up to those I've known for years.'

'There's less risk that way. Less risk of feeling judged. Less risk of possibly losing someone you care about,' Tish remarked. 'But now that you have opened up, what about Edwin? I think he deserves to know.'

'I'm so scared of how he's going to take it.' Augusta burst into tears again.

'I don't know your husband, but he seems to love you a great deal. He certainly worries about you.'

'Too much,' Augusta laughed betwixt the tears.

'I think he'll be angry that you didn't talk to him sooner, but I also think that if you explain your sense of shame, he'd understand. Maybe not at once, maybe not in a day or a week, but eventually. This all happened before you'd ever even met him. Before the term "date rape" had even entered our country's vocabulary,' Tish explained. 'I can't see him holding this against you for the rest of your life.'

Augusta nodded. 'You're probably right. Edwin

flies off the handle if he thinks someone is out to harm me, but apart from that, he's a kind and reasonable man.'

'It's also probably best that he hears this news from you instead of the police.'

'The police? How would they find out?' Augusta leaned forward in her seat, her grief having turned, quite rapidly, into anxiety.

'They're investigating Binnie Broderick's murder, Augusta. If she knew about your attack and the subsequent pregnancy and threatened to tell the board and the police find out, you're a prime suspect.' A thought occurred to Tish. 'Was Doctor Livermore aware of your pregnancy all those years ago?'

'No. He wasn't even here in town when it happened. And now – well, not to cast the man in a bad light, especially when he's down, but I don't think he's ever treated anyone like me,' Augusta recounted. 'If you know what I mean.'

Tish nodded. She understood the tacit meaning of Augusta's statement, but she was still unclear about some things. 'What I don't get is, if you didn't report your attack to the police, Doctor Livermore didn't know about the subsequent pregnancy, and you stayed out of Hobson Glen until you were ready to deliver, then how did Binnie Broderick know about the existence of your son?'

'Because my son's father, the boy who raped me, was Ashton Broderick. Binnie's husband.'

Sixteen

'Binnie Broderick's husband raped Augusta Wilson?' Mary Jo repeated, her expression a mix of both horror and astonishment.

'Yes, but that's to stay just between us and Augusta,' Tish replied, still seated in the chair she had occupied when Augusta visited an hour earlier.

'And then Binnie used that knowledge to blackmail Augusta into resigning?' Jules, who had, since morning, slipped into a pink T-shirt and beige linen trousers, was incredulous.

'Yes,' Tish answered again, this time her voice reflecting the weariness she felt.

'So Augusta Wilson was a double victim. The first time of rape and the second of blackmail,' Mary Jo inferred as she pulled up the hem of her blue floral-printed maxi-dress and sat across from Tish.

'Thus giving her one hell of a motive for wanting Binnie Broderick dead,' Jules concluded while he rummaged through the refrigerator.

'Or Edwin,' Tish offered.

'But Edwin didn't know about either the rape or the blackmail,' Mary Jo corrected.

'That's what Augusta tells us,' Tish asserted. 'But how do we know that's true? Perhaps Binnie had spilled the beans to dear old Edwin without Augusta knowing about it. But

162

then, if that's the case, what about Doctor Livermore?'

'What about Doctor Livermore?' Jules repeated as he shut the refrigerator door with a frown.

'Augusta told me that she was never Doctor Livermore's patient. Therefore, he had no knowledge of Augusta's rape and subsequent pregnancy. If that's true, then neither Augusta nor Edwin had reason to shoot him.'

'Easy,' Mary Jo pronounced. 'Augusta was lying and the good doctor had, in fact, treated her. Augusta has no other children, but it would be clear from a physical exam that she had, at some point in the past, given birth.'

Tish refused to believe this was the case. 'I don't think so, MJ. Augusta isn't stupid. She knows the police could easily prove if she and Edwin were patients of Doctor Livermore. There's also the fact that everyone I've spoken to made a point of describing Doctor Livermore as being expensive and rather elitist. Augusta and Edwin may be reasonably well-off financially, but they're not part of Binnie Broderick's country club crowd. Oh, I also checked Doctor Livermore's website. He's affiliated with Virginia Commonwealth Hospital.'

'Meaning?' Jules challenged as he poured himself a glass of water from the tap.

'Meaning Augusta went to Bon Secours St Mary's Hospital the night before the benefit. If she had called the emergency line of her doctor's office first, she would have been referred to VCU.'

'Clever,' Jules purred. 'Pretty soon we'll see

you as the detective in one of those made-for-cable murder mysteries.'

'I don't think so,' Tish opined. 'I probably drink too much wine. And say the word "hell" far too often.'

'Wait,' Jules pulled a face, 'I thought that was me.'

'Where'd you think I picked up those habits?' Tish winked, much to Jules's amusement.

'Oh, you guys,' Mary Jo sighed, as if trying to corral her teenage children. 'What I want to know is how did Binnie find out about the rape? It's not like her husband would have told her.'

'While cleaning up her late husband's things, Binnie found his journal. In it, he described the guilt he felt for attacking Augusta. Apparently, his frat brothers put him up to "trying it on" with a black girl. Although Augusta never told him about the pregnancy, when his frat brothers told him about her absence during the fall semester and her reappearance in the spring, Ashton Broderick wondered if he might not have accomplished more than just "trying it on." A woman as well connected as Binnie only had to place a few select phone calls to discover the fate of Augusta's child.'

'Wow!' Mary Jo shook her head. 'Could you imagine being Binnie Broderick and finding something like that? Poor thing.'

'It must have been a devastating discovery, to be certain, but any sympathy I might have felt for that "poor thing" would have evaporated the moment she used the information to intimidate Augusta Wilson into dropping her complaint about the book purging.'

'You're right, of course. But what if Binnie Broderick hadn't always been so mean? What if she always knew something was wrong with her husband? What if this wasn't the only case of assault in Ashton Broderick's background? That could easily take its toll on both the marriage and Binnie herself.'

'I admire your determination to give people the benefit of the doubt,' Tish commended Mary Jo. 'And I agree that there were probably other issues between Binnie and her husband. However, there's a big difference between harboring bitterness about one's betrayal of trust and committing emotional extortion.'

'What a pair,' Jules lamented, clicking his tongue. 'As much as I may complain about my folks, Cordelia must have had it rough.'

'Cordelia,' Tish mused. 'Yes, I might need to check in on her again. Just to see if she knew about any of this.'

'You think Binnie might have told her daughter that her father was a rapist?' Mary Jo was skeptical.

'Maybe. By all accounts, Cordelia and Binnie were quite close. It's not like either of them had many friends in whom to confide.'

'So what will it be this time?' Jules posed. 'You've already given away Finnegan's Cake and madeleines – which were a hit with the news guys, by the way.'

'Hmm, tomorrow's Monday. Cordelia's grieving. Augusta's probably talking to Edwin as we speak and the two of them will then tell the police. It sounds as though we need

165

something substantial, doesn't it? Like sandwiches,' Tish offered, still thinking of the lunch she had never consumed. By the time she had finished with Augusta, the fish she had left on the counter was at room temperature and most likely unsafe to eat.

'Oooh, I could charge more for sandwiches.' Jules rubbed his hands together in anticipation.

'They'd also be great marketing tools. You know, teasers for your café menu,' Mary Jo suggested.

'Good idea.' Tish jolted out of her seat and took a pad of paper and a pen from a kitchen drawer. Returning to the table, she began to scribble a list. 'Let's see . . . three varieties of sandwiches should suffice, don't you think?'

'Any more than that and people can't decide,' Jules warned.

'We'll start with a veggie option. The Rudyard Kipling. Curried hummus with cumin-spiced roasted red peppers served in a pita with arugula. Then there's the Zelda Fitzgerald.'

'Oh, something decadent and naughty, no doubt.'

'Pimento cheese and sliced fried chicken breast on a buttermilk biscuit.'

'Pimento cheese *and* fried chicken? That's crazy.'

Tish looked up from her pad of paper and pointed a finger at her friend. 'Exactly.'

Mary Jo laughed. 'Leave it to you.'

'And, finally, the Animal Farm sandwich,' Tish announced.

Jules and Mary Jo exchanged questioning

166

glances as they awaited a description. 'OK, we give up,' Mary Jo declared.

'In theory, a variety of luncheon meats in equal parts; in practice, just a plain ol' ham sandwich. With condiments, of course.' Tish grinned.

'Zelda isn't the only crazy one.' Jules giggled. 'You don't really want me to use those names and descriptions when I sell them tomorrow, do you?'

'Of course she does,' Mary Jo insisted. 'That's how people will know what to order when the café opens.'

'OK. OK. I'll print out the names tonight and stand them by the stacks of sandwiches. We're going to have to hit the store before they close, though. Your refrigerator's pretty bleak.'

'Bleak doesn't even begin to describe it.' Tish's stomach growled. 'I can pop out to Publix with you right now if you want, but I need to be back here well before six.'

Mary Jo raised a questioning eyebrow. 'Why? What's going on at six o'clock?'

'I'm meeting Schuyler Thompson for dinner,' Tish spat out before her brain could even estimate the consequence of her words.

'A date?' Mary Jo and Jules exclaimed in unison.

'No. I'm going to see if Schuyler can shed any further light on Binnie's death and Doctor Livermore's shooting.'

'I have no doubt that the fine Mr Thompson can illuminate a great many things,' Jules teased.

'Ugh, here we go.' Tish sighed.

'Hey, you can't blame us. We're simply excited

167

to see you back in the dating game again,' Mary Jo explained.

'I'm not dating,' Tish maintained. 'I was about to call Schuyler to arrange a time to meet and discuss . . . everything going on . . . but he beat me to it.'

'So, wait, he called you?' Jules asked, his eyes wide with excitement.

'Settle down, will you? Yes, he called me. He'd heard about the shooting and wanted to make sure I was OK.'

'Ohhh,' Mary Jo and Jules sang.

Tish flung her head back and covered her eyes with her hands. 'He was just being a decent human being.'

'A decent human being who asked you out for dinner on a Sunday.' Jules folded his arms across his chest as if he had won his case with a single statement.

Tish narrowed her eyes. 'Yes?'

'Hello? It's Sunday. He could have taken the brunch route. Fun, but less committal, less chance for romance. Instead, he invited you out for dinner. Dinner means he plays for keeps.'

Mary Jo nodded her head. 'Truth.'

'Truth? How do *you* know?' Tish playfully balled up a paper napkin and lobbed it at Mary Jo's forehead. 'You haven't dated in nearly twenty years.'

Mary Jo caught the napkin ball. 'I may be married, but I'll have you know that I read *Allure* and *Red Book* every time I have my hair done. Oh, and I also check out Kayla's *Teen Vogue* from time to time.' With that, she threw the ball back at Tish, hitting her directly in the cleavage.

'*Teen Vogue*? Well, then, please accept my apologies for doubting your credentials. Now I know the next time I have dating questions or I'm simply in a state of alarm over the future of the Justin Bieber/Selena Gomez relationship, I can call upon you for guidance.'

'Ladies, ladies. There are more important things to discuss,' Jules called his friends to order. 'Like, what are you wearing tonight?'

Tish looked down at her Capri pants and flip-flops. 'This. I was going to freshen my make-up, of course.'

'Is this dinner out or your kids' soccer game?'

'Ouch! OK, OK. I'll wear something else. But, first' – Tish raised her left hand in superhero style – 'to the grocery store.'

Seventeen

IT'S NOT A DATE!

Julian Jefferson Davis cackled maniacally at Tish's most recent text message.

'You shouldn't torment her like that,' Mary Jo scolded in motherly fashion from behind the driver's wheel of her SUV. 'Particularly right now. She's either driving or on her way into the restaurant.'

'It's not like I forced her to answer me,' Jules replied in his defense.

'Yeah, but you know she can't help herself.'

Jules's phone suddenly chimed. He pulled it from his pocket and glanced at the screen. 'It's Tish. Oh, wait . . . it *is* a date. Whoo-hoo! I knew it!'

Mary Jo reached over to the passenger seat and gave Jules a high five. 'So now that that issue's been resolved, you mind telling me why we're heading to the rec park instead of staying at the café to make sandwiches?'

'I figured since baby bird has flown the nest for the evening, mama and papa bird would do some detective work.'

'OK, first off, I already have a papa bird at home. I need another one like a blind man needs sunglasses. Second, detective work at the rec park?'

'Mayor Whitley is there to open the new skate park. The dedication starts at six,' Jules answered excitedly.

'Lovely. Greg and Kayla and their friends will be some of the first to check it out, I'm sure. But what does the new skate park have to do with us or the case?'

'Nothing at all. But the opening will give us a chance to ask the mayor some questions about Binnie Broderick and why he was about to pardon her for the book purge.'

'And don't forget Doctor Livermore,' Mary Jo reminded him. 'Oh hey, maybe the mayor was his patient.'

'Good call, MJ. I'd never even given that a thought, but it's quite possible.'

'Motherhood hasn't rendered me completely

crazy. At least not yet. Problem is, this is a public event. How on earth are you going to ask anything about the book scandal or the murder without the mayor's handler escorting you, or the mayor, away?'

'Simple.' Jules produced a set of passes suspended on red lanyards. 'VIP passes to get us to the front of the crowd. There's one for each of us.'

'That's brilliant!' Mary Jo exclaimed.

'How soon you forget that I work in a newsroom and, therefore, have connections.'

'I do sometimes. Sorry. How did you manage to get them so quickly?'

'Oh, I bribed Sarah, our admin person with free madeleines and coffee. She called a bestie of hers at the mayor's office and voilà!'

Mary Jo flashed him a distrusting look.

'What? Oh, please! Don't worry, I put the money in the till for coffee and madeleines,' Jules insisted. 'I wouldn't steal stuff from Tish's café. Except for the few madeleines I may have eaten, of course. There was, however, just one little teensy lie involved.'

'Oh no . . .'

'I told Sarah that I wanted the passes for you because you're a devoted parent who wanted the mayor's ear to discuss other youth-oriented projects. Sarah has kids so she completely understood your concern. She wished you luck.'

'Jules,' Mary Jo sang.

'It was all for the greater good. The mayor's office isn't open until tomorrow morning. By the time Tish called and made an appointment, she

171

wouldn't have gotten in to see him until Tuesday at the earliest. And that's if she was lucky.'

'You're assuming we're just as lucky and that we'll learn something useful this evening.'

'Oh, we will learn something, honey. We will,' Jules avowed as the SUV pulled into the rec-center parking lot. 'I'm not giving up until we do. Now let's go ferret out the truth. Oh, and bring something you can film with.'

'What?' Mary Jo panicked.

'Well, I'm going to be doing the questioning. I can't film at the same time.'

'I have my iPad.' Mary Jo remembered having the device in her purse.

'Perfect! Let's go.'

Mary Jo pulled the car keys from the ignition and threw them into the side pocket of her over-sized handbag before reaching an arm into the main compartment of the bag to retrieve her iPad. As she fumbled to extract the gadget, she simultaneously jogged to keep up with Jules while also endeavoring to keep her silver slip-on sandals fixed to her feet. Had she known there would be physical activity involved in the day's schedule, she'd have changed into a pair of running shoes and capris instead of visiting the café in her Sunday best.

Mary Jo, her shoes and dignity intact, finally caught up with Jules as he introduced himself to Mayor Whitley's burly, dark-suit-clad handler. Jules flashed his VIP pass and was admitted to the front of the makeshift outdoor briefing room that had been erected on the edge of the skate park.

Mary Jo followed Jules's lead and flashed her pass to the handler. After a search of her bag and a scan of her iPad, she was waved through to join Jules and the smattering of other local journalists and political supporters gathered approximately twenty feet away from the center podium.

'Shall I start filming now?' Mary Jo whispered in Jules's ear.

'No,' Jules answered in a soft voice. 'Not until the Q and A session. I don't want to record Whitley's boring speech.'

'But he's bound to say something about Binnie's murder and Livermore's shooting this morning,' Mary Jo stated. 'It might be interesting to capture how he handles the situation.'

Jules heaved a long and particularly heavy sigh. 'Yes, I suppose you're right.'

'Of course I'm right.' Mary Jo was matter-of-fact. 'By the way, since when does a small-town mayor need a handler, a Lincoln, and VIP passes?'

'Since said small-town mayor is a shoo-in to be elected to the next Virginia General Assembly this fall.' As Jules scratched his chin, a sudden gleam came into his eye. 'Unless, of course, through sharp, focused questioning, I discover that Mayor Whitley was involved in both Binnie Broderick's death and Doctor Livermore's shooting.'

'Yeah, well, even more reason to record the speech. To capture your sharp, focused questioning in action. You know, in case you want to quote from the video footage or something. For a lead story. Or an op-ed. Like journalists do.'

'That's brilliant.' Jules finally got the hint. 'But stop the camera and start it again before the Q and A so that I don't have to wade through the speech to get to the good stuff.'

Mary Jo was about to point out that, technically speaking, the speech was, insofar as Jules's job as a journalist was concerned, the 'good stuff,' but Mayor Whitley's aide came to the podium before she had the opportunity.

The aide introduced the head of the skate park, a thirty-something man dressed in board shorts, a bright tropical-printed shirt, a backwards baseball cap, and flip-flops. After a brief round of applause, the man in the cap gave some background on how and why the concept of the skate park came about and named the people responsible for the funding, design, and build of the space. He then welcomed Mayor Whitley to the podium and stepped aside.

If the skate park founder looked outrageously casual for an opening ceremony, the mayor looked unduly conservative for an event on an early Sunday evening at a small-town park in the middle of August. Dressed in his standard navy suit, light-blue shirt, red tie and black dress shoes, Jarrod Whitley approached the podium with slicked-back auburn hair and a broad smile, and proceeded to deliver a thirty-minute speech that rambled between such subjects as the skate park, the values of today's youth, how his term as mayor had improved the local economy, how the improved economy had enabled the skate park funding, the need for donations for December's holiday light display, and, finally, a reminder that last year's Santa was retiring.

As Whitley droned on, Mary Jo struggled both to stay awake and to keep the iPad steady. Her eyelids were about to droop when she felt Jules's right index finger poke her in the shoulder.

Mary Jo improved her posture and did her best to look alert, but Jules's shoulder tap wasn't meant to awaken her: it was to draw her attention to the back of the crowd. There, behind the rows of occupied wooden folding chairs, a female figure could be seen furtively peeking over the shoulders of standing spectators.

Mary Jo sifted through her memory to put a name to the woman's face, but did not succeed. As if on cue, Jules whispered, 'Cordelia Ballantyne.'

The figure vanished as quickly as it had materialized, leaving Mary Jo and Jules to turn their attention back to the mayor's speech, which was, thankfully, and awkwardly, drawing to a close.

'And in closing,' Jarrod Whitley stated, 'I'd like to thank all of you for being here today. Now skate – er, I mean, board. Um, skateboard? Skateboard on!'

From the looks on the faces in the audience, it was doubtful the mayor's speech was going to garner much in the way of applause, but Jules still wasted no time in stepping forward lest the moment get away from him. 'Mayor Whitley! Mayor Whitley, you've made no reference at all to the murder of Lavinia Broderick or the shooting of Doctor Livermore, two of Hobson Glen's most prominent citizens. Would you care to comment on the situation?'

Despite the look of surprise upon his face, Mayor Whitley responded in a timely fashion. 'I was saddened to hear of, first, Lavinia Broderick's passing, and then the mortal wounding of Doctor Roger Livermore this morning. I have expressed my condolences to both families and I trust that the Hobson Glen Police Department is running a thorough investigation to find the perpetrator of these terrible crimes.'

'You are saying Doctor Roger Livermore was "mortally wounded"?' Jules clarified.

'Yes.' The mayor's face flushed slightly. 'I'm not sure if the police have issued a statement yet, so I may be out of line here, but the good doctor passed away this afternoon.'

A series of gasps and cries rang out from the audience, and the few reporters standing behind Jules and Mary Jo began shouting questions, but it was Jules who maintained control of the debriefing. 'What are your plans for replacing Lavinia Broderick as executive director of the library?'

'I have no plans. The library board is in charge of selecting all executive staff. I have absolutely no say in the process.'

'Is that why you didn't act when Mrs Broderick destroyed hundreds of books at the Hobson Glen Library?' Jules challenged, to the audible satisfaction of several members of the audience.

'I not sure I like the tone of that question,' Whitley reprimanded, 'but yes. It was the library board's duty to deal with the problem and they voted against terminating Mrs Broderick.'

'But that vote was overturned and you were

176

called in to mediate, weren't you?' Jules continued to press.

'A member of the board consulted me about the problem, yes, but I upheld the board's decision to retain Mrs Broderick as executive director. There was no—'

Jules didn't give him time to finish his next statement. 'No, you didn't. I have it on good authority that your original choice was to fire Mrs Broderick. You only reversed that decision within the past few days. Why the sudden change of mind?'

'As I already stated in my announcement, my fact-finding commission found no wrongdoing on the part of Mrs Broderick.'

'No wrongdoing? She destroyed hundreds of books. Was Mrs Broderick blackmailing you? Is that why you changed your mind? You were seen having a heated conversation with the deceased just before she died.'

Another round of gasps sprang from the audience.

'I refuse to even acknowledge such ridiculous claims,' an indignant Jarrod Whitley seethed. Still, his face registered far more surprise and guilt than anger. 'I have always been completely honest and forthright in all my dealings with Mrs Broderick and the members of the library board. No more questions. This interview is over.'

The same security guard who had granted Jules and Mary Jo admittance reappeared to escort them out of the fenced-in area of the skate park. Mary Jo hovered a finger over the iPad's record button to pause filming, but when a second security guard appeared and grabbed her firmly by the wrist, she thought the better of it.

The way Jules was still carrying on, footage of their eviction might become useful at a later date.

'Don't force us out, Mayor. The people of Hobson Glen deserve the truth!' Jules shouted while the first security guard guided him out of the barricaded area and into the public area of the park.

He and Mary Jo walked in silence back to Mary Jo's SUV.

'Well, that's an hour of my life I'll never get back,' Jules exhaled as he climbed into the passenger seat and slammed the door behind him.

'What do you mean? You were terrific.' Mary Jo was seated behind the steering wheel, fiddling with the iPad.

'I don't know. I thought I'd do more to break the case open.'

'You kept him on the run, Jules. That was the face of a guilty man if I ever saw one, and you didn't let him go. You were relentless. A true investigative journalist in action.'

'Really? I thought I could have been tougher.'

Mary Jo put her iPad aside for a moment and looked Jules straight in the eye. 'If you'd been any tougher, we'd be in jail right now.'

'Maybe,' Jules moped. 'Still, I thought I'd get us farther along.'

'Yes, because Woodward and Bernstein broke the news of Watergate by shouting at Nixon across a town park.' She rolled her eyes and picked up the iPad.

'I guess you're right,' Jules chuckled. 'What are you doing?'

'I'm re-watching part of Whitley's speech.'

'Looking to cure your insomnia?' he quipped.

'This would certainly do it,' Mary Jo agreed. 'I could barely keep my eyes open. But, no, I'm looking for something.'

'Like what?'

'Well, remember when Cordelia Ballantyne showed up? I want to see if and how Mayor Whitley reacted to her presence.'

'I don't get it. Why?'

'Because what was Cordelia doing there? Tish described the woman as being nearly prostrate with grief this afternoon.'

'Prostate? Cordelia's a woman,' Jules was obtuse. 'Women don't have prostates.'

'Prostrate,' Mary Jo placed special emphasis on the second letter 'r.' 'Exhausted. Drained. Too tired to speak. You should try it some time.'

'And deny you my dazzling wit? Never.'

She rolled her eyes. 'Anyway, don't you think it's strange that she was there? And slinking around and hiding behind other people, to boot.'

'Mmm,' Jules grunted in agreement. 'Given that Doctor Livermore died this afternoon, it's even stranger that she'd be out and about and alone.'

'Cordelia may not have known the doctor died,' Mary Jo allowed. '*We* only just found out. But yes, even without that, it's difficult to believe she'd be at a skate park dedication, of all things. Unless . . .'

'Unless what?' Jules prompted.

'Hold on. If I recall correctly, when we spotted Cordelia, Whitley was nattering on about needing a volunteer seamstress to patch the Santa suit before the end of the year.' She rewound the footage of the speech to the spot in question and then pressed the play button on the iPad video player.

In the clip selected, the mayor was expounding upon the need for new lights for the park display and younger volunteers to help hang the decorations since the park caretaker, Mr Luft, needed hip replacement surgery in the autumn. From there, he embarked upon the subject of the poor state of Santa's trousers.

'There,' Mary Jo called out and stopped the video. 'Look at his face. That's clearly a grimace.'

'I see it,' Jules acknowledged. 'But we have no idea what or who he's looking at.'

'He's looking out above the seated audience and toward the back of the enclosure.'

'Agreed, but he could be focused on someone standing there making a funny face or looking at their phone instead of listening to him. There could be a hundred explanations for that grimace.'

'Maybe. Or maybe not. Let's find out.' Mary Jo replaced the iPad in her bag, which she put on the back seat before stepping out of the car.

'Where are we going?' Jules asked as he got out of the car and shut the door.

'To see if my suspicions are correct. You have your phone?'

180

'Of course. Why?'

'Because if my hunch is right, we'll need to capture something in a photo or a video, and my iPad isn't exactly designed for discretion.'

Giving the skate park a wide birth while at once keeping it well within view, Mary Jo led Jules to a copse of trees just behind the nearby baseball field. From their hidden location they watched as the opening ceremony attendees were served flutes of champagne and trays of canapés.

'Hors d'oeuvres? This is the gig Tish should have gotten,' Jules angrily declared. 'Who arranged the catering for this thing? They're going to hear from me.'

'There will come a day when we can concentrate on getting Tish catering jobs. This is not that day. Now, focus, will you?' Mary Jo chastised.

'I'll try, but it would help if I knew precisely what I was supposed to be focusing on.'

'Mayor Whitley,' came Mary Jo's immediate answer. 'And, if my intuition is accurate, Cordelia Ballantyne.'

'What? Cordelia? But why—'

'Listen for a minute, will you? Cordelia Ballantyne is grieving over her mother, her marriage is on the rocks, and her daughter is away from home.'

'Right.'

'On top of that, she gets news that Doctor Livermore has been shot. And maybe, just maybe, she also learns that he's died from his wounds.'

'I'm with you so far.'

'Despite all of this, she leaves Wisteria Knolls and comes down here. Given her emotional state, one would think that Cordelia would search out someone who might console her.'

'Makes sense,' Jules allowed.

'But who would that person be? According to you, her husband was in a motel with Roberta Dutton.'

'Well, I'm sure he's out of there by now.'

'Granted, but I doubt he'd check out and rush home to his wife's waiting arms. Not after the argument Tish said they had.'

'Tish also said that Cordelia has no friends in town, apart from her mother.'

Mary Jo nodded. 'So if she was here to meet someone, who could it be? Who else was guaranteed to be here this evening? And who suddenly decided not to fire Cordelia's mother?'

'Mayor Whitley.' Jules's mouth opened wide. 'You don't think . . .'

'I don't know what to think. But if Cordelia came here to see the mayor, now would be about the right time for him to duck out of the party. The day's cooling off, kids are skating, everyone's had a glass of fizz or two. Few people would notice if Whitley went off for a few minutes on his own.'

'Are we sure he's even still there? Maybe my questions scared him off?'

'You definitely had him on the ropes, honey, but if he wants skatepark sponsors to drop more money on his re-election campaign or Santa's trousers, he has to hang around for at least a little while. I also happened to notice that the

Lincoln he drives around in is still parked in the lot,' Mary Jo explained.

'Well, I hope he hurries up,' Jules complained.

'I know. We have a bunch of sandwiches to make.'

'Not just that, but I seem to be kneeling on a patch of thistle. Ow.'

Just as Mary Jo leaned over to examine the ground beneath Jules's knees, she heard a pair of shoes crunching along the gravel path a few yards away. She looked up to see Jarrod Whitley approaching from the left.

'It's the mayor,' Jules stated in a frantic whisper.

'Yes, I know. Shh!' Mary Jo and Jules huddled together and watched silently through layers of foliage as Whitley walked past them and farther down the path toward the baseball field.

'Get your phone out,' Mary Jo prompted, noticing a female figure approaching on the path from the right.

Jules did as instructed and they moved behind a second nearby bush so as to get a better shot of the pair as they united.

Mary Jo's hunch had paid off. The woman was, indeed, Cordelia Ballantyne. She rushed forward and embraced Jarrod Whitley with the ferocity of a woman who hadn't seen her lover in months.

'Are you filming?' Mary Jo tapped on Jules's arm.

'Yes. Shh!' Jules replied with an impatient nod of the head.

After their embrace, Cordelia and Jarrod exchanged a passionate kiss.

'You shouldn't be here, Cordelia,' Whitley reminded her. 'We're taking a huge risk.'

'I know, Jarrod, but I just had to see you. What with Mother and now Doctor Livermore dying, I couldn't bear to be alone. I'm just so scared.' Cordelia burst into tears.

'I know, but if we're seen together, my wife and your husband would—'

'Oh, I don't care what John thinks anymore. I know he's just waiting to get a divorce. I want you. You make me happy.' Cordelia reached up and stroked Whitley's cheek in a loving fashion.

Whitley responded by taking her hand in his and removing it. 'Cordelia, we can't be seen like this. Not with my re-election right around the corner. You knew the rules going into this.'

'Yes, I know, but I had no idea at the time that all this was going to happen.' She broke down again.

'Look, I know you're going through a rough patch right now' – Jarrod's voice was gentle, yet firm – 'but there are just two and a half months left until election day. I can't blow it now. If anyone were to discover we were seeing each other, it could all be over for me.'

'Well, then, what are you suggesting? We can't just stop now, can we? Not now. Not after—'

'No. No, I'm not suggesting that. I'm just saying that maybe we should take a little break.'

'A break?' Cordelia's voice rose sharply. Even from Mary Jo and Jules's vantage point, it was evident the woman was trembling.

'Just a short one. Just until this election business is over.'

'Election day? You want to stay apart until election day? That's . . . that's crazy.'

'Calm down, Cordelia.' Whitley placed his hands on her shoulders. 'I'll still be available by text and email should you need someone to talk to.'

Cordelia stopped crying. Without a sound, she reached up and forcibly removed Whitley's hands from her shoulders. 'Text? Email? How very big of you. My God, Jarrod. How could you be so insensitive? And how could I have been so stupid? Goodbye.'

'Um, goodbye for now, right?'

'I meant what I said,' Cordelia shouted. She marched back along the path from whence she came.

Jarrod Whitley threw his hands in the air and retraced his steps as well.

When the pair were gone from view, Mary Jo nudged Jules. 'Did you get it all?'

'Every incriminating, heartbreaking word.'

'Whitley was pretty harsh, wasn't he?' Mary Jo commiserated as she stood up and stretched.

'Positively frigid. He'd better hope that Santa suit doesn't get repaired because all he's gonna see in his stocking this Christmas is coal.' Jules rose to his feet and returned the phone to his back pants pocket.

'He'll see worse than that if he winds up in prison,' Mary Jo mused.

'You think he may have murdered Binnie Broderick?'

Mary Jo shrugged. 'She obviously found out about his affair with Cordelia.'

'And used it to preserve her job,' Jules added. 'Question is whether Whitley trusted Binnie to keep silent.'

'God only knows.' She shook her head. 'But we'd better head back to the café. We have a flock of sandwiches to assemble.'

'Yeah, and I could really use a drink.'

Eighteen

IT'S NOT A DATE, Tish insisted in the all-caps text message she sent Jules from the parking lot of the Hobson Grille. As much as she loved Jules and his outrageous sense of humor, there were times when the man could take a joke too far.

Having heeded Jules's and Mary Jo's fashion advice by ditching the Capri pants and tee in favor of a cream-and-red rose-printed dress with a coordinating red shrug sweater, Tish teetered into the restaurant in a pair of cream ankle-strap stiletto sandals that she hadn't worn in over a year. She prayed she didn't embarrass herself by falling head first into someone's dinner.

The door opened into the bar part of the restaurant where a young woman in a pale-blue Hobson Grille logo polo shirt and black shorts greeted Tish upon entering. 'May I help you?'

'Yes, I'm meeting Schuyler Thompson here tonight. Tall man, blond hair, fortyish.'

'Oh, yes, I know Mr Thompson. He's in the

186

dining room, third booth by the window.' She gestured to the door at the back of the bar with a smile.

'Thanks.' Tish followed the route the hostess indicated. From the doorway, she spied Schuyler in the booth in question, looking as attractive as ever in a pinstriped azure button-down shirt, linen blazer, and, in keeping with the casual weekend vibe, a pair of blue jeans. On the table before him rested a cellophane-wrapped bouquet of pink roses.

At the sight of the flowers, Tish retreated back into the bar and texted Jules. *OK. Maybe it is a date.*

Fearful Jules would press her for details, Tish switched her phone off and placed it in the bottom of her red Coach handbag before drawing a deep breath and proceeding into the dining room.

As she drew near, Schuyler smiled and gallantly rose to his feet. 'I'm so glad you could make it. These are for you.' He presented the bouquet.

'Oh, thank you. They're lovely.' Tish tried to conceal her discomfort, but Schuyler saw through her plastered-on smile.

'I hope you don't think me presumptuous. I was actually going to bring you some vegetables from my garden, seeing as you're a cook, but I was afraid a bag of squash might send the wrong message.'

Tish's discomfort melted into genuine laughter. 'Oh, I don't know. Optics aside, a bag of squash would have made a great pairing for the five pounds of rib roast left in my refrigerator.' She

187

sat across from Schuyler, on the side of the booth nearest the bar-room door.

'Five pounds? Note to self: next time bring potatoes,' Schuyler teased and returned to his spot opposite Tish. 'I hope the restaurant is OK for you. It's not the best around, but it's decent. And it's open Sundays.'

'Oh, no, it's perfectly fine. That rib roast I told you about? Aside from a half gallon of skim milk and superstore-sized sacks of flour and baking powder, that's all the food I have in my kitchen.'

'Well, we'd best get you a menu, then.' He passed her a brown faux-leather folder stamped with the Hobson Grille logo. 'I also goofed a little bit. I forgot there's no bar service to the dining room on Sunday. If you want a drink, I need to buy it at the bar and bring it out.'

Tish narrowed her eyes. 'Blue laws?'

'No, underage wait staff on Sundays. The eighteen and overs put in extra hours on Fridays and Saturdays.'

'Oh,' Tish chuckled.

'So,' Schuyler clumsily segued, 'I have to admit I had an ulterior motive for inviting you to dinner tonight. I mean, apart from giving you a break from cooking.'

'I suspected as much.' Tish smiled.

'The roses kinda gave it away, didn't they?'

'Maybe just a little.'

'I knew I should have stuck to the squash.' He gave a playful snap of his fingers. 'All joking aside, I've liked you from the moment I saw you. I mean, there you were, this beautiful blonde

188

looking to rent a property from me. And there I was, sweaty and stinky after an evening run.'

'I wouldn't say you were stinky.' Tish blushed in reaction to Schuyler's use of the word 'beautiful.' 'Perhaps "not so fresh" would be a better description.'

'That's very generous of you,' Schuyler thanked her. 'But after getting to know you these past few weeks and seeing how passionate you are about your business, how determined you are to make it a success, and how you've kept your chin up these past few days, my admiration for you has moved beyond the physical. I um . . . well, I'm just going to say it. You're quite the woman, Tish, and if you'd allow, I'd like to get to know you better.'

An obviously anxious Schuyler leaned forward in his seat.

Tish took several moments to choose her words before responding. 'I would like to get to know you better too, Schuyler. However, I must be honest. I haven't given much thought to cultivating a love life in quite a long time. I don't know if that's because I'm not ready for it, or I've been so focused on the café that there's no room for it, or if I'm still healing from my divorce, or if I'm quite simply scared. That's not me saying "no" or making excuses should things not work out between us. Nor am I warning you off because I anticipate doom. That's just me asking you if we can move slowly while I figure things out.'

Schuyler's tense facial expression thawed into a broad grin. 'Yes. Yes, of course we can move slowly. Any woman I become romantically involved with needs to be my friend first. We need to be able to laugh with each other and support each other during any crisis. And, um, well truth be told, despite my suave, sophistic- ated demeanor' – he issued a self-deprecating clearing of the throat – 'I'm pretty rusty at this dating thing myself. The past several years have seen me focused on ramping up my father's law practice and cleaning out my mother's bakery. I'm looking forward to getting together with you and talking . . . about life and films and books, and whatever else might come our way.'

'I look forward to that too.' Tish did not pass the comment out of politeness.

'Good.' Schuyler leaned against the backrest of the booth. 'Whew! For a minute there, I thought I was going to wind up in the bar area alone, eating soggy fries.'

'Are the fries soggy here?' she asked. At this point, she was so hungry that getting saddled with a plate of greasy food would be not just disappointing but borderline disastrous.

'No, not at all. They're actually quite good. Mine would have been soggy because I'd be crying into them.'

Tish laughed. 'I'm glad I rescued you from that fate.'

'You and me both.' He leaned forward again and smiled. 'So, when I called you this afternoon, you were about to call me. Is everything OK with the café and the apartment?'

'Oh, yes. Wonderful. Couldn't be better.' A sheepish Tish nodded and smiled. How on earth was she supposed to question him about a murder investigation now?

'Great. Then what did you want to discuss?'

Maybe she should just leave that to Sheriff Reade. 'Oh, it was nothing. Let's enjoy our evening.'

'Sounds good to me. May I get you something to drink?'

'Um, a glass of Chardonnay, please.'

'Coming right up.' Schuyler excused himself from the table.

Tish leaned against the back cushion of the booth, kicked off her ridiculous shoes, and deliberated her next move. Yes, she would leave Schuyler to be questioned by Reade, she resolved. That way she could get on with her evening. And enjoy her time. With a potential murderer . . .

A man suddenly appeared beside her. A man who wasn't Schuyler.

Tish looked up to see Sheriff Reade standing by the table, as if her thoughts had somehow summoned him from out of the ether. 'Oh, Sheriff Reade. How are you?'

He was dressed in a black T-shirt, ripped jeans and motorcycle boots. 'Fine. And you?'

Tish was still more than a bit rattled by the sheriff's sudden tableside appearance. 'Good. Um, busy. Good. What brings you here?'

'The boys and I use the back room for rehearsals on Sunday. We took a break to grab a beer and I saw you sitting out here. Mr Davis meeting you for dinner?'

'Mr Davis?' Tish's face registered confusion.

191

'No, Jules is back at the café. I'm here with Schuyler Thompson.'

It was Reade's turn to be confused. 'I'm sorry. I just thought from this morning and the way you both were dressed that . . .'

'We were an item?' Tish filled in the blanks with a boisterous laugh. 'Yeah, um, no. He and Mary Jo are old college friends of mine.' She dropped her voice to a whisper. 'You're actually far more Jules's type than I am.'

'Oh.' Reade nodded and then shook his head. 'I really got that wrong, didn't I?'

'It happens.' She shrugged.

'Guess so. May I sit down?'

'Well, Schuyler will be on his way back any minute.'

'I won't be long,' Reade promised. He had already taken Schuyler's seat. 'Augusta May Wilson visited me this afternoon. Thank you.'

'Thank me for what?'

'For talking to her and getting her to confide in me. That couldn't have been easy for her.'

'I can't imagine how difficult it must have been for her to open up to me,' Tish reflected. 'But then to repeat the same story to you?'

'I know, but she did and she was quite brave. So thank you.' Reade smiled.

'All I did was listen and give her my opinion on how to proceed. Speaking of which, was Edwin with her when she gave you her statement?' She hoped that she hadn't misread the Wilsons' marriage and given Augusta faulty advice.

'He was. Naturally, he has a lot of information

to digest, as I gathered that he only just learned of his wife's story shortly before I did. But by the end of our interview, he was holding Augusta's hand and behaving in a supportive manner.'

'Well, that's a relief. I hope they can move past this together.'

'Yes.' Reade shifted in his seat. 'Unfortunately, I also have some bad news for you. Doctor Livermore died this afternoon.'

Tish felt a sudden chill. Two people dead in as many days. When was it all going to stop?

Schuyler had returned and, after placing their drinks on the table, draped his linen jacket over Tish's shoulders. 'They always seem to turn the air conditioning up to "freeze" in this place.' His sympathetic smile made it clear he understood Tish's goose bumps weren't from the temperature of the room.

'Hey, Schuyler,' Sheriff Reade greeted.

'Hi, Clem.' Schuyler handed Tish her glass of wine and took a sip from his glass of beer. 'Can I get you anything from the bar?'

'No, thanks. I have a running tab I should probably settle up. I'm sorry for disturbing your . . . um, date.'

'No problem. How are things?'

Tish slid over to allow Schuyler to sit beside her. 'Sheriff Reade gave me some terrible news. Doctor Livermore died this afternoon.'

Schuyler accepted the seat. Tish found the proximity to the attorney not at all unpleasant.

'Yeah, I heard the sheriff on my way back from the bar. I can't believe it. Why would anyone want to kill a small-town doctor like

Livermore? I mean, Binnie Broderick had her enemies, but I never heard a negative word uttered against Livermore.'

'Speaking of Mrs Broderick, Schuyler,' Reade spoke up, 'I'd like to see you in my office tomorrow.'

'Sure thing. What time?'

'Whatever works best for you. I know you typically take appointments in Richmond.'

'Yeah, let's see. My first appointment is at ten so I could meet you at the station at, say, eight o'clock?'

'That would be fine. You know, Ms Tarragon, I've heard you've been busy spreading your baked goods around town,' Reade changed the subject.

Tish took a sip of wine. 'Yes, I had leftover cakes from the fundraiser that needed to be eaten. Oh, and I brought some madeleines to Cordelia Ballantyne. I thought she could use the visit and the food.'

'That's kind of you,' Schuyler praised.

'Yes, very kind,' Reade agreed. 'Miss Cordelia was an awful mess at the shooting scene this morning. How did you find her?'

'Calmer, but still not in a good place. She's terribly lost without her mother. And not having her daughter around isn't helping things.' Tish saw an opportunity to gather some information. 'What happened to Charlotte Ballantyne anyway? Cordelia mentioned private school, but it seemed that Charlotte was somewhere far less accessible.'

'Binnie always told me her granddaughter was at St Margaret's School just outside of Richmond,' Schuyler stated. 'It's a boarding school with a fairly illustrious reputation.'

Tish shook her head. 'That can't be right. I overheard John Ballantyne mention something about Charlotte being in Williamsburg.'

'Williamsburg? That's a forty-five-minute drive from here.'

Sheriff Reade, meanwhile, questioned Tish's phrasing. 'Overheard?'

Any trace of a chill disappeared as she felt the blood rise to her cheeks. 'Yes, I happened to overhear John and Cordelia having an argument in front of an open window. I was on their doorstep, about to press the bell so I could deliver those rosemary cornmeal madeleines I told you about.'

'Yes, those madeleines of yours seem to have made their way to more than a couple of interesting places around town,' Reade smirked.

'Well, they are one of my most popular baked items.' Tish gave an innocent smile before taking another sip of Chardonnay.

'Uh-huh. Well, as far as Charlotte Ballantyne is concerned, I heard she left St Margaret's last Christmas. The story goes that she got into some kind of trouble.'

Schuyler frowned. 'I heard that rumor too, but Binnie still spoke of Charlotte being at St Margaret's. Though it would have been just like Binnie Broderick to try to keep up appearances.'

'Or Cordelia underplayed her daughter's

troubles and never told her mother that Charlotte had been pulled from St Margaret's,' Tish ventured.

'You have a suspicious mind, Ms Tarragon,' Reade observed. 'Are you sure you didn't hand out those baked goods as a way to run a little investigation of your own?'

'I'm not sure I'd know how to run a criminal investigation,' Tish replied honestly. If she happened to learn about Binnie Broderick's murder while creating goodwill, it was simply because she listened. 'No, I'm just trying to do some damage control and build some buzz for my baked products. Having a woman poisoned during one's first catering gig doesn't exactly do wonders for business.'

'I might have some good news on that front.' Reade was cryptic.

'Anything you're able to share with us?'

'Sure. The reporters probably have their hands on it by now anyway. Lab reports show that there were no traces of poison in the food on Binnie's plate, in her glass, or in the bottle of hot sauce.'

Tish sipped her glass of wine pensively.

'Um, Tish. Did you hear that?' Schuyler prompted. 'That's great news for your business.'

'Hmph?' Tish snapped from her reverie. 'Oh, yes. Yes, it is great news. I was simply remembering something . . .'

'What?'

'There was a half-empty case of sriracha in the butler pantry at Wisteria Knolls. I noticed it this afternoon.'

Reade gave this information a few seconds' worth of consideration. 'Clearly Binnie Broderick had a taste for the stuff. Hence why she asked for it the night of the fundraiser.'

'If she ate that much of the stuff, someone she worked with or lived with or ate with would have known about it,' Schuyler noted.

'You're right, they would,' Reade acknowledged. 'But it doesn't matter. The hot sauce at the party wasn't poisoned.'

'That's right.' Schuyler frowned and took a swig of beer.

Tish recalled another odd detail regarding the butler pantry. 'Perhaps someone tampered with the hot sauce, or some other food product, at Wisteria Knolls. I saw Enid Kemper sneaking out of there yesterday afternoon. She came out through the pantry door and wandered off into the woods behind the house. Might she have been in the pantry to cover her tracks by removing the tainted hot sauce?'

'Enid Kemper? You're positive?' Reade questioned.

'Yes, I'm positive. Unless there's someone else in Hobson Glen who travels with a parrot – sorry, conure – and wears cardigan sweaters in ninety-degree heat.'

'I'll talk to Enid tomorrow and find out what she was doing lurking around Wisteria Knolls. But I highly doubt it had anything to do with Binnie. There's absolutely no motive.'

'But there is,' Tish and Schuyler insisted in unison. Each looked at the other.

'You go first,' Tish invited.

197

'No, please. I happen to be a gentleman,' Schuyler insisted, much to Tish's delight.

'It's obvious, isn't it?' a tickled Tish blurted excitedly. 'Binnie banned Langhorne from the library.'

'This again?' Reade shook his head.

'Yes, "this again,"' Tish fired back. 'Enid said she would make Binnie pay. What if she had and then returned to Wisteria Knolls to discard the evidence?'

'Langhorne aside,' Schuyler began, 'and I know how important that parrot—'

'Conure,' Tish and Reade corrected in harmony.

'How important that *conure* is to Enid, but she had an even greater motive than that for killing Binnie Broderick,' Schuyler asserted.

As Reade and Tish leaned forward in their seats, awaiting Schuyler's next words, the lawyer took a long draught of beer.

'Oh, come on,' Tish urged, fighting the impulse to give him a playful slug in the arm.

'OK, OK,' Schuyler laughed, having brought his audience to the unbearable brink of suspense. 'Binnie's family – the Darlingtons – bankrupted Enid Kemper's family back in the day. According to Binnie, her father, Wade Darlington, a brilliant businessman – Binnie's description, not mine – played the market and wound up purchasing Kemper Pharmaceuticals for a song. To hear it from the locals who were around at the time, Wade Darlington took advantage of Enid's father, Jerome Kemper. Ol' Jerome was more interested in his inventions than running a manufacturing plant, so he hired Wade Darlington to manage the business. Wade allegedly dragged the business into the ground and then bought up the majority of the shares. Jerome Kemper took a tremendous hit and wound up selling his shares entirely. He never recovered from the loss. He died a few years later, leaving his wife and Enid to sell off belongings in order to stay in their home.'

'Some brilliant businessman,' Tish mumbled. 'Sounds more like a completely heartless scoundrel.'

'That's a sad story and I feel badly for Enid and her family,' Reade began, 'but, as you said, that must have been – what? – forty, fifty years ago. People don't seek vengeance after nearly half a century. Besides, it was Wade Darlington who bankrupted the Kemper family, not Binnie Broderick.'

'True,' Schuyler admitted, 'but Binnie Broderick wouldn't allow the story to die. She rubbed it in Enid's face every opportunity she got. That silly rule about Langhorne not entering the library? Merely a power play on Binnie's part.'

Schuyler wasn't the first person to have described Binnie Broderick as a braggard and a bully. Tish recalled the Wilsons' story of how Binnie even lorded the Darlington name over her own husband. Although that might have been more a result of Ashton Broderick's lack of character than true haughtiness on Binnie's part.

'As I said, I'll talk to Enid tomorrow and see what's going on.' Reade rose from his side of the booth. 'Looks like the band's getting back to rehearsing. I'll see you both around. Goodnight.'

'Goodnight,' Tish and Schuyler responded.

Schuyler stood up and took the seat previously occupied by the sheriff. 'I can only guess that you probably have some questions for me.'

Tish narrowed her eyes. 'What do you mean?'

'Well, if you're "running your own investigation," as Reade suggested, you probably want to ask me about Binnie Broderick.' He grinned.

'I already told Reade I'm not running my own investigation.' Tish tried to look casual as she sipped her wine.

'Uh-huh,' Schuyler smirked.

'OK, maybe I am investigating. Just a little. And maybe that was the reason I was about to call you,' Tish sheepishly admitted.

'You shouldn't be embarrassed. I'm sure, by now, you've probably heard all about Binnie and her treatment of my mother. Besides, if we are to ever move beyond friendship, you need to have absolutely no questions or doubts about me.'

'And you about me.' She took another sip of wine and smiled admiringly at Schuyler before chiding herself for acting like a lovesick little girl. There were important questions to be answered. 'So are the stories true about your mother's illness being brought on by Binnie's behavior?'

'Um, yes and no,' Schuyler hemmed. 'Sorry if that sounds evasive. It's just I don't think it's fair to lay the entirety of my mother's cancer on one woman's doorstep. My mother was a strong, resilient woman. However, she also was extremely soft-hearted. My father's death crushed her, but she was just thirty-nine years old and had a seven-year-old boy to raise. My uncle was my dad's partner in the law firm, and he would send my mother money, but she wasn't one for handouts, so she invested her cash in a business that would allow her to work from home. She started out by baking pastries and delivering them in the mornings to local businesses. People loved them so much that she eventually had to expand into a bakery. Then she met Celestine – and the rest is history.'

Schuyler took a swig of beer. 'When Binnie tried to undermine that business, it angered my mother, but she also found it incomprehensibly hurtful. She couldn't fathom how a woman could want, quite literally, to take food out of the mouth of another woman and her child. There was a complete disconnect there that my mother never understood. The legal battles with the zoning commission and the endless back-and-forth with Binnie certainly weakened my mother's health, but I believe she had already been ill for quite some time.'

'Why do you think that?' Tish asked and then thought better of it. 'I mean, not to be nosy, of course.'

'No, you're not being nosy at all. When my mother was admitted to the hospital, her cancer was quite advanced. The doctor marveled over the fact that she hadn't experienced any pain. After she passed, I cleaned out her belongings – with Celestine's help – and discovered that she had been in considerable pain. Her bathroom cabinet and nightstand were chockablock with over-the-counter painkillers of every description.'

'Why didn't she see a doctor?'

'I wondered that too until I saw the account she left in my name, with strict instructions that it should be used for the law school of my choice. I suspect – although I have no concrete evidence – that my mother feared that treatment for her illness would drain that bank account dry. She was a business owner and had no health insurance to speak of – just a life insurance policy to cover her funeral costs.'

'I'm so sorry, Schuyler.' Tish reached an outstretched hand toward his. He clasped it and smiled.

'It's OK. I miss her still, but not like I did. I also got over my hatred for Binnie Broderick. My mother never blamed anyone for her disease or for her impending death. She was happy with the life she had led and was looking forward to being reunited with my father. She was full of forgiveness – even for Binnie. She said that "anger is like taking poison and expecting the other person to die." It's a lesson I took to heart.'

'You're a far better person than I am,' Tish conceded. 'I'm not sure I'd be able to forgive someone who did that to someone I loved.'

Schuyler shrugged. 'What was I supposed to do? Let my hatred and anger rule my life? My mother sacrificed herself so that I could live life to the fullest. She wanted me to have a career and a family. I have the first of those and eventually, with some luck, I'll have the second.' His eyes slid toward Tish, who colored slightly and averted her gaze. 'I'd have neither if I were to allow revenge to consume me. Also, harboring grudges doesn't tend to work well with clients.'

'That's right. Binnie was a client of your law firm, wasn't she? You met with her the day I moved into town.'

'I did. That was our last meeting.'

'What did you discuss? I mean, if you're able to tell me, that is. I know you're bound by attorney–client privilege.'

'Attorney–client privilege ends when the client is murdered over something that may or may not have to do with the client's legal dealings. I should consult with Reade before I tell you. Then again, it will all be out soon enough, I suppose,' Schuyler reasoned, before swearing Tish to secrecy until he spoke with the police. 'Binnie Broderick came to see me regarding her will.'

'Was she drafting a new will or changing an old one?'

'Changing the will she made after her husband died.'

'Hmm, was Binnie feeling OK?'

'Yeah, I wondered the same thing. Aside from a headache, Binnie said she was strong as an ox.'

'I don't suppose you can tell me about the changes she made.' Tish smiled.

Schuyler drew a deep breath. 'Oh, what the hay,' he exhaled. 'Whereas her original will favored Cordelia and John Ballantyne, the new will left everything to her church.' Schuyler raised his eyebrows to demonstrate that he was as shocked as Tish by the modification.

'Her church? You mean the one next door to my café?' Tish took a drink.

'No.' Schuyler shook his head and took a swig of beer. 'Some ultra-conservative church ten miles out of town. Binnie had attended services there for years.'

'Still, a woman as shrewd as Binnie signing over her entire fortune? Are you certain they're a church and not a cult?'

'Ninety-nine percent positive. I raised the same issue with Binnie, who assured me they were fine, but then I did some nosing around on my own. Apparently, they're a legitimate Born Again parish with absolutely no history of forcing members to tithe their assets to the church. Moreover, Binnie stipulated that no one from the church was to know about the will change. She was genuinely excited at the prospect of surprising her minister as well as her fellow parishioners.'

'What about Cordelia and John Ballantyne? Were they aware they'd been written out of the will?'

'I may have misled you with my statement about the will favoring the church. Cordelia wasn't completely written out per se. According to the revised will, she was still due to inherit Wisteria Knolls and all of its contents. In addition, Binnie set up a trust to ensure Cordelia could continue to maintain the property. John, however, was out completely. No mention of him whatsoever in the new will.' He drew a deep breath. 'As to whether or not Cordelia and John were aware of the changes, I couldn't say. However, something significant must have

204

transpired to initiate such a drastic action. It's difficult to imagine neither of them would be aware of any actions on their part that might have precipitated such revisions.'

Schuyler's statement made sense, yet was there not more than a bit of a malicious streak in Binnie Broderick's nature? 'Do you really believe something serious incited the change?'

'I'm not following.' Schuyler's face registered confusion.

'Well, given her treatment of your mother and several other people around town, it's clear that Binnie Broderick was quite capable of vindictiveness. I don't think it's unfathomable that Binnie might have changed her will over an issue you or I would have considered trivial.'

'Can't disagree with you there,' he stated.

Tish nodded. 'And what about Charlotte? Did Binnie make any provisions for her granddaughter?'

Schuyler shook his head. 'Not a one.'

'How odd,' Tish mused. 'One would think she'd want to provide for or at least contribute to her sole grandchild's education.'

'Most grandparents would, but we're not talking about most grandparents. I may have made my peace with Binnie Broderick, but that still doesn't mean I liked her much or respected her views on the world.'

Tish fiddled with the stem of her wine glass and smiled. She appreciated not just Schuyler's integrity but his complete and utter honesty. 'Enough about Binnie and murders. Shall we order some food?'

205

'Absolutely. And then, perhaps, we can discuss more pleasant things?'

'Why, Mr Thompson, I thought you'd never ask,' Tish purred and took another sip of wine.

Nineteen

After a second round of drinks and a lovely meal of pesto chicken with tomato pasta and Moroccan salmon over vegetable couscous, respectively, Schuyler and Tish made their way to the Hobson Grille parking lot where, without even realizing it, Tish had parked her car beside that of her date.

'See? Kismet,' Schuyler joked as he gestured toward the Matrix and his black BMW sedan.

'I didn't notice. Might be time for me to get glasses,' Tish joked.

'Nah,' Schuyler dismissed. 'You're perfect.'

'Well, I'm not sure about that, but this night certainly was perfect,' she replied. 'With the exception of Sheriff Reade popping by.'

'Even that served a purpose. It got things out in the open,' Schuyler reasoned. 'Do you think maybe we can do this again sometime soon?'

'I'd like that. I'd like that a lot.'

'Me too. There's a great farmers' market over in Fredericksburg. You'd love it. Especially this time of year. Perhaps we can drive over one morning, have a picnic lunch, and explore the town.'

'And maybe, a day or so later, I can cook you dinner with the ingredients we pick up there?'

'That would be . . . wow.' He shook his head as in disbelief. 'I'll give you a call to check in and we'll set things up. In the meantime, if you need me for anything, just let me know.'

'I will,' she promised before bestowing him with a hug and a kiss on the cheek. 'Goodnight.'

'Goodnight.' Schuyler walked backwards to his car, his eyes fixed on Tish the entire time.

Tish, meanwhile, played it cool. Pulling her car keys from her bag, she admitted herself into the Matrix with nary a backward glance. With a brief wave in Schuyler's direction, she pulled the car out of the Hobson Grille parking lot and on to Main Street. From her side-view mirror, Tish could see Schuyler watching after her as she drove away.

Perfect. Tish replayed Schuyler's words through her mind. It had been nearly twenty years since she had been on her first date with her ex-husband, Mitch. Had Mitch ever described her as perfect? Had he ever even called her beautiful?

No, he hadn't. No one ever had. A tear trickled down Tish's cheek. Inwardly, however, she felt like dancing a jig or getting on the phone and detailing the event to Mary Jo and Jules. Perhaps she might pull over to do just that – only Schuyler had pulled out of the restaurant parking lot just a few cars behind hers.

Knowing that Schuyler would keep straight on Main Street, Tish hung a left on to the bypass road. Round the bend past the road that led to

207

Celestine's house, she once again noticed a figure in the gathering twilight skulking on the grounds of Wisteria Knolls.

Tish turned on her headlights and, seeing no other car parked outside the house, pulled into the driveway. As she reached the top of the drive, the lights of the Matrix's headlamps picked out the familiar form of Enid Kemper. Upon being discovered, Enid jumped and set off toward the woods, but Tish was too fast for her.

Springing from behind the steering wheel, she took off in chase and quickly took hold of the elderly woman's arm. Tish's grasp was firm but forgiving. The last thing she wanted to do was to hurt the woman.

Enid gave one last tug in an effort to gain independence, but Tish's hold upon her was unyielding. In the end, Enid's last-ditch attempt to escape only caused the contents of her cardigan sweater pockets to go tumbling on to the driveway pavement with a dreadful clatter.

'Silverware?' Tish asked in astonishment as she released Enid's arm and bent down to collect the items from the pavement.

'Not just silverware – *my* silverware. My family's silverware,' Enid corrected. 'It belonged to my great-grandmother, but I had to put it up for auction last year to pay for updated plumbing and a new furnace back at the house.'

'But if you auctioned your silverware, what was Binnie doing with it?'

'What do you think she was doing with it? She bought it.'

'Bought it? To help you?'

'Help me?' Enid erupted in boisterous laughter. 'Heavens, no. She did it to rub it in my face. Just another souvenir of the Darlingtons' triumph. Another reminder of how her father crushed my father into the ground.'

'And this is your revenge? Stealing back her – I mean, *your* – silverware?'

'Beats murdering her, doesn't it?'

'Yes, well I . . .' Tish frowned. 'I suppose it does.'

'Think about it. You can only kill someone once. But you can steal back your stuff gradually over time. It's like gaslighting. Binnie goes looking for a fork and can't find it. She'd never guess it's back in my own dining room.'

This was the only time Tish had ever seen Enid smile. She felt horrible for pointing out the obvious flaw in the woman's plan, but someone had to snap her back to reality before she got into trouble with the law. 'But Binnie's dead, Enid. You could take the entire set in one fell swoop and she wouldn't know. She's no longer here for you to gaslight.'

'I'm not senile, you fool,' Enid said indignantly. 'I know Binnie's dead. And I admit that not being able to get under her skin does take some of the fun out of the whole exercise. But dang it, even if Binnie never knew I was taking my silver back, *I* know. And my family's silver will finally be back where it belongs.' Enid's facial expression switched from defiance to fear. 'You won't tell Clemson Reade, will you?'

'Not if you put the silver back,' Tish stipulated.

'What? Now?'

'No, not right now. I'm not sure when Cordelia or John might come back.' Tish glanced worriedly over each shoulder. Indeed, Tish didn't even wish to be caught in the driveway of Wisteria Knolls on her own, let alone with a woman whose pockets were full of antique silver. 'Tomorrow. You keep an eye on this place, as you seem to do on a regular basis. Sneak over when no one is home, and instead of taking the rest of your family's silver, you replace what you've taken.'

'Replace it? But it's mine.'

'And it will be yours again once we ask Cordelia if she would kindly return it to you.'

'What makes you think she'd do that?' Enid posed.

'Because Cordelia Ballantyne strikes me as being a reasonable woman.'

'Reasonable? With that mother of hers? Not sure how that's genetically possible.'

'Now, I'm sure she'd work out some sort of arrangement with us.' Tish calculated, in her mind, just how she'd approach Cordelia about 'loaning' the silver to Enid Kemper. The details weren't clear, but she was certain she'd come up with *something*.

'Why should I trust either of you?' Enid clutched at the silver and brought it to her bosom. 'The Darlingtons destroyed my family.'

'I do understand everything Binnie has done to demean you over the years, but what her father did was decades ago. I heard it said recently that holding on to anger is like drinking poison and expecting the other person to die.' As the words

210

of wisdom crossed Tish's lips, she realized the flaw in applying Schuyler's maxim to this particular situation.

Enid was quick to point it out. 'The other person *did* die.'

'Yes, she did,' Tish sighed, 'but not because of your anger.'

'No, because of someone else's.'

Clearly the philosophy of Schuyler and Cynthia Thompson was not going to work on this fine summer evening. She decided to try a different tack. 'Well, if you don't want to think of yourself, at least give a thought to poor Langhorne.'

The introduction of her beloved bird to the conversation gave Enid pause. 'Langhorne? What on earth does my sweet boy have to do with any of this?'

'Who's going to look after him while you're in jail?'

'You're not going to tell anyone—'

'No, but Binnie Broderick is dead and her estate will be handed down to her family. There will, inevitably, be an inventory performed to ensure the contents of the house are intact. Your silver service – or anything else that may have gone missing – will be questioned by Binnie's attorney, the insurance company, and, eventually, the police.'

Enid's face went gray and Tish wondered if she might have overplayed her hand. 'Are you OK?' she asked.

Enid didn't answer. 'How . . . how would Clemson know it was me?'

'Sheriff Reade may be a small-town policeman, but he's not stupid. The records of your auction would indicate that Binnie bought your silver-ware, and he'd easily learn about the animosity between the two of you.'

'Do you think Sheriff Reade would send me to jail?'

Clemson Reade didn't strike Tish as the type of man who'd happily incarcerate an elderly woman, and she said so. 'I think he'd do his best to prevent that, Enid, but the law isn't entirely in his hands. He has to answer to laws of Virginia, where I'm pretty sure burglary is considered a felony. Also, if Binnie's killer still hadn't been apprehended by then, you'd probably be added to the suspect list.'

Enid frowned. 'Langhorne doesn't take kindly to strangers.'

'No, and he shouldn't have to. That conure loves you,' Tish stated, glad that, this once, she used the correct ornithological term. 'You're his family.'

'And he's mine.' A tear trickled down Enid's cheek. 'I'm not sure what I'd do without him.'

'Then don't find out.' Tish placed a consoling arm upon the woman's shoulder. 'Put the silver back tomorrow and then we'll come up with a proper time at which we might be able to talk to Cordelia about it. OK?'

Enid nodded. 'And the library? Will I be able to bring Langhorne there again?'

Tish recalled that both Roberta Dutton's and Daryl Dufour's reactions to Langhorne had been positive. 'You can ask them, and I'm fairly

212

certain they'd say yes. But for now, how about one step at a time, huh?'

Enid nodded and headed off toward the woods. 'Goodnight,' she called over one shoulder before disappearing. Considering the woman had never once in the past few weeks greeted Tish with a hello, the caterer viewed the gesture as progress.

Climbing back into the driver's seat of the Matrix, the engine still running, Tish left Wisteria Knolls as quickly as possible and headed straight for the café.

As she pulled into the parking lot, her driver's side window rolled down to catch the evening breeze, she was surprised by the sound of loud music. Spying only Mary Jo's SUV and Jules's Mini Cooper in the parking lot, she wondered if the pair had forgotten about tomorrow's sandwiches and had, instead, decided to throw a party to celebrate her date.

After shifting into park, closing the window, and taking the key out of the ignition, Tish walked up the worn wooden steps to the front screen door and opened it. Inside, Mary Jo was in the kitchen area sipping wine and smearing pimento cheese on a platter of buttermilk biscuits, while Jules danced and twirled to The Smiths' 'This Charming Man,' while simultaneously sprinkling a garnish of chopped cilantro over a tray of Rudyard Kipling hummus-stuffed pitas.

'This is quite the jolly scene,' she remarked, relieved to see that the pair had made great progress. 'I don't think I've ever seen two people so happy to make sandwiches. You put the elves to shame.'

'I doubt Santa's elves have a couple of bottles of dry Long Island rosé on hand to help them along.' Mary Jo raised her glass. 'We've finished two types of sandwiches and just need your help frying chicken for the third.'

Jules retrieved a glass from the pantry and placed it in Tish's hand while he poured the beautiful pink liquid. 'All this food prep – and MJ and I have discovered that we might be the greatest detectives since Holmes and Watson, Poirot and Hastings, Wolfe and Goodwin, and Nora and Nora.'

'Um, I think that's *Nick* and Nora,' Tish corrected.

'You have your favorite mysteries, I have mine,' Jules explained before waltzing back to the refrigerator.

'Morrissey *and* White Zinfandel? You must have made a very big break on the case for you to party like it's 1993,' she teased.

'It's not White Zinfandel,' Jules faux-seethed.

'1993?' Mary Jo objected. 'OK, just for that, we're not telling you a thing until *you* spill all the details of your date.'

'Oh, come on! That's not fair,' Tish complained.

'It's more than fair,' Mary Jo interjected. 'You texted Jules hours ago saying you were on a date, and we haven't heard a peep from you since.'

'Um, because it was a date,' Tish was confused. 'You didn't actually expect me to text a play-by-play, did you?'

'No, but you could have left your phone on for a few minutes, just so we could overhear,'

Jules suggested while Mary Jo nodded in agreement.

Tish pulled a face and said nothing.

'No? OK, then, why don't you just tell us?'

As she prepped the chicken, buttermilk batter, and oil for the fryer, Tish recounted her evening with Schuyler Thompson.

'Perfect? He said you were perfect?' Mary Jo asked, her hands clutched together as if praying.

Tish's eyes welled with tears and she nodded her head.

'You *are* perfect.' Mary Jo embraced her dear friend. 'It's about time someone said that. I'm so happy for you.'

'I am too.' Jules joined in on the hug. 'I hope you gave him a big wet sloppy kiss for it.'

'Ewww,' Mary Jo and Tish squealed as the embrace between friends broke apart. 'Jules!'

'What?' Jules placed his hands on his hips. 'I'm just saying it might have been nice to reward that sweet man for his good behavior.'

'I kissed him on the cheek and hugged him before saying goodnight,' Tish explained.

'Boring,' Jules sang.

'And I agreed to go with him to the farmers' market in Fredericksburg,' she continued.

'Oh, that should be great fun for you,' Mary Jo remarked.

'Yeah, I said I'd cook dinner with the produce we purchase there. I'm really looking forward to it.'

'And where's your third date going to be? Winn-Dixie? Or maybe you'll go the whole hog and drive to see the Super Kroger up north?'

Jules teased. 'I hear you can get a gasoline discount if you spend over a hundred dollars.'

'Jules,' Mary Jo reprimanded.

'Sorry. I'm happy for you, Tish, really. But I'm just wondering how we got to the age where a glorified grocery run can be considered a first date. Where's the romance? Where are the fireworks?'

'I'm fine without fireworks,' Tish replied. 'Sweet, slow, and easy-going suits me to a tee.'

'I'm glad, honey.' Jules embraced her tightly. 'You deserve someone who treasures you. And if a farmers' market is your idea of relationship nirvana, then go for it. Oh, and buy me some fresh cage-free eggs while you're there, will you?'

Tish rolled her eyes and nodded as Jules pulled away and folded his arms across his chest. 'I'm just sayin' that when I meet that special someone, you can bet it's going to be fireworks, magic, glitter, and wining and dining.'

'Was there ever a doubt?' Tish teased.

'Seriously,' Mary Jo commiserated. 'You probably travel with a mirrored disco ball in your trunk.'

'Trunk? No, it's too big for the Mini Cooper. I need to keep my emergency rain and snow gear in there, so I moved it to the back of my closet,' Jules stated matter-of-factly.

'So, Tommy and Tuppence' – Tish used Jules's bizarre confession as an opportunity to move the topic of conversation away from her love life – 'why don't you tell me about your crime-fighting escapades this evening?'

'Tommy and Tuppence?'

'Beresford. From the *Partners in Crime* books.' As both Jules and Mary Jo gaped at her with nary a glimmer of comprehension in their eyes, Tish added, in exasperation, 'By Agatha Christie? You two really need to turn off the TV and read more.'

'I do read,' Mary Jo maintained.

'I think she means books. Not *Teen Vogue*,' Jules advised his friend, sotto voce.

Mary Jo simply shrugged and launched into the tale of her and Jules's investigative adventure before playing Tish the video of Jules questioning the mayor and the subsequent rendezvous near the baseball field.

'So Mayor Whitley and Cordelia Ballantyne,' Tish stated in wonderment when the video clips had finished.

'You seem surprised,' Jules noted.

'I am. This morning at Wisteria Knolls, Cordelia seemed so . . .' She struggled to find the right words. 'She seemed so desperate to keep her family together. To keep John Ballantyne at home with her and their daughter. She even wanted to bring Charlotte home, so they could start over together, but John wouldn't allow it.'

'If John's been too busy for Cordelia because of his affair with Roberta Dutton, it wouldn't be unusual for Cordelia to find comfort elsewhere,' Mary Jo opined.

Tish and Jules eyed their friend worriedly. 'Not that I'd do it, of course,' Mary Jo defended. 'I realize Glen isn't always home and that he should be doing more to help around the house, but he's working, not checking into cheap motels with librarians. Besides, I have my kids. Poor Cordelia doesn't even have her daughter around for company or solace or just to mother and shower with affection. I'm sorry, but the love for your children keeps you going during tough times. If Charlotte were here in Hobson Glen, I doubt Cordelia would have been catting around with Mayor Whitley.'

Tish nodded. 'Well, now we know why the mayor didn't fire Binnie Broderick.'

'You really think Binnie found out about the mayor's fling with her daughter?' Jules asked.

'I do.'

'And what about Cordelia? If Binnie was the holy roller everyone claims, she couldn't have been very pleased with her daughter's behavior either.'

'The night of the fundraiser,' Tish recalled, 'Binnie made a crack about Cordelia being "easy." It didn't make sense to me at the time, but now it does.'

Tish thought about the modifications to Binnie's will. Was Cordelia and Whitley's affair the event that prompted the changes? And if so, why would John Ballantyne be left out in the cold? Unless, of course, Binnie had learned of his affair as well. The whole scenario was rife with 'ifs' and no concrete answers.

'Wait a minute,' Mary Jo begged excitedly, 'what if Cordelia and the mayor planned to bump off Binnie Broderick and then run away with the inheritance?'

Tish narrowed her eyes. Cordelia might not

have known about her mother's change of will, but there was something else about Mary Jo's hypothesis that seemed rather unlikely. 'Then why would Whitley break up with her now? It was nearly pay day. He only had to hold out a short while longer.'

'Mmm.' Mary Jo frowned. 'You're right. It doesn't make sense, does it?'

'The mayor said he wanted to take a break, that's all. Maybe he wanted to slow things down until the day they actually could be together full-time,' Jules offered. 'There is a murder investigation going on, you know.'

Mary Jo and Tish both gave Jules a look.

'What?' he questioned.

'I sometimes forget you're a man and then you pass a comment like that and it all comes roaring back to me,' Mary Jo quipped.

'When a guy says he wants to take a break, Jules, it typically means break as in "break up." It's not like a coffee break where you return to work once you feel refreshed,' Tish explained.

'Really? Wow, that stinks,' Jules reacted. 'Well, there goes that theory, then. Although it wasn't exactly solid anyway, was it? It leaves absolutely no explanation for Doctor Livermore's murder.'

'No, it doesn't.' Tish sighed and began frying the chicken breast cutlets. The sandwiches, at least, were something she could control.

'Well, I'm sure we'll get it figured out, but I'd best be on my way. I'm on the early show tomorrow.'

'Oh, is there a storm on the way?'

'No. Gus, the usual morning weather guy, is still recuperating from his brother's wedding weekend out in Tahoe. I told him I'd take over. Putting his green face in front of a green screen would make all of Richmond think they're getting their weather from a headless dude in a suit.'

'A headless weatherman would certainly help explain the inaccuracy of the Channel Ten forecast.' Tish laughed and dropped a heavily battered chicken breast into the fryer.

'You're not going to try to drive home, are you?' Mary Jo reproached. 'You've had a few glasses of rosé.'

'Of course not, Mom,' Jules teased. 'I've already texted a cab.'

'Texted?'

'Yeah, the new cab service in town has a hunky driver who works on Sundays. I'm far too civilized to hit on him, but I can at least have some fun watching him in the rear-view mirror. Mind if I leave my car here overnight, Tish? I'll catch a bus after my shift and pick up the sandwiches.'

'Of course not.' Tish slipped another piece of chicken into the fryer.

'Instead of taking the bus, how about I stop by the station with the sandwiches and we sell them together?' Mary Jo offered.

'That would be great.' Jules was appreciative. 'But I don't want to take you out of your way.'

'You wouldn't be. I was planning on staying here for the night and hotfooting it over to you. That is, if Tish doesn't mind some company.'

'You and Jules are always welcome here,' Tish affirmed.

'At least until a certain Mr Thompson decides to stay over,' Jules announced with a wink before bidding the ladies adieu.

Tish mock-threatened him with a pair of metal tongs as he exited through the screen door of the café, before turning her attention to Mary Jo. 'You know I love having you here and I enjoy a good girls' pajama party every now and then, but is everything OK at home?'

'Yeah.' Mary Jo sighed. 'Glen and I had a fight last night. He was miffed about the fact I'm rarely home. I told him he's the one who's never home. It just happens that whenever he is home, I'm out hauling the kids everywhere.'

'But he's OK with you being here tonight?' Tish questioned.

'Yeah, I guess my words must have resonated somehow. He called in a personal day for tomorrow and said he'd take care of the kids tonight and in the morning, while I went out and took care of "me."'

'Cool. Then why don't you look happy?'

'I am. I'm enjoying my wine and it's been ages since you and I have watched a good chick flick together, but, well, when Glen gets the kids he's the hero. He takes them out for fast food and a movie and then treats them to pancakes for breakfast before taking them to work. I get the mom-jeans jokes, the skirt-too-short arguments, the loud, angry music, and complaints about there not being enough Doritos in the house. After tonight, Glen will say, "They're great kids,

221

I don't know why you complain." And they *are* great kids, but he doesn't have to parent them on a daily basis.'

Tish took a moment from her frying to offer her friend a hug and top her glass with wine.

'Thanks, honey. You always seem to know the right thing to do.' Mary Jo smiled. 'Oh, and on top of my argument with Glen, there's Kayla.'

'Is she OK?' Tish returned to the task of cooking chicken.

'Yeah, just your typical moody, snotty fifteen-year-old girl. Whenever I go off to do something that doesn't involve her or the family, she gets upset that I left her with the boys. Even though those boys are her father and brother, and even though I'm sure she has a great time with them.'

'She'll grow out of it, I'm sure. Fifteen is an ugly age all round. I remember my mother and I butted heads quite often, but then the rest of the time we got on like a house on fire. Just like you and Kayla, we were too much alike. It's that way with mothers and daughters,' Tish advised.

'Yeah, mothers and daughters.' Mary Jo sighed.

A rap came at the front screen door of the café. 'Who's that?' Tish pondered aloud.

'Probably Jules wanting a glass for the road now that he's realized he isn't driving.' Mary Jo giggled.

Tish laughed along, but she didn't anticipate seeing Jules's face at the door. He might enjoy a night of revelry with friends, but Jules was a consummate, and sober, professional when a studio call beckoned. Still, despite preparing herself for any number of local visitors, Tish

222

was completely and utterly flabbergasted to see the face of Daryl Dufour peering through the door at her.

Tish opened the main door to the café but remained behind the screen, with her hand on the latch. 'Yes?'

Dufour's unremarkable face was red and clammy. 'I'm so sorry to trouble you at this hour on a Sunday, Miss Tarragon.'

At the sound of Dufour's voice, Mary Jo moved from the kitchen to a position close behind Tish in a display of girl-power solidarity meant to deter the possibility of any bad behavior on the part of the librarian.

'Evening.' Dufour acknowledged Mary Jo with a nod of the head. 'Anyway, I would have called, but your café isn't in any directory I could find.'

'That's fine, Mr Dufour. How can I help you?'

'I was in the bar at the Hobson Grille and I couldn't help but notice you in the dining room, having supper with Sheriff Reade.'

Two hours had passed since Tish had spoken with Sheriff Reade. It was clear from both Dufour's speech and somewhat flustered appearance that he had only just left the bar of which he spoke. 'I was in the dining room, yes, but I was having dinner with Schuyler Thompson. Sheriff Reade only stopped by for a brief chat,' Tish clarified.

'During that brief chat, you didn't happen to mention our conversation at the library, did you?' Dufour asked nervously.

'I beg your pardon?' Tish asked. She would

require far more information from Mr Dufour before she would make any attempt at an answer.

'Yesterday at the library – goodness, it seems like ages ago, doesn't it? – I said some things I probably shouldn't have.'

'Such as?' Tish angled.

'It doesn't matter what. I just don't want what I said getting back to anyone. My social media accounts have already been hacked once this year.'

'I'm sorry to hear that, but I fail to see how that has anything to do with me.'

'I was just wondering if you might have let something slip to the sheriff. Something that might have cast suspicion in my or some other innocent person's direction?' Dufour remained as vague as ever.

Tish egged him on. 'I still don't understand.'

'You see, when confronted with baked goods, I sometimes get to rambling. That was the situation when you brought the cakes to the library. Nothing I said yesterday afternoon should be taken seriously. It was all stream-of-consciousness.'

Tish nodded. 'You needn't worry about me, Mr Dufour. Your name was never mentioned during my conversation with Sheriff Reade. I assumed that if you had information about Binnie Broderick's murder, you'd have told the police directly.'

'Y–yes, I would have. I . . . I met with them this morning.'

'Ah, very good, then. Goodnight.'

'Goodnight, Miss Tarragon.' Dufour gave

Mary Jo another nod of the head in farewell. 'Goodnight. Sorry for bothering y'all.'

'Not a problem,' Tish excused as she checked the lock on the screen door and bolted the main.

'What was that all about?' Mary Jo asked.

Tish shrugged. 'Don't know, but I wouldn't be surprised if Mr Dufour stops by again tomorrow to apologize for stopping by tonight.'

'He was awfully creepy.' Despite the warm weather and the heat given off by the deep fryer, Mary Jo shivered.

'And more than a little buzzed,' Tish added.

'Mmm, what did he want you to keep from the police?'

'Could be one of three things. First, he may be fearful that I told the sheriff just how much he despised Binnie for destroying books and making him a glorified clerk, that he holds a certain affection for Celestine Rufus, and that he believes Binnie's murderer is a worthy recipient of a Governor's award.'

'Makes him a pretty strong suspect. And, heaven knows, he's certainly creepy enough,' Mary Jo noted.

'Second, he's afraid I told the sheriff about his accusations against Roberta Dutton. That I mentioned how Daryl saw her slip the note into John Ballantyne's pocket the night of the fund-raiser and how he suspected that she's capable of murder.'

'Jules has proven Roberta and Ballantyne have been having an affair. Plus, she sounds like the type to hack Daryl Dufour's social media accounts in revenge.'

'Very much the type.' Tish nodded. 'Especially if Daryl threatened to excel at work where she didn't.'

'You think she was the hacker the first time around?'

'I wouldn't be surprised. And then there's a third possibility behind Dufour's visit. He's worried his comments about Celestine being devastated by Cynthia Thompson's death might have put her in the hot seat. Remember, they both met with the sheriff today.'

'Do you think she's the innocent party he mentioned?'

'I'm almost sure of it. However, it seems I may have to give Celestine another visit tomorrow just to be positive.'

'Well, be careful,' Mary Jo urged. 'All I can say is that with two people dead and everyone doing their best to keep their skeletons in the closet, I'm glad I'm here tonight.'

Tish gave Mary Jo a hug. 'I am too, honey.' She frowned. 'I am too.'

Twenty

With windows and doors locked and bolted, air conditioning switched on to combat the shortage of ventilation, and charged cell phones at the ready, Tish and Mary Jo spent an uneasy, restless night above the café.

Choosing to rise shortly after dawn rather than

toss and turn another hour, Tish quietly pushed back the bed covers and tiptoed past the guest bedroom and downstairs into the kitchen to brew some coffee.

She was surprised when, less than an hour later, Mary Jo appeared at the bottom of the stairs. 'I'd ask you how you slept,' Tish greeted, 'but I think I already know the answer.'

'Ugh. More sleep than I got when Greg and Kayla were babies, but still . . . ugh.' Mary Jo yawned and drew her hands through her mangle of uncombed brunette hair.

Tish rose from her seat and poured some coffee out of the French press carafe keeping warm on the stove. She passed the mug to Mary Jo and pointed to the milk and sugar on the nearby counter, before refilling her own cup. After several wordless minutes had elapsed, Tish and Mary Jo went on to discuss and plan their day, consume another pot of coffee, and then, in turns, shower and dress.

It was eleven o'clock by the time they each set off to their designated appointments. Mary Jo, with platters of sandwiches in hand, drove to the Channel Ten news station to collect Jules. Tish, bearing a smaller disposable plate of sandwiches, headed to Wisteria Knolls to check in with Cordelia Ballantyne. Before leaving the café, both women urged the other to be safe, promising to reunite there in the mid-afternoon and to phone or text should either of them be delayed.

Tish, feeling cooped up after nearly twelve hours spent in air conditioning, rolled down the driver's side window on the Matrix and enjoyed the sounds of birds chirping and children, still a week away from the start of school, playing in the warm, unusually dry August air.

Having spent the night fearing, analyzing, and attempting to resolve two murders, the noise of ordinary life provided Tish with much-needed comfort. This soothing sense of solace, although therapeutic, was short-lived, as she soon found herself pulling up at Wisteria Knolls. Seeing two cars parked in the driveway, Tish brought the Matrix to a stop beside the curb just before the house and, sandwiches in hand, walked up the gravel-lined front walk.

She was met along the path by John Ballantyne, who huffed and puffed as he dragged one tall wheeled suitcase, and then another, through the narrow colonial doorway and on to the slate steps.

'Hello,' Tish greeted, her voice tentative.

'Hi,' Ballantyne growled. It was clear from his tone that the huffing and puffing had little to do with the physical act of hauling the luggage out of the house and everything to do with the exhausting reasons behind his move. 'She's inside. In the bedroom. Not sure she'll come out to see you.'

'Oh. I'll try anyway. Maybe she'll change her mind. Um, are you going on a business trip?' Tish asked, hopeful that was the explanation behind his departure. Deep down, she already knew the answer.

'No. I'm leaving town. It's time I got away from Hobson Glen, Wisteria Knolls, and those damned Darlingtons for good,' Ballantyne declared.

'Have you told Sheriff Reade you're leaving?' Tish blurted out.

'What?' Ballantyne was incensed. 'Why should I? This is a *personal* matter.' He placed special emphasis on the fourth word of his statement.

'Yes, I understand it's deeply personal, but, um, your mother-in-law and the doctor are dead and there's an active murder investigation going on. I'm not sure what the protocol is, but you might want to have a word with Sheriff Reade. Just so he knows you're not skipping town or anything like that . . .' Tish's voice trailed off.

'Don't you have a café to run?' he challenged.

'Not for another two weeks,' she replied in earnest.

With a dirty look in Tish's direction, John Ballantyne huffed one last time and turned on one heel, dragging the two suitcases toward one of the cars in the driveway.

Another potential customer bites the dust, she thought to herself as she watched him drive off. Between the murder victims, those citizens of Hobson Glen who were annoyed with her for trying to find the killer, and those citizens who believed Tish herself to be the killer, she wondered if there would be anyone left in Hobson Glen who would actually dine at her café. Perhaps she should give up the investigation, abandon the concept of a literary café, and simply open a diner in New Jersey.

Recalling that she wasn't particularly fond of the idea of living in New Jersey, Tish lurched onward, toward the house. Plate of sandwiches firmly in hand, she gave the doorbell a steady ring and, with the door still ajar following John's departure, leaned her head into the hall and gave a shout. 'Cordelia?'

There was no answer. Tish stepped into the hall and called again. 'Cordelia? Cordelia, it's Tish. I came to check in on you. Cordelia?'

Again receiving no answer, Tish went into the kitchen, past the sink which was filled with a collection of Mason jars in need of cleaning, and placed the sandwiches in the near-empty refrigerator. Spying a pen and a napkin on the table, Tish left a note instructing Cordelia that food was in the fridge and that she could call if she needed anything. Tish signed off on the note with her cell number, just in case Cordelia had misplaced the last napkin upon which Tish had jotted it. Satisfied with her handiwork, she placed the note under one of two silver salt cellars that someone had been in the process of refilling before the scene of quiet domesticity had been rudely interrupted.

With this task done, Tish retraced her steps into the hall and headed toward the door. Before she even set foot outside, a horrifying thought crossed her mind, stopping her cold in her tracks. What if John Ballantyne was, in fact, running from the police? It would explain why he got so cross with her for mentioning Sheriff Reade. What if he was the murderer and was leaving town before the police caught on to him? What if Cordelia wasn't grief-stricken, angry, and hiding in her bedroom? What if she was dead?

Dead because Ballantyne had killed her.

Tish felt her skin go clammy and her stomach churn. Reluctantly, she turned around and gazed at the flight of stairs that led to the second floor and the Broderick/Ballantyne family bedrooms. Tish drew a heavy sigh and thought of the phone in her pants back pocket. She would notify Sheriff Reade of John Ballantyne's departure as soon as possible, but what about Cordelia? Should she call Reade and have him and his officers come to the house?

No, if Cordelia was despondent – who could honestly blame her? – and locked up in her bedroom, hiding from the world, the last thing the woman needed was the Hanover County police dragging her from her bed and asking a thousand questions. No, Tish decided, she would go upstairs and try calling at the bedroom doors. If there was still no response from Cordelia, then a call to 911 would be in order.

Confident she had made the right decision, yet fearful of what she might find upstairs, Tish moved along the wide wooden planks of the hall, grasped the handrail of the circa-1700 staircase, and placed an apprehensive red-sandaled foot upon the first tread. As expected, the old wood creaked loudly under the slightest amount of pressure. The sound echoed in the sparsely furnished hallway and resonated up the stairs, causing Tish to shudder.

Pull yourself together and just get upstairs, she berated herself before taking the stairs two at a time and on her toes. Upon reaching the top step, she once again called, 'Cordelia? Are you here?'

Again, there was no reply.

The upstairs landing, like the entry hall below it, featured a neutral color scheme – this time in pale yellow – a whitewashed chair rail, picture rail, wide wooden floorboards, and minimal furnishings. However, this being a living space for family, some concessions for modern-day comfort had been made – namely the presence of plush scatter rugs and a hall table featuring an abundance of family photos.

Tish stepped on to the landing, the floor again creaking beneath her feet. 'Cordelia?' she called outside the first closed door she encountered. 'Cordelia?'

As she waited – nay, prayed for – some sign of life, Tish wandered over to the center table and examined the photos assembled there. Taking main stage was a faded eight-by-ten color photograph of a young Lavinia Darlington at her wedding to Ashton Broderick. Ashton, as Augusta had described, was tall, dark-haired, and handsome, albeit somewhat serious, while Lavinia, in her high-neck 1970s-style gown, her red hair piled high upon her head and topped with a cathedral veil, beamed for the camera. Lavinia's right arm was wrapped around her husband's waist, her left hand placed on his chest in a possessive gesture that suggested Lavinia might have been less excited about being Ashton's wife than she was about claiming the Broderick name as her own.

To the left of the wedding photo stood a smaller dual frame featuring Cordelia, first as an infant, giggling and happy in a white lace baptismal gown, and then another wearing a backpack and hugging her father outside a two-story brick building on what appeared to be her first day of school. In front of the dual frame stood a small wallet-sized photo of Cordelia and John Ballantyne on their wedding day. Cordelia, with her mane of teased hair and high-neck fishtail gown, bore more than a passing resemblance to her mother, yet in contrast to Binnie's wedding photo, Cordelia gazed at John adoringly.

To the right of Ashton and Lavinia's photo was displayed a portrait of the Broderick family when Cordelia was approximately nine years old. With her layered, suddenly blonde hair curled into 'wings,' Binnie sat in an upholstered wingback chair and stared imperiously at the camera while Cordelia, dressed in a smaller version of her mother's diagonally striped shoulder-padded frock, her natural blonde hair brushed into a similar early-1980s' flip hairstyle, stood nearby, a frown upon her face and a hand on her mother's knee. Ashton, in a three-piece brown suit with ultra-wide lapels, stood alone behind the two female members of his family and seemed so disconnected from his surroundings and the two women in his life that one might have thought him an interloper who had wandered on to the set.

In front of this odd family portrait stood a candid shot of Cordelia, in her hospital bed, swaddling a new-born Charlotte as an ecstatic John looked on with obvious tears in his eyes. Beside this shot was yet another dual photo frame. The left side bore a photo of a pigtailed

Charlotte posed outside a yellow school bus flanked by Mom and Dad. The second featured a recent snapshot of Charlotte. So recent, in fact, that Charlotte looked quite similar to the way she did in the picture on Cordelia's phone.

In the recent shot, Charlotte rested her chin on her hands while seated at a red picnic table set in the middle of a grassy field. In the background stood a single-story brick building with metal grates on the windows and a tall chain-link fence which surrounded the nearby environs. Smiling for the camera, Charlotte appeared to be relaxed and happy, so what was it about the photo that made Tish feel so ill at ease?

'Cordelia?' she called. 'Cordelia, are you here?'

This time, Tish's shouts were met with the sound of rustling covers from a nearby room.

'Cordelia,' she cried again in the hope of better determining the woman's location. 'Cordelia, it's Tish. Are you OK?'

'I'm all right,' a groggy voice answered from a room at the other end of the hall.

Tish drew closer. 'You're not physically injured or ill are you?'

'No . . . I just need to rest.'

Tish pondered her next move. 'I'd feel better if I could see you. Even if for just a moment or two.'

'I'm not in the mood to see anyone, Tish. Please go.'

'OK . . . there are some sandwiches in the fridge if you get hungry, and my phone number is in the kitchen should you need me. I could

234

also call Charlotte for you if you'd like . . . I know things are crazy right now but—'

'No.' Cordelia's voice, previously weak and frail, grew radically stronger. 'No, I don't want to burden her with this right now. I need to find the right words to tell her about her grandmother and her dad and . . . and me.'

The forcefulness of Cordelia's words took Tish by surprise, but she supposed it made sense. Cordelia was having difficulty enough processing recent events in her own mind. Organizing that information and then presenting it so that it was digestible for a sixteen-year-old must have seemed an insurmountable task.

Still, part of Tish strongly believed that Charlotte deserved to know about her grandmother's passing and of her parents' decision to separate. Now, however, was not the time to broach the subject. 'OK. I'll check in with you later.'

Tish beat a hasty retreat down the stairs, out of the front door, and back to the Matrix. Not wishing to be seen on the phone, she drove the car approximately one block down the road, then pulled over and placed a call to Sheriff Reade.

Unfortunately, she got his voicemail. Detailing John Ballantyne's departure as quickly as she could, she then asked the sheriff if he might check in on Cordelia – without mentioning that Tish had sent him, of course – just to ensure that the despondent woman hadn't taken a sleeping pill or done anything equally drastic.

With the message complete, Tish disconnected

the call and, after pulling away from the shoulder of the road, proceeded to drive toward Celestine's house. She had driven only another block when she noticed a spandex-clad figure on a bicycle approaching from the opposite direction.

Tish put her foot on the brake pedal of the Matrix and, once again, veered right, so as to allow the biker to pass. She then waved the biker, unrecognizable in a helmet and dark wraparound sunglasses, forward.

Rather than accept the invitation, the biker waved back, and stopped outside the driver's side window of the Matrix. 'Tish,' the familiar voice greeted. 'Just the woman I was looking for.'

'Oh, hello . . .' Tish squinted as she shifted into park and endeavored to put a name to the voice. The biker, as if on cue, pulled aside her sunglasses and yanked the helmet from her head, revealing a tangled mane of silver hair. 'Opal. You wanted to see me?'

'Yes, I wanted to ask you about cucumbers.'

'Huh?' Tish glanced in her rear-view mirror to check for any vehicles that might be stuck behind her. Fortunately, the road was clear.

'Cucumbers. My garden is overrun with both the regular and pickling varieties, and I was wondering if you could use them for your café.'

'Well, I'd love to buy some off you. I want to use local produce exclusively. But my café isn't quite up and running yet.'

'That's OK. I'll bring over some samples for you to try. If you like them, we'll talk about price and delivery schedule,' Opal proposed.

'Are you sure? I don't expect you to give me food for free,' Tish argued. 'Even if it's only a sample, I'm sure you could put them to good use.'

'Nah, it's fine. Like I said, I have more than I know what to do with. I'll give you some and then take the rest to the farmers' market. A friend of mine has a stall there. He'll sell them on my behalf. Thing is, selling them to you is a sure thing whereas the market can be sketchy. If it's raining or too hot, people don't come out to buy.'

Tish nodded. 'I understand.'

Opal gave a sardonic chuckle. 'It's funny. You know, Binnie Broderick used to be my best customer. Before she purged my books, I mean. She was a pickle fanatic. Just about every cucumber I put up for sale ended up in her kitchen. Poor things . . . to wind up as the feature ingredient in Binnie Broderick's bread-and-butter pickles.'

Tish's ears pricked up. 'So, her pickles were the talk of the town?'

'Joke of the town, more like it. I swear, they were infamous. She brought them to every single social function in Hobson Glen. Mind you, they weren't too bad at first. Not the best bread-and-butter pickles I'd ever tasted, but certainly not the worst. However, the last few times she brought them? Horrid. Absolutely horrid. Edwin Wilson, Doctor Livermore and I were on the planning committee for the annual town picnic and barbecue this June, and we were tempted to ban her from bringing them. We were soon sorry we didn't. They were so terrible that I thought she was playing some bizarre practical joke. I honestly expected a film crew to jump out from behind the trees and tell us we were going to be on a new version of *Candid Camera* or *Punk'd*. The even stranger thing was that while few of us at the barbecue would even venture a bite, Binnie was eating them as if they were going out of style.'

'Hmm, a new recipe, perhaps?'

'Something like that, I guess.'

'Yes . . . something like that.' Tish bit her lip. 'So you and Doctor Livermore were on the picnic planning committee, huh?'

'Yes.' Opal colored slightly. 'We were friends. Hobson Glen won't be the same without him.'

'Oh?'

'Yes, "Oh." You asked me if he was my physician. You never asked me if he and I might have been "friends with benefits."'

Tish felt her jaw drop open, much to Opal's amusement.

'As my mama said, just because there's snow on the roof,' the novelist chortled. 'I'm widowed; he was single, never married. Townsfolk used to speculate he might be gay. I can safely state that he wasn't.'

Tish nodded and tried to think of a way to politely extricate herself from the conversation. She needn't have bothered.

Opal replaced the helmet on her head and slid her sunglasses back on to the bridge of her nose. 'Well, I'd better get pedaling. Riding and writing – the only times I don't smoke. Well, maybe not the *only* times. Anyway, I'll stop by later with the veg.'

'Sounds good. If I'm not there, just leave it on the porch swing,' Tish instructed before the two women said farewell and went their respective ways.

So Livermore and Opal had been lovers, Tish mused. But what bearing did that have on the murder case, unless, perhaps, Binnie was also involved with the good doctor and Opal killed them both out of jealousy? The theory made Tish slightly nauseous.

The bigger question was whether Binnie had been experiencing memory issues before her passing. The unexpected downturn in the quality of her bread-and-butter pickles sounded highly suspicious. For a cook to suddenly tweak or change a recipe she'd been making for years seemed unlikely, especially when that cook was as conservative as Binnie Broderick. Memory loss would, indeed, explain the pickles as well as the modifications to Binnie's will, but it still did nothing to explain her murder or that of Dr Livermore.

Tish pulled the Matrix into the familiar toy-littered driveway of the Rufus' home. This time Celestine did not greet her at the door. Standing on the weathered wooden deck, Tish could hear the whir of a vacuum cleaner working its magic on a carpet or piece of upholstery somewhere deep within the house.

Tish pressed hard on the doorbell for several seconds. The vacuum switched off, followed by the sound of heavy footsteps. Celestine, dressed

239

in flip-flops, denim capris, and an oversized *World's Best Grandma* T-shirt, appeared behind the screen door. 'Why, hey there, Tish. I wasn't expecting to see you today. Come on in.'

Tish thanked Celestine for her welcome as she stepped behind the screen door and followed her into the kitchen.

'Tea?' Celestine offered and extracted a pitcher from the refrigerator.

'No, thanks,' Tish declined. She felt self-conscious accepting the hospitality of the woman she would soon be questioning for the second time in three days.

'What's on your mind, girlfriend? Got more questions?' Celestine poured herself a large glass of tea with ice and plopped down in the chair at the head of the table, same as she had during their last chat.

Tish assumed the same seat as well. 'Yes, I do . . .'

'Well, don't pick at it, honey. Rip the Band-Aid off.'

'Did you happen to see Daryl Dufour at the police station yesterday?'

Celestine's face registered surprise, but she quickly collected herself. 'Yes. Why do you ask?'

'Because he showed up at the café last night.'

'Oh, brother.' She sighed. 'He'd been drinking, hadn't he?'

'He had,' Tish confirmed. 'He was also extremely anxious about something he told me when I spoke with him at the library on Saturday.'

'Never could hold his liquor.' Celestine clicked her tongue. 'So what was he so upset about?'

'I have no idea. He mentioned several things that afternoon.' Tish looked Celestine squarely in the eyes. 'You were one of them.'

'Me?' Celestine laughed.

'Yes. It would appear that Mr Dufour admires you a great deal.'

'Oh, I wouldn't pay that no mind. Daryl and I were just childhood sweethearts.' Celestine dismissed the topic with a wave of her hand.

Tish would have nothing of it. 'That may have been many years ago, but I don't think his affection for you has dissipated much.'

'Oh, I don't know about that . . .'

'It sounds as though he was quite worried about you after Cynthia Thompson died.'

'Yeah, well, lots of folks were concerned. My family most of all. Like I told you, I wasn't myself for a long time.'

'I think Mr Dufour is still rather concerned about you. Knocking on my café door at nine o'clock on a Sunday night to ask a woman he barely knows if she spoke to the police?'

'Is that what he did? Oh.' Celestine covered her face with her hands.

'Yes, he did. I found it rather odd at the time.'

Celestine uncovered her face and shook her head. 'I'm sorry if Daryl scared you, but he's harmless. And I wouldn't listen to a word he says if he's had a tipple.'

'Oh, but I did take Daryl's words to heart. If he had doubts about anyone else in this town, he'd have gone directly to Sheriff Reade and told him everything he knows. Coming to me means he's not just afraid of being implicated

241

in the murders but he's looking to shield someone from the sheriff.'

After a lengthy pause, Celestine finally spoke. 'I don't know why you're so afraid of your café not taking off, honey. You're certainly clever enough to pull off just about anything.' Celestine guffawed and shuffled off to the refrigerator.

'Where are you headed?' Tish asked.

'If I'm gonna tell you the whole story of Daryl and me, you're gonna need refreshment.' Celestine poured Tish a glass of iced tea and topped up her own, then eased her heavy frame back into the seat at the head of the table. 'So . . .'

'So?' Tish volleyed.

'Daryl Dufour and I were, as I said, childhood sweethearts. He was a year older than me. Still is, I suppose,' she chuckled. 'From the time I could crawl and Daryl could walk, we were thick as thieves. All through our toddler days and on into grade school we were the closest of friends and confidants. I don't think we spent more than a day or two apart, and that was usually only because one of us had been dragged somewhere by our parents. We even came down with the same illnesses at the same time, most likely because one of us had given it to the other or our mothers wanted us to catch something – like chicken pox. I remember being sent to Daryl's house so I could catch it and get it done. It was a good way to get sick because you still had someone to play with.'

'Sounds like fun,' Tish remarked and took a sip of tea.

'When high school rolled along and Daryl and

I came of age, it seemed only natural that he and I should become boyfriend and girlfriend. My mother loved Daryl and Daryl's mother had taken a liking to me. We went steady a full three years before Daryl went off to college. It was understood by both our folks that we'd be married just as soon as Daryl got out of school.'

'So what happened?'

'Lloyd Rufus. That's what happened. Six feet tall, curly brown hair, brown eyes, and a boyish grin capable of giving a girl goosebumps.'

'And he swept you off your feet with his youthful good looks,' Tish presumed.

'It was more than that. He was a loner, who had just arrived from West Virginia, and even though he was only two years older than I was, he had a car, a job with a plumbing and heating company, and a pack-a-day cigarette habit. For a girl of eighteen who'd rarely traveled outside her home town and never been – save for a weekend trip to Washington, DC, with her parents – outside the state of Virginia, Lloyd was an adult. To me, he was worldly, exciting.' Celestine shook her head and laughed. 'Worldly. Hard to believe that now, to look at him here on a Saturday night. Stained white T-shirt and boxer shorts, snoring in his recliner, watching the NASCAR he's saved on the DVR.

'But back then,' Celestine continued as the smile ran away from her face, 'back then Lloyd was like a breath of fresh air in my very limited world. First time I saw him, he was at the gas station filling up his car, a dark-green 1977 Oldsmobile Toronado. He'd bought it second hand but it was still new enough to be impressive. It was just before Christmas and I was across the street at the Foodland market picking up whatever my mother had asked me to fetch on the way home from school. I never expected Lloyd or any other fella to ever notice me. I'd only really known one boy my entire life and that was Daryl Dufour. Everyone in town knew I was with Daryl and that we were fixing on getting married, so I'd never encountered anyone wanting to ask me out on a date. Besides, as I told you when we met, I take after my daddy's side of the family, which my mother made clear would never win any beauty contests.'

Tish cringed at Celestine's mother's rather harsh condemnation of her daughter's physical appearance. Why were some parents so critical of their own children? Even her own mother – who was otherwise supportive and kind – had been known to pass the odd comment about Tish having gained a few pounds over the holidays, or her hair being too light or too dark, or her taste in clothing being inappropriate for her age. Why her mother felt the need to criticize her only child, Tish never knew, but it was a personality trait that only worsened as her illness progressed.

'You could just imagine my surprise when the boy at the gas station looked up to see me watching him and then smiled,' Celestine went on with her story. 'And my complete and utter shock when he gave a whistle as I walked away.'

'He wolf-whistled at you?' Tish raised an eyebrow.

244

'Yeah, I know it wasn't proper. Still isn't. If some guy was to do that to my granddaughters, I'd smack 'em senseless with my mama's cast-iron skillet. But I was young and naïve and he was beautiful,' Celestine rationalized. 'I didn't see Lloyd again until well into the new year. Daryl had come home from college for the Christmas break and it was glorious. Dinner with both sets of folks, time with family, my first beer – this was before they raised the drinking age – outings with friends. Looking back, it was my last childhood Christmas and it was magical, but part of me wondered from time to time about the boy at the gas station. Not for very long, mind you, because I was too busy having fun and, quite frankly, I never thought I'd see him again.

'Daryl went back to school the second week of January and we had a great big tearful romantic send-off. I was already back in school – my senior year – and wouldn't see him again until the term ended in May. Weeks dragged on. It was an unusually cold winter and my girl-friends all had boyfriends, which made me feel something like a third wheel, so instead of hanging out, I stayed in and read books and baked with my sisters.'

'And Daryl?'

'We'd talk on the phone once a week. Sunday was our day since he worked at the campus bookstore part-time,' Celestine replied.

'Preparing for his librarian job,' Tish remarked.

'Yes, he's always loved books. Me too, but not as much as he does. Thing is, though, when you're eighteen and looking to explore the world, books only incite you to move forward rather than stand still. Does that make sense?'

Tish nodded as she thought about her café. 'It does.'

'It was an odd snowy Friday in February when I saw Lloyd again – not that I knew that was his name at the time. I was running another shopping errand for my mama and he was at the gas station again, filling the giant tank of that Coronado. This time, however, he didn't just smile or whistle at me. Nope, he stopped what he was doing and ran across the road to greet me. He said he'd been admirin' me and asked me if I had a boyfriend. God help me, I don't know what came over me that day. I don't know if I was missing Daryl or it was the loneliness of being cooped up in the house with family, or seeing my friends have fun while I stayed home, or the excitement that a boy I didn't know thought I was wonderful, or the deep brown of his eyes, or that I'm just a terribly wicked woman and always have been, but I said no, I didn't. Me, the girl who'd had a boyfriend before she could even crawl, said she was available. See? Wicked.'

'I don't think you were wicked at all. You were young and had lived a sheltered life. The boy at the gas station was something different,' Tish allowed. 'Also, what about you and what you wanted? What about college instead of getting married right away?'

Celestine shook her head. 'Never was very good at school, so my parents thought it a waste of money to try to send me. We didn't have much money at all and Evangeline, the older of my two sisters, was smart as a whip. She's the one my folks were saving for. It was best for me to go out and get a job to help the family or to leave the nest and get fed elsewhere.'

'What about a student loan? They mustn't have been as difficult to pay off as they are now,' Tish suggested, as if Celestine could somehow go back in time.

'Nah. To be honest, I didn't like school very much. Only thing I've ever loved to do is bake, so I figured I'd get a job after school, get married, and maybe open up a little bake shop once we got enough money tucked away. Still, it was scary to think that Daryl was *it*. I cared about him, sure, but he – our marriage, kids, Hobson Glen – was going to be *it* for the rest of my life.'

Tish leaned back in her chair and crossed one leg over the other. 'Daunting thought for an eighteen-year-old.' She sighed.

Celestine nodded and took a sip of tea. 'So, after telling Lloyd that I didn't have a boyfriend, he asked me if I would join him for coffee. I said yes, but I had to get the groceries back home. Honestly, I didn't even drink coffee at the time, but I wanted to seem older and more mature than I was. Lloyd followed in his car as I walked home and then parked down one of the side streets while I dropped off the groceries. I put away the shopping and then went back out, telling Mama that I was meeting some friends and would be home for dinner. Then I got in Lloyd's car and we went to a diner on the edge of town where I didn't know too many folks.'

'You got in his car?' Tish was incredulous, especially after hearing Augusta's heart-wrenching tale. 'You'd only just met him.'

'Things were different back then, honey.' Celestine laughed.

'Not that different. I've heard stories.'

'Those stories weren't as common as they are now.'

'That's not true. I was – what? Six years old. I was told never to get in a car with a stranger.'

Celestine laughed even harder. 'Hush yourself. OK, I know I was reckless, foolish, and all those other things, but I obviously survived. Now, will you let me finish telling you about *all* my past sins before you start criticizing me for one or two of the minor ones?'

Celestine was right. Tish needed to decide whether she was questioning Celestine about a murder or listening to a good friend share a secret. The problem was, deep down in her gut, she still couldn't believe that Celestine might be guilty. 'Sorry.'

'No problem, honey. As I was sayin', we went to the diner. As it would happen, Lloyd didn't care much for coffee either. He said it just to impress me, so we both had a Coke and some nachos, and we talked about what we wanted to do with our lives. I told him I was finishing up school and dreamed of opening a bake shop. He liked that I wasn't going to college. He'd dropped out of high school in favor of technical school training. After he graduated, he spent his time traveling through the South and picking up odd jobs along the way for food and gas money. He'd seen palm trees in Florida, beaches in the Carolinas, and hanging moss on the live oaks in Georgia. It sounded like the most exciting life in the world, traveling from place to place, seeing things, meeting new people.'

Celestine stared off into the distance, a smile upon her face. 'I left the diner that evening completely smitten and with a promise from Lloyd that we would spend Valentine's Day together. Valentine's Day was on a Saturday, so our school held a dance. It was the perfect excuse for getting out of the house. I remember my mama was so pleased I was going out with friends instead of languishing in my room. If only she'd known I had gone for burgers and then the movies with Lloyd and that after . . . well, she soon found out about the "after," didn't she? It was the beginning of March that I found out I was expecting my eldest, Lacey.'

'That's her and her family, there.' Celestine pointed to a Christmas photo card on the refrigerator depicting a pretty blonde, a dark, bearded man in a Santa hat, and three children ranging in age from approximately eleven years old to five.

'Beautiful family,' Tish admired.

'They are. My Lacey's done well for herself. Works part-time as a dental technician at the clinic on Main. Took some time off to start a family and just went back now that the little one is in school. Her husband's a builder. He takes good care of her and the kids, and checks in on us too.'

'That must be a great comfort.' Tish paused. 'Forgive me for being obtuse, but I don't understand what any of this has to do with Daryl Dufour. I mean, you obviously dumped him for Lloyd and lived happily ever after, but aside from that . . .'

'I'll make it clearer for you. My night with Lloyd was just two weeks after Daryl left town and went back to school,' Celestine remarked. 'My Lacey – our Lacey – might be Daryl's daughter.'

Tish caught her breath and then fortified herself with some cold tea. 'Might? You mean you don't know?'

The World's Best Grandma gave a solemn shake of the head. 'I was in love with Lloyd. My "bad boy," as Mama called him. You ever fallen for a bad boy?'

'Yes, once. And divorced him.'

'Yeah, well, once I told my mama about Lloyd, my fate was sealed. He and I were married as soon as I graduated school. I was three months along and sick as a dog at our wedding. He and I still talked about traveling, even after the baby, but it never happened. He got a job here in Hobson Glen, and before you know it, three more kids came on the scene.'

'Do you have any regrets?'

Celestine shrugged. 'I regret that I caused the pain I did, but I have a loving family and I like to think I've learned my lessons the hard way. Aside from that, what's the point of "if only"? Did Lloyd and I go through some tough times? Sure. Did I occasionally wonder what life would

250

have been like if I had married Daryl? Yes. But I wasn't going to undo everything and hurt my kids just to find out.'

'What about Lacey? Didn't you ever want a paternity test?'

'Oh, I'd thought about it. And Daryl pressed me on it several times, but what good would it have done? I'd already hurt Daryl and both our folks. Wouldn't have accomplished a damn thing hurting Lloyd too.'

'So Daryl wanted a paternity test?' Tish was surprised, given that if he were the father, Daryl would most likely have had to give up school.

'Oh, yes, the minute he heard I was marrying Lloyd, and why, he insisted upon one. I begged him not to complicate things. By then Lloyd knew I'd had a boyfriend when we met and it didn't bother him none, but I also never told Lloyd about the timing of my last farewell to Daryl either. In my mind, Lloyd was my baby's father and that was that. To his credit, Daryl didn't push the subject, but up until the day I married Lloyd, he told me he was still in love with me and offered to raise the baby – no matter who was the father – as his own.'

'And now? How's your relationship with Daryl Dufour?'

'I already told you, we're friends. We chat when we pass each other at the grocery store, and we often see each other when I bring the grandkids to the library. He checked in on me after Cynthia's death. We're friends, and if he says he's happy, I'm happy.'

'And he never brings up Lacey's paternity?' Tish was dubious.

'No, although he has looked after us, in a way, through the years,' Celestine added.

'Looked after you?'

'Years ago, when Lloyd was out of work due to a back problem, Daryl floated me some cash to make sure my kids had new clothes for school. I paid him back, of course,' Celestine was quick to note. 'And he gave Lacey a very generous gift for her wedding. All my kids got nice wedding presents, come to think of it, but Lacey might have gotten a little more. And then . . .'

'Yes?' Tish prodded.

'There was a time a couple years back, when I found out Lloyd had stepped out with one of the pretty young receptionists at his company's call center. I was jealous and angry, and I went storming out of the house. I have no vices to speak of, so rather than going to the bar, I went to the Publix and shopped for baking supplies. It was there that I ran into Daryl. I tried to hide what was going on, but that was no use with him. I remember it clear as day. He said, "Celestine, if you're not happy with Lloyd and need somewhere to go, I'd take you, the dog, the kids, the grandkids – all of it – in a heartbeat."'

Tish watched as Celestine's eyes welled up. 'Wow. After all these years.'

'After all these years,' Celestine repeated, blinking back tears.

'What did you say?'

'I told him the idea was silly. I mean, how could I possibly go back to Daryl after what I did to him? He deserves more than the likes of me.'

'I take it Daryl Dufour never married or had children,' Tish presumed.

'Nope. He graduated top of his class at UVA, went on to get his master's, and then returned to Hobson Glen to take care of his mother. His father had passed away soon after my Lacey was born, and Mrs Dufour didn't take his passing too well. She'd been sick on and off the whole time Daryl was away at school – physical ailments, you see? Mama and I would go over and help with the housekeeping and cooking. But once Daryl got his degree and got back home, Mrs Dufour kinda fell off her rocker. Believed Daryl was her husband returned to her. She was harmless to herself and others, but she required round-the-clock care and supervision. Daryl hired nurses for whenever he was working at the library but, as her only child, he was essentially her primary caregiver.'

Tish leaned forward and rested an elbow on the table. 'Did Binnie Broderick know all this?'

'About Mrs Dufour's dementia? Of course she did.'

'No, not the dementia. About you and Daryl Dufour. About Lacey.'

'Daryl never could handle his liquor,' Celestine lamented once again before leaning forward to meet Tish's gaze. 'It was just this past April, the day before Easter, and the library sponsored an egg hunt and story time for the kids, accompanied by a thank-you lunch for the library staff sponsored by the Lions Club ladies auxiliary, of which I'm a member. The lunch, unfortunately, featured wine and Daryl, feeling emotional over the holiday, picked up the box of Riesling like it was his own personal Capri Sun sippy thing. Well, it wasn't long before he was telling some of the auxiliary members his life story.'

'And Binnie Broderick was there?'

'Naturally. You know, I swear that woman was part bat. She had sonar hearing whenever gossip was concerned. Her ears could detect a rumor drop from a mile away.'

'And at this lunch, Daryl mentioned that Lacey might be his daughter?'

'I didn't hear what he said. I was too busy in the kitchen. But after the lunch, on Easter Sunday, he caught me at church and apologized for mentioning that he may have a child floating around out there. That's the expression he used – "floating around out there." Man's only ever lived in Hobson Glen his whole life. Where in Sam Hill did he think people would expect that child to be?' Celestine shook her head in exasperation.

'So Binnie figured it out,' Tish surmised.

'Of course she did. Binnie Broderick was many things, but a fool wasn't one of them. I thought, maybe, Daryl had dodged the bullet, because Binnie was quiet for while after that luncheon, but then right before Mother's Day I bumped into her at the bank and she asked me how Lacey was doing. Not Lloyd, not my family, just Lacey. I tried to pay it no mind, but then at our annual barbecue she cornered me while I was away from my family's table and said she thought it was fascinating how all my children resemble Lloyd. All my children apart from Lacey. Lacey, Binnie determined, didn't look like either of her parents or her siblings.'

'Ouch,' Tish winced.

'Yeah.' Celestine sighed.

'Did she do anything else with this information?'

'Nothing other than innuendo and the occasional offhand remark.'

'But there was a risk that she'd expose you to Lloyd or Lacey, wasn't there?'

'Of course there was. Binnie was a loose cannon. One never knew what she'd say, to whom, or when. Or when she might decide that the information she had could help her get something she wanted.' Celestine's normally cheerful, friendly face grew grim. 'But that doesn't mean I killed her.'

Tish sighed. As much as she wanted to believe Celestine and, in her heart of hearts, actually did, the information was extraordinarily damning. 'What about Daryl? You said he's been protective of you through the years. How far would he go to keep you safe, Celestine?'

'Not murder, if that's what you're implying,' Celestine insisted. 'Never murder. Daryl is a kind, wonderful, sweet man with integrity. He hasn't the temperament to do such a thing.'

'Even if Binnie was threatening to destroy your

life? Your reputation? Your relationship with Lacey?'

'He still wouldn't. Daryl is not a murderer, Tish. I know he isn't.'

'How can you be so certain?'

A tear trickled down Celestine's cheek and dropped on to her upper lip. 'Because, after all the years he's been alone, all the time he spent as a sole caregiver to his mother, all the Christmases spent with whatever friends invited him, all the children he's read to at the library without a hope of reading to his own, if there was anyone on this earth Daryl would have and should have murdered, it's me.'

Twenty-One

Mary Jo, the tray of sandwiches balanced upon one arm, arrived at the Channel Ten television news studio at five minutes after twelve. While still in the station lobby, she was greeted by a breathless Jules. 'Oh, thank goodness you're here. I am positively famished.'

Jules peeled back a corner of the plastic wrap protecting the sandwich tray and reached a set of greedy fingers beneath it. Mary Jo promptly swatted away his hand. 'That'll be four dollars, please.'

'Four dollars?' Jules exclaimed. 'You're making me pay four dollars for a sandwich?'

'You know what? You're right.' Mary Jo set

the tray of sandwiches down on a nearby magazine table. 'The chicken and pimento cheese is five dollars.'

'What? After all I've—'

Mary Jo burst into laughter. 'I got you.'

'Ha ha,' he mimicked. 'It's not fair to tease a starving man.'

'Yeah, yeah. You sound like one of my kids. So, why did you call and ask me to bring the sandwiches here? I thought we were going down to the police station to sell these to the reporters in the parking lot.'

'Change of plan. You're going to sell them to the reporters and staff in our lunch room,' Jules explained as he crammed a Zelda Fitzgerald biscuit sandwich in his mouth. 'Good Lord, how does the woman come up with these flavor combinations? So good.'

'Mind telling me why we're staying here, or do you need some time alone with your sandwich?' Mary Jo wisecracked.

'Sorry . . . just so good,' Jules mumbled and wiped his mouth on his sleeve. 'We're here because I found something that might help solve Binnie's murder case.'

'What did you find?'

'Phil in the newsroom.' Jules punctuated the statement by taking another bite of the fried chicken and pimento cheese sandwich.

'And? I swear if you don't tell me everything right now, I'm going to grab that sandwich of yours and stomp on it,' an impatient Mary Jo threatened.

Jules giggled between chews. Even in college,

257

Mary Jo never liked being kept in suspense. It was clear that some things never changed. 'Phil does camera work for us, along with some other odd jobs. I found out today that he was hired by Binnie to film the fundraiser Friday night. I thought we'd stay here, sell our sandwiches, and then watch his footage.'

'Shouldn't that footage go to the police?'

'It has, but Phil has a copy of the file here at the studio.'

'I don't understand. What do you think we're going to get out of it that the police won't?' Mary Jo was skeptical.

'Townspeople are sharing all sorts of things with Tish. We might see something that doesn't line up with what they've told her. And if not, no harm done.' Jules shrugged and took another bite of sandwich.

'I suppose you're right. How long is the footage?'

'Hour and a half. Two hours. Somewhere around there.'

'So like a feature-length film, only starring a few well-heeled Hobson Glen inhabitants and wealthy people from Richmond. Sounds absolutely riveting,' Mary Jo quipped.

'Oh, come on.' Jules led her to the lunch room. 'You'll love it.'

The station lunch crowd had long disbanded from the studio cafeteria and returned to their desks when Mary Jo, a leftover fried chicken and pimento cheese sandwich in hand, sat beside Jules, who was now digging into a hummus pita, to watch the fundraiser footage on his laptop.

'OK,' she commanded, as she drew her chair closer to the long folding table. 'Let's get this over with.'

'Oh, come on. It will be fun.' Jules was upbeat as he munched on his pita. 'Like watching those cheesy award shows and mocking the red-carpet fashions.'

'Only this red carpet isn't for Hollywood celebrities. It's for a bunch of people who requested a Dixieland band for entertainment and probably own every single episode of *Hee Haw*, *Bonanza*, and *The Big Valley* on DVD.'

'Not *The Big Valley* – Stanwyck was far too stylish. Hello? Fashion icon.'

'True,' Mary Jo agreed. '*Gunsmoke*?'

Jules shook his head in the negative. 'Miss Kitty was a saloon girl.'

'Really?'

'Really. Not exactly the family-values show, huh? Personally, I think that fundraiser bunch has *Matlock* in their video library. I could see some of those big-haired ladies swooning over ol' Andy Griffith back in the day. Come to think of it, some dude came to the bar wearing the exact same rumpled gray suit Matlock did. He must have been trying to conjure up those old "magic Andy" feelings.'

Mary Jo scowled. 'If you wanted my fried chicken sandwich, you could have just asked. You didn't need to try to make me ill, OK?'

Jules chuckled and pressed the play button. Almost immediately, a parade of formal-attired bodies became visible on the computer screen. Mary Jo and Jules watched the display attentively as the fundraiser guests entered the reception area of the lodge through a set of double doors and then along Tish's old carpet runner.

As they viewed the footage and consumed their sandwiches, either one or both of them would break the silence with a comment ('Look at that crowd; it's as if everyone just got off the same bus'), a snicker ('Up until now, I'd only seen a bouffant hairdo in photographs'), or accolades ('The cut of that man's suit is exquisite') for someone's evening wear.

'Oh, look, there's Binnie rushing off to greet someone,' Mary Jo noted as she pointed to the image of the dead woman herself flitting across the screen. 'Strange to watch her now that we know . . .'

'Yeah,' Jules agreed with a slight shiver. 'Chilling.'

The pair inhaled sharply as the video switched to footage of Binnie's speech.

'This is far creepier to watch than I thought it would be,' Jules noted.

'Let's just focus on the audience. Someone out there is bound to let their emotions show,' Mary Jo suggested. 'If the camera ever pans there, that is.'

'Oh, it will. Phil is excellent at his job. He won't be here in Hobson Glen for very long. Some DC station is sure to pick him up.'

True to Jules's word, the camera panned to the rows of tables in front of the speakers' podium.

Jules and Mary Jo leaned in and scanned the sea of unfamiliar faces.

Spotting a sneering Roberta Dutton in the crowd, Mary Jo cried out, 'Oh, there's Binnie's table. Pause the video!'

Jules promptly obeyed.

'I'd say that's the face of anger, but Roberta Dutton always looks like that,' Mary Jo noted.

'I can't imagine what she looks like if you bring a book back late. Or ask her to reserve something,' Jules commiserated. 'Daryl Dufour, in the meantime, is all of us.'

Mary Jo moved closer to the computer screen. The assistant librarian was clearly yawning. 'I must admit, I was glad I was in the kitchen while this was going on.'

'I was happy to be near the booze while this was going on,' Jules half joked. 'Check out Edwin and Augusta.' He pointed at their faces on the screen. 'They look like they're just not having any of it.'

'John Ballantyne too.'

'He looks annoyed with the entire world. And Cordelia just looks plain . . .'

'Miserable,' Mary Jo stated.

'Painfully so.'

Jules hit the play button, allowing the video to pan to the next table before pausing again. 'There's Mayor Whitley. Semi-conscious and quasi-caring. Nothing new there.'

'And two seats away is Opal Schaeffer. She looks—'

'Drunk,' they declared in unison at the image of the writer with her eyes closed and mouth open and a balloon-shaped glass of wine in her hand.

'And where's Hobson Glen's answer to Matlock?' Jules squinted at the computer screen.

'If you mean Schuyler Thompson, he's right there, right in front of your face.' Mary Jo pointed to the attorney, who was at the mayor's table in the seat closest to John Ballantyne. 'It might be time to look into glasses. You know your eyes can change dramatically once you're past forty.'

'Thanks. That makes me feel simply marvelous,' Jules deadpanned. 'Hey, is it me or is Schuyler smiling in this shot?'

'He is. He had just visited Tish in the kitchen.'

'Ooh,' Jules sang. 'Cozy. Speaking of cozy, poor Schuyler looks like he's shoulder to shoulder with Mr Happy himself – John Ballantyne. I really don't get these kinds of functions. I understand the ticket sales go to charity, but the comfort of the guests should still play a factor in how many seats are available.'

Mary Jo nodded her head in silent agreement and gestured to Jules to press the play button. He complied without hesitation.

Their stomachs full and Binnie's speech less than spellbinding, Jules and Mary Jo fought hard to stay awake during the next few minutes of footage, lest they miss another view of the audience. The second shot never came.

As the speech came to a close, they yawned, stretched, and sighed in relief – until Mary Jo noticed Celestine's granddaughter, Melissa, in the background, emerging from the kitchen bearing a round tray. 'Here we go. Dinner is getting underway.'

'Oh, I'm not sure I'm ready to see this.'

'I know, but if it helps put Tish's business in the clear, then we need to watch.'

Jules agreed and rested his head on his hands as he and Mary Jo viewed the subsequent footage intently. 'There's the mayor heading to Binnie's table.' He pointed to the image of the tuxedoed man on the screen. Within a matter of moments, a rather heated exchange transpired between him and the late library director. The mayor could be seen waving his finger and shaking his head emphatically. 'Wow, who knew he had it in him. I've never seen him fired up like that.'

'I suppose there had to be some passion in him to keep Cordelia Ballantyne intrigued.'

'She's not exactly a powder keg herself,' Jules observed. 'But, as my mama always said, still waters run deep.'

The mayor charged off from Binnie's table, nearly upsetting the tray of a passing member of the wait staff who was serving the main course. 'He practically knocked over that waitress. There's a vote he won't be getting this fall,' Mary Jo joked.

'Here comes Opal.' Jules singled out the writer as she careened across the dance floor and staggered up alongside Binnie's chair just as she was being served her plate of prime rib. 'Oh, boy. How'd you like to see that coming at you?'

'Are we certain Binnie was poisoned by arsenic? It looks as if Opal only had to breathe on the woman to put her out.'

'Maybe we should have Sheriff Reade put that to the coroner,' Jules suggested with a hearty laugh. His amusement soon dissipated. 'MJ, look.'

A stunned Mary Jo followed Jules's gaze to the computer screen and watched as the image of Schuyler Thompson rose from his chair, pushed between Binnie and Opal with his back to the camera, and then walked off camera.

Jules immediately replayed the scene. 'What the . . . Do you think he might have done something?'

Mary Jo was nonplussed. 'I don't know, but he certainly had the opportunity. Opal was too buzzed to notice anything and Binnie was probably too focused on the conversation. What do you think? I mean, do you really suppose he might have poisoned Binnie?'

Jules shrugged. 'No, but I don't know him that well. Tish doesn't seem to find him suspicious at all. She obviously accepted his explanation about that evening and his feelings about Binnie Broderick.'

'Question is, did he tell her that he was at the very next table? And did he mention being one of the last people to see Binnie alive that night?' Mary Jo posed.

'Somehow I doubt it. Tish wouldn't be so quick to plan another date with him if he had. She'd wait until the case was solved.'

'You're right. She's always been extremely cautious.'

'Cautious? Honey, it's been two years since that jerk of a husband left her for that *Nunsense* understudy, and the first date she plans is to a farmers' market so she can select some seasonal squash. That's not cautious; that's downright restrained.'

'Well, then, we'd better tell her about the video.' Jules picked up his cellphone and began punching at digits on the keyboard.

'What are you doing?' a frustrated Mary Jo asked.

'Sending her a text.'

'No, you're not.' Mary Jo snatched the offending device from his hand. 'Tish has developed quite a crush on Schuyler. This is something we need to tell her in person.'

'Excuse me, but if the guy I was macking on turned out to be a potential murderer, I'd like to know right away, by any means available.'

'Duly noted.' Mary Jo remained stern.

'Is this part of the female dating code, like that whole men "taking a break" thing?'

'Yes.' Mary Jo grabbed her bag and the tray of leftover sandwiches. 'Now, come on.'

Jules obediently picked up his laptop and followed Mary Jo out of the lunchroom. 'I'm glad I don't date women. Y'all are so complicated.'

Twenty-Two

Tish climbed behind the wheel of the Matrix sometime after one thirty in the afternoon and, from Celestine's road, made a left on to the bypass to return to the café. Halfway down the thoroughfare, she spotted Sheriff Reade's police-issued SUV parked outside Wisteria Knolls. Tish hit the brakes and, after pulling into a nearby driveway, backed on to the bypass road, this time facing the opposite direction.

She hit the accelerator, all the while feeling a complete idiot for trying to avoid the sheriff the way she was, but she didn't want to speak with him, or anyone, at this particular juncture. Celestine's story, coming on the heels of Augusta's confession, had left her with a distinct and overwhelming sense of self-loathing. Who was she to be prying into these people's personal lives?

What had started out as a grassroots goodwill campaign to preserve her café's reputation had become a full-blown investigation causing angst and discord to nearly everyone it touched. Daryl and Celestine, Augusta and Edwin, and, most of all, poor Cordelia and John. Some things, it would appear, might have been better off buried.

Tish pulled over on to the shoulder of the road as her eyes welled with tears. As she rummaged through her handbag in search of a tissue, her cell phone rang. It was Sheriff Reade.

Finding nothing to serve as a handkerchief, Tish dabbed at her eyes with her fingers and took a deep calming breath before answering. 'Hello?'

'Hey, you know U-turns are illegal on this road, don't you?' Reade teased.

Tish was not in the proper mindset for such playfulness. 'Really? Oh, I'm sorry.'

Sheriff Reade paused. 'I just left Wisteria Knolls and see you parked up ahead. Mind if I stop?'

Tish desperately wanted to answer, *Yes, I do mind*, but figured that ticking off the local police would only serve to make her present situation even less palatable. 'No, of course not.'

Within seconds, the flashing lights of Reade's SUV appeared in Tish's rear-view mirror. The sheriff stopped on the shoulder behind where Tish was parked and kept the truck idling as he exited the vehicle and approached the driver-side window of the Matrix. 'Hey,' he greeted and leaned his arms on the edge of the window. It was a move he had clearly perfected after years of traffic stops.

'Hi,' Tish returned the greeting. 'How's Cordelia?'

Reade shook his head. 'I want to thank you for checking in on her and then calling me. I really appreciate you taking action the way you did. She was in a bad way when we arrived. I have an officer trained in grief counseling with her right now, but she can't stay there all day. Maybe you wouldn't mind checking in with Cordelia again later?'

'Of course,' Tish agreed. It was the very least she could do after barraging the poor woman with so many questions.

'Good. She said she doesn't have too many friends here in town, so your kindness means a lot.'

'Ah,' Tish replied distractedly.

'You OK?' Reade asked.

'Fine,' Tish quickly dismissed. 'Didn't sleep much last night.'

'Yeah, there's a lot of that going around, but don't worry. We'll get to the bottom of it all,' he assured. 'By the way, I got in touch with John Ballantyne – another thing I need to thank you for. He's filing for divorce from Cordelia, and he and Roberta Dutton are on their way to visit his daughter.'

'In Williamsburg?' Tish instantly forgot about her bad mood.

Reade confirmed the location. 'They're going to spend a few days to break the news about the divorce and her grandmother, and give her a chance to get to know Roberta better.'

'Throwing the new girlfriend in there with the dead grandma and the "Mommy and I won't be living in the same house anymore" speech. Ballantyne's looking to win the Father of the Year award, isn't he?'

'In hockey, I think that's what's known as a hat-trick.'

'I would have thought it'd be more akin to skating into the wall.'

'Maybe,' Reade chuckled. 'Unfortunately, I can only tell them how to avoid violating the law. I can't tell them how to avoid violating the principles of good sense.'

'If only you could,' Tish said wistfully.

'I'd probably be out of a job. In most instances, people commit crimes because they've completely taken leave of their senses.'

'Is this one of those instances?' Tish asked.

'With two killings under the murderer's belt?'

'Well, the killer obviously "took leave of their senses," as you put it, when they murdered Binnie. Then they were faced with covering their tracks by killing Doctor Livermore.'

'Interesting. I'd have bet it was the other way around,' Reade interjected. 'Shooting someone outside a church in broad daylight is a lot more reckless than slipping them poison and quietly walking away.'

'Plus the killer would have to remember to take the poison with them and then, somehow, arrange to dispose of the bottle,' Tish reflected. 'Or jar or plastic baggie or something.'

'Off the premises, obviously, since we didn't find anything in the washroom or kitchen trash cans or in the dumpster out back.' Reade placed his hand to his forehead as if tipping an imaginary hat. 'Well, I'd best get back to the station. Thanks again for your help.'

Help, Tish thought to herself. *Sure, I helped all right.* 'Yeah . . .'

'Are you headed back to the café or do you have more investigative work ahead?' he smirked.

Tish squinted at him. 'I'm not investigating. I've been delivering baked goods and sandwiches.'

'Ah.' The smirk morphed into a look of consternation. 'I just hope the ingredients of those sandwiches don't disagree with anyone. You never know who may be sensitive to what.'

'Is that a warning, Sheriff?'

'Just a reminder. There's all sorts of allergies out there these days. Just be careful.'

'I will. Thanks.' As Reade turned to walk back

to his SUV, Tish stopped him. 'You know, you just reminded me of something.'

Reade sauntered back to the Matrix. 'Yeah?'

'Do you remember Binnie Broderick's bread-and-butter pickles?'

'I remember her bringing them to all sorts of local functions. But I don't remember the pickles themselves. Never ate them. Where I come from, pickles are made with garlic and dill.'

'Yeah, same here. Opal Schaeffer did remember them, however.'

At the sound of Opal's name, Sheriff Reade heaved a heavy sigh. 'Mrs Schaeffer . . .'

'What? Can't I trust her observations?'

'Oh, no, she's very astute. Great eye for detail. Problem is, she's always after me and everyone else in town over eighteen and under fifty to pose for her book covers.'

'Yes, she asked me too,' Tish confided.

'See? Go on,' he urged.

'Well, Opal said that at this June's town barbecue the quality of Binnie Broderick's pickles, although never fantastic, took a serious downturn. She actually used the term "bizarre practical joke" to describe their flavor.'

'So?'

'So you said that there were no traces of arsenic found in the food she ate at the fundraiser.'

'Nor in her drink,' Reade added.

'What if someone had been poisoning Binnie prior to the fundraiser? And what if that person had done so by tampering with her beloved bread-and-butter pickles?' Tish proposed.

'Was this someone also trying to kill off half the town?' Reade countered.

'Huh?'

'The killer couldn't be certain who would eat the pickles. Mrs Broderick brought them to every potluck function within a ten-mile radius of town. Maybe even farther. Popular opinion was she was too cheap to bring anything else, and I'm not about to disagree. Still, they were available to anyone and everyone, even if the people who wanted to eat them were far and few between.'

'Exactly. The only person who ate the pickles at the barbecue was the maker of the pickles herself, Binnie Broderick.'

'And you're suggesting that the "off" taste of the pickles was due to them having been spiked with arsenic,' he concluded.

'Yes. It does make sense, doesn't it?' Tish was optimistic.

'No. No, it doesn't.' Reade was quick to dash her hopes. 'If the flavor of the pickles was off, why didn't Binnie detect it?'

It was a question Tish hadn't anticipated. 'Well . . . everyone's taste buds are different. Some people can't taste sour things while others revel in eating lemons and sour candies.'

'Yes,' the sheriff allowed, 'but Binnie's taste buds were different to the point where everyone else tasted something that she didn't? Sorry, but I don't buy it.'

'Then how do you explain the pickles tasting so different?' Tish challenged.

'I don't. Just as taste buds vary from person

to person, they also change over time. Mrs Broderick may have changed the seasoning of the pickles to reflect her current tastes or, let's be honest, she may even have forgotten the recipe and added too much or too little of an ingredient. The same goes for Mrs Schaeffer. We only have her word for it that the pickles were markedly different. Her tastes may also have changed due to age, medication, or any number of reasons.'

Tish frowned. The sheriff was right. Poisoning a jar of bread-and-butter pickles, on the off chance your intended victim would consume not just one or two slices of cucumber but enough pickles for the poison to take effect, was a ridiculous way of killing someone. Still, there was something about those pickles, and particularly their flavor, that aroused suspicion. 'Well, it was a theory,' Tish said wistfully, pretending to abandon the idea entirely.

'And not a bad one either,' Reade praised. 'But it's far more likely that Mrs Broderick had a bit of a bad memory when making those last few batches of pickles. She was getting to "that age." I'm twenty years younger than she was and even I walk into a room sometimes and forget why I'm there.'

'Yes.' Tish would not validate his theory with a corroborating story or a 'me too.' 'Well, I'm going to go home and take a short nap. The air conditioning will feel good. It's starting to get muggy again.'

'Yep, be another two months before it cools down much. See ya around,' Sheriff Reade issued his farewell. 'And, again, be careful, huh?'

272

'I will. Bye,' Tish gave a wave before rolling up the side window. Rather than immediately moving away from the curb, Tish idled in place until the sheriff drove past her. She smiled and waved again and then, as the sheriff drove off into the distance, she turned the Matrix around and took off for the café.

Tish had absolutely no intention of having a nap. She had only said that for Reade's benefit. Tish was not easily rankled, but the sheriff's warning to be careful had hit a nerve. Had Tish been careful, the sheriff wouldn't know about Augusta's pregnancy, John Ballantyne leaving town, Cordelia's depression, or Binnie Broderick's possible memory issues. In time, the sheriff would have eventually uncovered these things on his own – he was not by any means a stupid man – but her influence in the case had done much to expedite matters.

Tish accelerated along the bypass road. The café was her destination, and she longed for a cold glass of water with lemon and some quiet time alone in which to think. It was, therefore, a disappointment to find that Mary Jo and Jules had already returned from their sandwich run and were awaiting her on the front porch.

'Ah, well,' she whispered to herself before stepping out of the Matrix and on to the gravel-lined café parking lot. 'Hey,' she greeted. 'You two are back early. Did you sell out already?'

'Um, not entirely,' Mary Jo hedged. 'There's a couple of ham sandwiches and a few hummus pitas left in the fridge.'

Amid all the hoopla over John Ballantyne's

departure, Cordelia Ballantyne's despair, and Celestine and Daryl Dufour's secret past, Tish had completely forgotten to eat either breakfast or lunch. 'Hmm, I do believe those may have my name on them,' she announced as she mounted the front steps.

'Oh, I'll fix you a plate, honey.' Jules sprang from his perch on the porch railing and scurried into the café.

'What's gotten into Jules?' Tish asked. 'I usually have to ask him something three times before he looks up from that phone of his.'

'Nothing,' Mary Jo replied abruptly. 'I'll get you something to drink. Tea?'

'Um, water and lemon, but you don't need to—'

'Nonsense. You just sit on this here porch swing and relax.' Mary Jo got up from the swing and gestured to her friend to take her place. 'I know you got hardly any sleep last night.'

'Yeah, but neither did you.'

'Uh, yes, well, that's true, but I have teenagers. I'm used to staying up and staring at the ceiling, worrying. Now you sit and I'll be right back.' Mary Jo disappeared behind the storm door, leaving Tish in bewilderment.

The situation was not unlike those cheesy sitcom episodes where somehow the wrong doctor's report is discovered or a conversation is overheard, leaving the cast of the show thinking that a major character is dying, pregnant, or seriously ill, thereby compelling said cast to be unusually nice to said main character. Only, in this instance, there was no laugh track playing and Tish had absolutely no idea how Jules or Mary Jo might jump to any such conclusions.

Jules returned with two hummus pitas on a plate and a tea towel. 'I couldn't find a napkin,' he explained as he deposited the meal in Tish's lap.

'I'm out. Augusta used them all yesterday.'

Mary Jo soon followed with a tall glass of iced water in which several slices of lemon were suspended. 'Here you go, honey. Drink up. It's important to keep hydrated.'

Tish stared back at the two sets of eyes watching her intently. 'Why are you both still standing there? Why do I need to keep hydrated? What's going on here?'

'Nothing,' Jules insisted despite erupting into a nervous titter.

'Just eat your lunch,' Mary Jo urged. 'You need to keep your strength up.'

'Strength? OK.' Tish moved the plate of food on to a nearby wicker table. 'My lack of a love life means I can't possibly be pregnant, I went for a physical just last month so I'm not dying or ill, and my father texted just this morning to complain I hadn't called him in two weeks, so I haven't lost a family member. Why are you two being so nice to me?'

'We're *always* nice to you,' Jules upheld.

'Yes,' Mary Jo concurred. 'Well, at least *I'm* always nice. Jules can be a bit snarky at times.'

'Says the woman who once Googled "Does eye rolling burn calories?"'

'That was a legitimate question,' Mary Jo insisted.

275

'Having been friends with you both for over twenty years, I can safely say that if sarcasm and sass were Olympic events, portraits of the two of you would grace every box of *Wheaties* across the country,' Tish announced. 'Now, will you stop bickering, stop waiting on me, stop talking about hydration and strength, and just tell me what's going on?'

'Schuyler Thompson,' they blurted out in unison.

'We think he's the murderer,' Jules clarified.

'Well, I'm glad you didn't go out of your way to try to sugar-coat it,' Tish said sarcastically. 'Pray, tell me how you came to this remarkable conclusion.'

Mary Jo and Jules told Tish of their lunch hour spent at the television station and the fundraiser footage they both viewed.

'There's a moment in that video where Schuyler gets up from his chair and walks between Binnie and Opal,' Jules described.

'His back is to the camera, totally obscuring Binnie from view. He might have dropped something in her drink,' Mary Jo explained.

'Or in her food,' Jules countered.

'And Binnie wouldn't have noticed because she was focused on what Opal was saying, and Opal wouldn't have noticed because she was drunk,' Mary Jo volleyed.

'As a skunk,' Jules added.

'Just because Schuyler's back was to the camera doesn't mean he was doing something malicious,' Tish argued. 'He probably didn't know the camera was even there. I'm sure most

276

of the people at the fundraiser were completely oblivious to it. You were monitoring the floor, Mary Jo – did you notice a camera?'

'No, but . . . but I was busy watching the servers,' she stammered.

'Just like everyone else in that reception hall who was busy doing something other than staring at a video camera,' Tish stated. 'I'll also point out that the sheriff made it clear that there were no traces of arsenic in the food Binnie ate or in the glass from which she drank.'

'Maybe it wasn't arsenic,' Jules suggested. 'It's not like the boys in blue of this county – or the coroner, for that matter – have much experience with this sort of thing. Schuyler is an intelligent man, an attorney, who no doubt has connections in the world. He could have found a tasteless, odorless poison that's impossible to trace and used it on Binnie Broderick.'

'And Doctor Livermore?' Tish crossed her arms across her chest in defiance. 'What's the connection?'

Jules became uncharacteristically quiet.

Having won the battle, Tish collected her sandwich and drink and went inside to eat her lunch in solitude. She was not alone for long.

Mary Jo, followed by a sullen Jules, swung open the screen door and stepped inside. They silently approached Tish, who was ensconced at one of the whitewashed café tables, munching a pita and looking out of the window.

As if on cue, a roll of distant thunder indicated that yet another afternoon storm was on the horizon.

'Look, I grant you that we may have been hasty in accusing Schuyler of murder,' Mary Jo admitted after several minutes had elapsed. 'But I do take issue with the fact that he wasn't completely honest with you.'

Still gazing out of the window, Tish swallowed a bite of her sandwich and opened her mouth to argue.

Mary Jo stopped her before she could utter a word. 'Wait. Hear me out.'

Tish closed her mouth and faced Mary Jo with a nod of the head.

'You told us that what you like about Schuyler is that he was open and upfront with you even when you questioned him about his dislike for Binnie Broderick.'

'Yes, he had no qualms about telling me everything regarding Binnie and his mother's death,' Tish explained.

'But did he actually tell you everything?' Jules countered. 'It's great for him to say he's being above board about the whole thing, but you only have his word for it that he is.'

'Exactly,' Mary Jo agreed. 'So, on that note, did Schuyler tell you he was seated at the table next to Binnie's? Did he mention that he walked directly past Binnie while she was talking to Opal and, therefore, he was one of the last people to see Binnie before she died?'

Tish's eyes turned down as if searching the table for an answer. 'No, he didn't.'

A voice came from the doorway. 'I came back into town for a meeting and thought I'd bring by some croissants from the Sub Rosa Bakery

278

that a client of mine gave as a thank-you, but I can see you're all very busy.'

Schuyler Thompson's voice was harsh and embittered. He tossed a white paper bag on to the table adjacent to the one where Tish was seated and turned to bid a hasty retreat.

'Schuyler.' Tish pushed her chair back, causing it crash to the floor. 'Wait.'

Schuyler stepped back inside the doorway. Tish rushed to his side.

'You know, if you had any questions about that night and where I was or what I was doing, all you had to do is ask,' he reprimanded her. 'I said I wanted things to be out in the open between us, and I meant it.'

Schuyler slid an eye in Jules's direction, causing the color to rise in the weatherman's cheeks.

'OK, if all we have to do is ask,' Mary Jo took Schuyler up on his offer, 'we have footage of you at the fundraiser, leaving your table and pushing between Binnie Broderick and Opal Schaeffer just as the main course was being served. Where were you going? And why did you go that way?'

'I had to go to the men's room. Cutting past Binnie's table was the shortest route because the other way was blocked by a waitress. A waitress who happened to be serving the main course you just mentioned.'

'That's the best you can do?' Mary Jo remained accusatory in tone.

'MJ,' Tish scolded.

Schuyler held a hand aloft as indication that

279

he could handle the situation without Tish's assistance. 'Yes, that is the best I can do because it's the truth. If you have a Bible handy, I'd be happy to swear on it.'

'That's nice—' Mary Jo's response was cut short by the appearance of Opal Schaeffer, who swung open the screen door of the café and poked her head inside.

'Hello,' she sang. 'I have some goodies for you.'

'Doesn't anyone in this town knock on doors?' Tish complained.

'It's a café,' Opal explained. 'Why would I knock on the door of an eatery?'

'Because it's not open for . . . oh, never mind.' Tish realized it was best to deal with Opal as quickly as possible. 'What can I do for you, Opal?'

'I've brought you that bag of homegrown cucumbers I told you about and threw in some cherry tomatoes,' Opal announced as she extracted two brown paper sacks of vegetables from her hemp tote bag. 'And since you may be using my garden produce in your restaurant, I figured why not offer you the full Marjorie Morningstar package?'

'The full what?'

'Morningstar romance package.' Opal reached into her tote and pulled out two books and an assortment of jars. 'Here are my two latest novels. *The Young and the Vestless* features scandal and seduction in the men's fashion industry, and *A Scot in the Dark* is a fun historical romance timed to coincide with the success of the *Outlander* series.'

'To think I was blown away by the cheesiness of your menu titles, Tish. You may have been out-punned,' Jules acknowledged.

Opal looked up to see who had spoken. Cocking her head to one side as she gazed upon Jules's face, she asked, 'And who is this striking young man?'

'Julian Jefferson Davis, ma'am.' Jules extended his hand in greeting.

'Do I know you from somewhere?'

The smile ran away from Jules's face.

'He's the Channel Ten weatherman,' Tish explained.

'The one taken out by the snowplow last winter,' Schuyler was more than happy to add.

'Don't be catty, Thompson,' Jules warned.

'That face,' Opal declared. 'You should be on my next book cover.'

'Really?' Jules was agog.

'She asks everyone to be on her book covers,' Tish said to Jules, aside.

'She's never asked me,' Mary Jo pouted.

Tish flashed her friend a look that was the nonverbal equivalent of *Seriously?* 'I'd be happy to sell your books, Opal, with suitable warning labels. As for the produce, I'll give it a taste and get back to you.'

'Oh, but that's not all. I also have my line of homemade aphrodisiac bath bombs – I call them sex bombs,' Opal giggled, 'and massage oils. Just a little nudge to get my readers to spice up their own love lives.'

'Yeah, I, um, I'll have to think about those.' Tish cleared her throat.

281

'Don't be such a worrywart. They'll sell. Not everyone in this world is wrapped up as tightly as Binnie Broderick was. You'd think I was running a meth lab in my house the way she carried on about this stuff. Thankfully, the police saw I had all the appropriate certificates and paperwork and let me be.'

'So Binnie knew about your scent business?'

'Tish, my dear, Binnie Broderick made it a point to find out about everything. *Everything.*' She winked. 'For someone to have slipped arsenic into Binnie's food without her knowing, that person had to have known precisely what they were doing. One slip and it would have been curtains for them.'

Again, Tish's mind returned to the subject of Binnie's bread-and-butter pickles. And the empty jars in the kitchen sink at Wisteria Knolls.

Opal clicked her tongue. 'Well, that's it for me. Storm's coming in and I'd better go home and make sure my computer's plugged into the surge protector. I have a deadline looming.'

As Opal grabbed her hemp bag and headed through the screen door and out into the world, Mary Jo's phone rang. 'Sorry, I have to take this. It's Kayla.' She excused herself behind the counter and moved to the opposite corner of the café.

Tish stared after Opal as if in a fugue state. *The hot sauce . . . the pickles . . .*

'Well, if you're all finished interrogating me, I'd best be going too,' Schuyler announced.

Tish immediately snapped out of her reverie. 'What? Wait. Are we OK?'

'I honestly don't know.' Schuyler sighed and ran a hand through the back of his hair.

'I'm sorry about what happened today. Jules and Mary Jo kind of blindsided me, and what with the murders, and the café being involved . . .'

'Relationships are based upon trust and it seems you have some questions about me.'

Tish felt as though she might cry. 'No, I don't think I do. I . . . I defended you.'

From the opposite corner of the café, another drama was playing out. 'No, you were just in Williamsburg a few weeks ago to go to Busch Gardens with your friends. You can't go again. You have a summer job, remember?'

'Nice defense, letting Mary Jo question me about the video footage.' Schuyler's reply dripped with sarcasm.

'Well, you might have mentioned walking past Binnie's table when you did,' Tish rebutted. 'Even you have to admit the timing is odd.'

Mary Jo's voice grew louder. 'Yes, I know this is a concert and not a theme park. That's precisely why the answer is no. Funhouse Fest takes place on the front lawn of the old mental hospital where there's absolutely no shelter nearby. You're only fifteen years old. I'm not letting you camp overnight in a tent in the mud with teenage boys and perverts all around.'

The mention of Williamsburg and an old mental hospital triggered something in Tish's brain. 'Is there still a psychiatric hospital in Williamsburg?'

'What?' Schuyler nearly shouted. 'We were talking about us.'

283

'Yes, I know. I'm sorry, I still want to talk about us, but for the moment, I need to know if there is still a psychiatric facility in Williamsburg.'

'Yes, Eastern State Hospital. Why?'

'Sheriff Reade said that Charlotte was at St Margaret's School until an incident occurred this past Christmas, remember?' Tish prompted.

'Yeah, I do. What about it?'

'What if the trouble Charlotte got into required her to be taken to Eastern State?'

'That's a stretch, isn't it?' Schuyler was skeptical.

'Is it? It would explain why Cordelia didn't call her daughter to notify her about her grandmother's death. It also explains why John and Cordelia Ballantyne were arguing about moving Charlotte to Baltimore. The question is, why is John Ballantyne going to Williamsburg to talk to Charlotte but not taking Cordelia with him?'

'I don't understand.' Schuyler shook his head and looked to Jules to decipher Tish's behavior.

'No idea.' Jules shrugged.

'Why isn't Charlotte's mother going to speak with her? Why is Roberta Dutton going in her place? Why did Binnie Broderick change her will?' Tish blurted.

'She changed her will?' Jules repeated.

'Tish, that was confidential information,' Schuyler shouted.

Tish paid no mind. 'It's like Sheriff Reade said. We've been looking at this the wrong way round. The hot sauce wasn't the cause of Binnie Broderick's poisoning. It was a symptom.'

Once again, Schuyler forgot about his indignation. 'A symptom?'

'Didn't you tell me that Binnie was suffering from a headache the day she came to your office?' Tish reminded Schuyler.

'Yes, she asked me for a Tylenol and then insisted I close the blinds in my office because the light was bothering her.'

'Headaches, photosensitivity, and a metallic taste in her mouth,' Tish listed, pausing between each symptom.

'How do you know about the metallic taste?' Jules quizzed. 'Did Binnie mention it at the fundraiser food tasting?'

'No, not at the food tasting, but Binnie did tell us. She told us when she asked for hot sauce at the fundraiser. She told us with the case of sriracha in the pantry at Wisteria Knolls. And, most of all, she told us when the pickles she made for the annual barbecue were so foul-tasting no one else could eat them. Binnie adjusted the seasoning of those pickles to mask the horrible taste in her mouth. To everyone at that barbecue, they were horrid. To Binnie, they were delicious. They were delicious because they were seasoned to cover up the horrible effects of long-term arsenic poisoning. And I think I now know exactly how that arsenic was delivered.'

Tish ran out on to the front porch and snatched from the swing the handbag she had left there seemingly a lifetime ago. Retrieving her car keys from the inside pocket of the bag, she hopped into the Matrix and pulled out of the café parking lot.

285

Schuyler and Jules watched as Tish took off toward the bypass road. By this time, Mary Jo had disconnected from her phone call. 'Where's she going?' she asked.

'She has a lead on the killer,' Jules explained.

'That's it. I'm going after her,' Schuyler announced.

'Not so fast,' Jules warned. 'Tish is an intelligent, independent, and strong woman. She does not need you or anyone else to rescue her.'

Mary Jo folded her arms across her chest and nodded. 'And, if she needed your help, she would have asked for it.'

'I'm not rescuing her,' Schuyler insisted. 'And I know Tish didn't ask for help, but don't you think someone should be nearby just in case something goes wrong?'

Jules pulled a face. 'Maybe. But you are not that person. We still don't know for certain what you were doing on that video footage.'

Again, Mary Jo nodded.

'I already told you. I was going to the men's room,' Schuyler shrieked.

'So soon in the evening?' Jules challenged.

'Yes. I drank two glasses of champagne before dinner and . . . well, what happens to you after you drink two glasses of champagne?'

'I dance,' Jules answered flatly.

Schuyler threw his hands up in the air and marched out of the café and into the parking lot. 'Look, with or without you, I'm going after Tish.'

'OK. OK, we'll go, but Mary Jo drives,' Jules insisted.

'Whatever. Let's just track down Tish before

anything happens,' an exasperated Schuyler shouted.

Jules followed, leaving Mary Jo to lock up the café.

'There's no time for that,' Schuyler shouted to Mary Jo as she fumbled with her keys. 'Shut the door and let's go. You know, you guys are a trip. You're ready to jump all over me, but meanwhile you let your friend—'

He was interrupted by a sudden gasp on the part of Jules. 'Is that a Series 3 BMW you have there?'

'Yes,' an angry Schuyler replied.

'MJ, honey. No need for you to drive,' Jules called to Mary Jo, who was still on the porch. 'We're taking Mr Thompson's car and I'm calling shotgun.'

Twenty-Three

Just before she reached Wisteria Knolls, Tish pulled the Matrix on to the shoulder of the road and shifted into park. As she pocketed the keys and stepped out on to the asphalt, the sky opened up, sending lightning bolts flashing through the treetops and heavy drops of water splashing down on to the earth below.

Running as fast as she could, Tish picked her way through the shrubs and trees that formed a natural fence around the property and also shielded her from being seen from inside the house. Dispensing with the polite convention of ringing the front door bell, she sprinted directly to the side entrance. As before, it was unlocked. Tish turned the handle as quietly as possible and admitted herself into the butler's pantry. There, she slipped out of her wet shoes and tiptoed into the kitchen to look for the items she had seen there earlier in the day.

Unfortunately, the objects in question had been moved and the kitchen table was empty.

Padding across the kitchen floor, Tish pushed open the door that led to the dining room and stepped inside. In the gloom of the unlit room, she examined the glass hutch of the mahogany-inlaid Chippendale breakfront, but the items she sought were not on display.

With trembling hands, Tish opened the left door on the bottom section of the cupboard and peeked inside. Dessert plates matching the pattern of the dishes on display were stacked high and topped with a glass trifle bowl.

A peek behind the cupboard door on the right side of the cabinet yielded a view of neatly stacked cups and saucers, also in the same delicate blue floral with silver trim.

Tish closed both doors and continued her search. Sliding out the center drawers of the cabinet produced two different sterling silver flatware sets – one of which most likely belonged to Enid Kemper's family and, thankfully, appeared to be complete – as well as a vast and varied array of table linens. Tish closed both drawers and took a sweeping glance over the Chesterfield dining-room set, consisting of a broad, impeccably lacquered table and a dozen ornately carved cherrywood chairs. This also yielded nothing.

Tish shook her head. They had to be somewhere in the house or this hunting trip had been for naught. Pushing open the door that led to the entry foyer, she placed a tentative toe on the nearest floorboard only for it to be met with a loud creak. Her heart in her mouth, Tish listened for an audible reply to the sound of her movements, but there was none.

Stretching her other leg into the hallway, Tish shut the dining-room door behind her and shuffled along the floorboards to minimize the production of further squeaks and scrapes. So focused was she on keeping silent that she failed to notice the presence of Cordelia in the front parlor, seated in one of two silk-upholstered antique wingback armchairs.

'Hello, Tish,' the woman said through the open parlor door.

Cordelia's voice might as well have been the sound of a gunshot, for its effect upon Tish was precisely the same. 'Cordelia,' Tish greeted, despite the tremor in her voice, racing heartbeat, and a queasy stomach. 'I didn't see you there.'

Cordelia did not apologize for frightening her visitor. 'Why have you been creeping around the house?'

'Creeping? Oh, no, tiptoeing maybe. I've been trying to be quiet so I didn't wake you. I know how much you need to rest right now.'

'What were you looking for in the dining room?'

Tish stepped into the parlor and cautiously approached Cordelia. 'Looking for? Nothing. Just admiring the house. Wisteria Knolls is a charming old—'

On the table before Cordelia, along with a box of tissues, writing paper and pen, and a carafe and glass containing alcohol, rested two silver salt cellars.

'I knew you'd seen them this afternoon,' Cordelia said. 'I heard you in the kitchen and then saw your note. Although I don't know what put you on to them.'

'It seemed strange to me that you had neither the time nor presence of mind to cut flowers for the entry hall – a task you do on a regular basis – but you could manage to empty the salt cellars. Of course, you had to empty them. They were filled with arsenic. But how did you keep from poisoning the entire household?'

'Only my mother used the salt cellars. Part of the Darlington family silver. John rarely uses salt, and if he does, he opts for the Tupperware picnic shakers in the kitchen. But Mother always insisted that I bring one salt cellar upstairs on a tray with her eggs at breakfast and that the other be placed on the dining-room table so she could use it with her supper. She salted food without tasting it, you know. Terrible habit.'

'And the fundraiser?' Tish asked.

'I gave her an extra dose of arsenic that afternoon at lunch, hoping that it might kick her off. I had no idea it would be so successful.' Cordelia smiled.

'Weren't you afraid she might die at home?'

'There was a concern, but, quite frankly, between her work at the library and the parties with her friends, my mother was always out and about. She only came here for a few hours' sleep, breakfast, the odd meal, and to deride me about every single detail of my miserable existence.'

'Did she do that to Charlotte as well? Criticize every detail of her existence?'

'Yes, and for all those years I allowed Mother to do it. My God, how stupid I was. I thought Charlotte would be OK as long as John and I were supportive parents. We told her to ignore what Grandma said and praised her as often as we could. We thought we'd been successful too, but then, while she was in middle school, Charlotte began cutting herself. John and I got her a therapist and sent her to St Margaret's. Away from here. Away from my mother. She started to do better until . . .'

'Until just before Christmas,' Tish completed the sentence. 'When the prospect of returning home for the holidays caused a setback. Did she try to commit suicide? Is that why she's at Eastern State?'

Cordelia turned her head sharply to look at Tish. Her eyes were wild with hurt and panic. 'You know about that?'

'I knew she was somewhere in Williamsburg. Everything else was an educated guess.'

Cordelia nodded. 'I didn't want her there. I wanted her to be treated, mind you. John and I both did. We knew her life depended upon it. But Williamsburg wasn't our first choice. We both agreed that Yale–New Haven's program

291

was the best for her. New York–Presbyterian was a close second. Either choice would have worked. Charlotte loves art and having New York City right on her doorstep would have made an exciting change for her.'

'The plan was that we'd all move north, as a family,' Cordelia continued. 'John, Charlotte, and me. We'd find a house near the hospital so that even if she was in treatment, we could see her regularly, have meals with her, maybe bring her home for weekends and limited stays. No one here would know the reason for the move. Charlotte would avoid the wagging tongues, the small-town, close-minded comments of the locals, and the stigma that still comes with depression and mental illness. It was to be a fresh, clean start for all of us. Of course, I should have known that such a plan wouldn't and couldn't work.'

'Your mother didn't want you to go,' Tish ventured.

'Didn't want? No, the more appropriate term is "wouldn't allow."'

'Even at the risk of her granddaughter's health?' Tish questioned.

'We didn't tell my mother about Charlotte's failed suicide attempt because my mother would have considered it a disgrace and a sin,' Cordelia explained. 'So we couched our move in the terms of a wonderful business opportunity for John. An opportunity we couldn't possibly fail to act upon. My mother appeared to believe the story and congratulated us on the move. It was, however, all an act. A few days later, on her way to the library, she slipped on the ice and fell. Although she hadn't broken any bones, she claimed she was in too much pain to walk unassisted. Doctor Livermore determined that she had muscular damage and put her on bed rest and also ordered a walker. Our move was postponed while I cared for her and ensured she was able to keep up with her work at the library. It was spring by the time she could walk and drive again.'

'What about Charlotte? What happened to her in the interim?'

'That's when we sent her to Eastern State. Temporarily, we thought.'

'And your mother? Why did you say she had been pretending?'

'Because, while she was laid up, she had John's supposed business opportunity investigated and discovered it was non-existent.'

'Investigated? You mean she hired a detective?' Tish was incredulous.

'That's precisely what I mean. She also found out about Charlotte's suicide attempt and decided that she should be kept at Eastern State instead of – and I quote – "one of those awful Yankee hospitals that brainwash their patients into hating their families."'

'But Charlotte was already at Eastern State.' Tish failed to see the connection.

'Yes, convenient, wasn't it? My mother staged her fall to keep us here temporarily until she could do so permanently. When she found out about Charlotte, she pulled strings to have Doctor Livermore sign her into Eastern State, supposedly under the pretense that it was the best hospital, but it was because she knew I wouldn't move north without Charlotte.'

'But Doctor Livermore had taken an oath,' Tish argued. 'An oath to protect his patients. Why would he do that?'

'Oaths were no contest for my mother's powers of persuasion. She knew everything about everyone and used it to her advantage.'

Tish recalled Opal's confession regarding her relationship with the good doctor. A kinky romp with the local romance novelist would not sit well with Dr Livermore's more conservative, wealthy patients. 'Once you figured out what your mother had done, why not move Charlotte out of Eastern State?'

'To what purpose? My mother would never have allowed us to move with her. Not while there was still breath left in her body. Besides, Charlotte was starting to do well there. For the first time in a long while she seemed happy. Me, on the other hand . . .'

'Is that why you shot Doctor Livermore? Because he signed Charlotte into Eastern State and consigned you to life at Wisteria Knolls?'

'That was a factor, but no. It's because he was going to tell the police about it. He called me the day after the fundraiser to discuss "the issue" between my mother and me. He wanted me to be aware that he felt the need to tell the police about Charlotte's hospitalization and his role in it. However, since Charlotte is still a minor, he needed my permission to disclose her whereabouts and condition. It wasn't simply a debriefing for the police, though; I could tell from Doctor Livermore's voice that he was suspicious of me.'

'So you shot him,' Tish inferred.

'One of the luxuries of being educated at a private girls' school in the South: the rifle team. It was an easy shot from the alley across the street, and our town laws meant all neighboring businesses would be closed until at least noon on a Sunday. After the deed was done, I wiped the rifle clean of prints, locked it in the trunk of my car, and ran to the church in a state of panic.'

'You took a chance. One of the church members might have seen you,' Tish pointed out.

'Yes, it was a bit risky, but it was fun – the element of danger, I suppose. I've spent most of my life here, chained to my mother and her concepts of propriety.' Cordelia stared out of the window at the storm.

'And yet when John mentioned moving Charlotte to Baltimore, you were against it. You wanted to bring her here.'

'Because Wisteria Knolls was going to be mine,' Cordelia shouted. 'Mine to decorate as I pleased. Mine to make into a real home, instead of some stodgy museum. Apart from Charlotte, I've never really had anything that belonged exclusively to me. John might have for a short while, I suppose, but my mother managed even to take that away from me. Just as she had everything else.'

'Like your relationship with Mayor Whitley? He's the one who sent you that text message when I was here on Saturday, not Charlotte.

Charlotte wouldn't be allowed a cell phone at Eastern State.'

'Well, well, you are on your toes, aren't you? First Baltimore and now this. Here I thought my mother was resourceful,' Cordelia sneered. 'Yes, I had an affair with Jarrod. I started it out of spitefulness for John's affair with Roberta. Over time, it filled the gaps in my life, and I eventually fell in love. Unfortunately, my mother found out and used it for her own personal gain. That's what scared Jarrod off in the end. My mother's blackmail put the fear into him that others might find out about us.'

Cordelia reached down to the coffee table, extracted a paper handkerchief from the box, and blew her nose, loudly, into it. After several seconds had elapsed, she spoke again. 'My mother took great pleasure in my deprivation. She took my father away from me years ago.' Her hazel eyes focused on an indeterminate spot on the other side of the room. 'I adored my father, but my mother drove him away. He wanted to move us to Washington, DC, you know. How different my life would have been if he had succeeded. When I was in high school, I asked my mother if I could spend the summer with him and, of course, come home with him on weekends, but she wouldn't hear of it. I was a Darlington and, therefore, needed to learn about the running of Wisteria Knolls. I so wish I had put my foot down and gone that summer,' Cordelia said wistfully. 'My father died too soon. Heart attack, my mother initially claimed, but I knew better. When she confronted me this spring about John's business opportunity being a sham, she told me I was no better than my father. I pressed her on it. My mother had always criticized my father, even while he was still alive, but this . . . this had a different feel to it altogether. She went on to tell me that my father was a womanizer, an abuser of women, and that, ten years ago, upon discovering his transgressions, she had decided to do something about it. Someone, she said, had to defend the Darlington name, so she tampered with my father's heart medication. He was dead within forty-eight hours.'

Tish drew a hand to her forehead as she felt the blood drain from her face. 'You mean, your mother . . .'

'Murdered my father. My wonderful father. And then she sullied his memory with lies,' Cordelia screamed.

Tish said nothing. Ashton Broderick had raped Augusta Wilson and left her pregnant and scared. One could only imagine what he might have done to other women through the years, but sharing that information with Cordelia at this moment served no purpose.

'It was then that I knew we needed to be free of her.' Cordelia rose from her chair and gazed out of the front window. 'My daughter and I needed to be free to live our own lives. We needed to be free of the Darlington evil, and the only way that was going to happen was if my mother was dead.'

Some time elapsed before either woman spoke again.

'After all your mother put you through – all the abuse you suffered at her hands – a court would sympathize with you. You may serve some time in jail but a good attorney could get your sentence reduced.'

'I'm not going to trial. I'm not going to jail. Not for a single day. Not for ridding the earth of that cruel, manipulative bitch.' Cordelia moved from the window and lunged for the glass on the coffee table.

Tish, fully aware of what the glass and perhaps even the carafe might contain, rushed toward Cordelia and tackled her to the ground. The glass, full and upright, was still glued to Cordelia's fingers.

'Let go of me,' she screamed as she struggled to reach the glass to her lips.

Tish, pinning Cordelia to the parlor floorboards with her body, grabbed at Cordelia's wrist with both hands. Cordelia countered the move by grabbing Tish's hands with her free hand and digging her nails into the skin.

Tish cried out in pain. 'No. No, Cordelia. Think of Charlotte. You can't do this to her.'

'Better this than let her live with a murdering mother,' Cordelia exclaimed.

With the full weight of her body, Tish lunged at the hand bearing the glass and knocked it to the floor. The liquid inside the glass spilled on to the ancient floorboards. 'No. You need to tell her your story, so she can learn from it, so she can understand, from you, what's happened. Don't fail her.'

With those words, Cordelia's body relaxed.

Her grip on Tish's hands loosened and her fingertips relinquished the glass, sending it rolling toward the hearth of the nearby fireplace. 'I've already failed her,' she moaned.

'No, you haven't, Cordelia. But if you force her to navigate through this alone, she may never recover.' Tish sat up, leaving Cordelia to curl into the fetal position.

Schuyler Thompson suddenly rushed across the threshold. 'We were waiting in the kitchen and heard screams. Are you OK?'

Tish nodded and rose to her feet. As a precautionary measure, she handed the carafe to Schuyler and instructed him to put it away somewhere.

'The police are on their way,' he whispered to her.

With a weary nod, Tish grabbed a bunch of tissues from the box on the coffee table and, getting down on her hands and knees, crawled back to Cordelia, who was now convulsed in sobs. Sitting beside Cordelia on the hardwood floor, Tish lifted her head on to her lap and silently stroked her hair as they awaited Sheriff Reade's arrival.

Twenty-Four

It was a clear, cool, early September Saturday when Tish and company celebrated the official grand opening of Cookin' the Books. As Jules stirred the punch and prepared the other beverages, Mary Jo and her kids decorated the shop with flag banners made from recycled book pages and colorful scrapbook paper.

Celestine, carrying a large parcel covered in aluminum foil, was the first to arrive on the scene. 'Well, good day, y'all. And I do mean *good* day. It's like you custom-ordered it, honey.'

Tish, dressed in a black T-shirt, black skirt with an embroidered floral border, and a white Cookin' the Books' apron, took the heavy package and placed it on the counter, and then greeted Celestine with a hug and peck on the cheek. 'I know. Seventy-five degrees and not a lick of rain in sight. Can you believe it?'

'Well, you deserve it,' Celestine replied. The smile on her face was genuine. 'After the rocky start you had.'

'Oh, I still feel badly about asking you so many questions,' Tish apologized.

'You know, it actually did me some good to reflect on things and open up about them. Sometimes we keep things inside for so long that we forget they even happened. So I thank you for those questions.'

'Hello.' Augusta Wilson, accompanied by Edwin, stuck her head in the door. 'I heard there's a party going on in here.'

'There is, come on in and join us, girlfriend,' Jules greeted her with a glass of punch.

'Don't mind if I do.' Augusta stepped into the café, resplendent in a bright pink dress and a wide-brimmed sunhat topped with peonies in coordinating rosy shades. She accepted the glass and immediately took a sip. 'Mmm. Oh, Tish, Edwin and I got you a little something for the café.'

Edwin, looking happy and relaxed in a blue polo shirt and plaid pants, presented Tish with a potted plant. 'It's bamboo, for luck.'

'Oh, thank you,' Tish exclaimed as she proceeded to bestow the Wilsons with appreciative hugs. 'You didn't need to bring me anything.'

'It's just a token of our friendship and appreciation,' Edwin explained.

'Well, thanks again. So, what have you two been up to lately?'

'Actually, Edwin and I have booked our first vacation in ten years,' Augusta announced.

'Good for you,' Mary Jo congratulated.

'We're taking a European cruise,' Edwin elaborated. 'We leave this evening from Virginia Beach.'

'Yeah, with everything that's happened – my illness, job stress, and other issues' – her eyes slid toward Tish in confidence – 'we decided it was time to celebrate life and each other.'

'That sounds toast-worthy.' Jules raised a glass and clinked it against those of the Wilsons.

'Do I hear some toasting going on?' Daryl Dufour called from the doorway.

'That depends,' answered Celestine. 'Does that punch have booze in it, Jules?'

'This one does, but I have a virgin version too,' he offered.

'Mr Dufour will be having the virgin,' she commanded with a wink in Daryl's direction.

'That's fine,' Daryl allowed. 'It's such a

glorious day, I don't need anything to add to the buzz.'

'It is beautiful out there, isn't it?' Tish remarked.

'It is, and not only are we lucky to have a wonderful new business and a most worthwhile new resident in our town, but I have some good news as well. I've been busting a gut to tell y'all, if you don't mind me sharing, Miss Tarragon.'

'Of course not. After what we've all been through, the more good news and celebration, the better.'

'Thank you, ma'am.' Daryl bowed slightly. 'I found out last night from Ms Augusta herself' – he indicated the woman in the pink dress – 'that I have been appointed the new director of Hobson Glen Library.'

A cheer went up around the café. Celestine, beaming from ear to ear, walked over to Daryl and gave him a warm embrace. 'That is wonderful news, Daryl. I cannot think of a single person more deserving than you.'

'Why, thank you, Celly.' Daryl wiped the trace of a tear from the corner of his eye.

'What about Roberta Dutton?' Tish asked.

'She withdrew from the running,' Augusta explained. 'Told me that Daryl was the better person for the position and that she'd lied about his conduct in the past. She feels she's been too competitive in her career and has decided to focus on her new life with John Ballantyne.'

'I hope things work out for her.'

'I do too,' Daryl agreed. 'Life is too short for unhappiness.'

'Hear, hear,' Edwin added.

'On that note, let's get this party started,' Jules announced as he, Mary Jo, Kayla, and Gregory disappeared behind the counter to set out the trays of sandwiches and pastries created just for the occasion.

As Tish instructed them on garnishes and presentation, a vaguely familiar face appeared from behind the screen door. She was young, perhaps sixteen or seventeen years of age. Her slender frame was dressed in jeans and a logo T-shirt, and her dark hair was trimmed into a playful Pixie cut. She looked around the room, her face registering confusion.

Tish welcomed her to the café. 'Hi, I'm Tish, the owner. I'm afraid we're not open for business today, so I can't give you a menu. But it's our grand opening, so you're welcome to help us celebrate by helping yourself to the food and drink we have available.'

The girl smiled. 'Oh, no, I didn't come to eat. I came here to see you. I'm Charlotte Ballantyne.'

Tish felt her jaw drop open. 'Oh! Oh, it's so nice to meet you, Charlotte.'

'It's nice to finally meet you too. My dad brought me up for a visit so I can help pack some things for the estate sale, but I wanted to stop by and say thank you.'

Tish looked at Charlotte in bewilderment. 'Thank me?'

'My mother told me what you did for her. She said she wouldn't be alive if it hadn't been for you,' Charlotte declared.

'Oh, I think you had more to do with that than I did. Your mother loves you very much.'

'I know.' Charlotte smiled. 'I love her, too.'

'How are you doing?'

'I'm OK. I decided to stay at Williamsburg for now. With everything that's happened, I didn't feel it was the right time for another big change. I have lots of friends where I am and I can be close by while my dad sorts things out here.'

'That sounds like a smart decision,' Tish stated. 'I've stayed in touch with your mom these past few weeks and she seems to be handling things OK, but if there's anything I can do for you . . .'

'There is, actually.' Charlotte blushed slightly. 'Um, I'm very much into cooking and art and creative things. My school and rehabilitation program has been going well, and my doctors have okayed me working a few hours over the weekend or during home visits. Do you think I might help out around here sometime when I'm in town?'

'Absolutely. Celestine and I would love to have you on board.'

'Awesome. There are some forms you need to complete,' Charlotte added nervously.

'No problem. Send the paperwork through and I'll get to it as soon as I can. I do have to warn you that since we're just starting out, the job may not be too glamorous at times.'

'That's fine. I don't mind if I have to push a broom around so long as I can squeeze icing on the occasional cupcake.'

'I think we might be able to work that into the schedule.' Tish grinned.

'Cool! Well, I'd better get back to Dad before he starts to worry.'

'Oh, grab some sandwiches to take back with you,' Tish ordered.

Mary Jo, having overheard the exchanged, ushered Charlotte behind the counter. 'Come on. We'll get some cellophane and I'll introduce you to Kayla and Gregory, your potential co-workers.'

As a few locals wandered in, the café filled with conversation and laughter. Tish gazed around the room in wonder.

She had done it. Her own eatery.

Out of the corner of her eye, she saw a figure enter through the screen door. Still beaming with pride, she turned around to see Schuyler Thompson.

He was dressed in jeans and a blue plaid shirt, and he was carrying a pie.

Tish approached him, her face a question. 'I don't think I publicized this as a bring-your-own event.'

'You didn't. I felt the need to bring this along. It's humble pie.'

Tish couldn't help but smile. She took the pastry and placed it on the counter behind her. 'Hmm, smells suspiciously like apple.'

'OK, it's a humble apple pie,' Schuyler amended. 'It comes with an apology and a request. Can we start over?'

'I'm sorry, too, Schuyler. And, yes, I'd love a chance to start over. It would be nice to get to know you without there being a murderer on the loose.'

'Or your café's future in jeopardy,' he added.

'Or two well-meaning but slightly insane

friends meddling in our business and accusing you of criminal activity.'

'Or you scaring the bejeezus out of me by wrestling killers to the ground in their own living rooms.'

'Or me violating attorney–client privilege.'

'Or me withholding ill-timed men's room visits from you.'

'Um, no, you can still keep that a secret.' Tish laughed.

Schuyler laughed with her. 'I was also thinking, since this is our first official date, instead of the farmers' market, maybe we should do something more exciting. Something with more' – he drew air quotes – 'razzle-dazzle.'

Something about the phrase 'razzle-dazzle' set off her internal alarm. 'Oh?'

'I was thinking maybe we can drive out to the wine country, see the mountains, enjoy some tastings, and then, for dinner, there's this restaurant in Charlottesville that has great reviews. It's not flashy or trendy or new, but it has good, fresh, well-prepared food, and a relaxing, cozy atmosphere.'

'That sounds terrific.' She held her arms open and the pair embraced.

From behind Tish's back, Schuyler flashed Jules a thumbs-up sign. Jules immediately reciprocated.

'Are you butting in again?' Mary Jo asked upon spotting the secret signal.

'I'm not butting in. I just made some recommendations to Schuyler to help give their date some sparkle,' Jules explained.

'Tish said she was fine without sparkles.'

'I know, but the girl deserves them anyway.'

Mary Jo leaned in and gave him a kiss on the cheek. 'You're irritating, but you're sweet, Mr Davis. You know that?'

'Stop!' Jules waved her away. 'You keep that up, you're going to make me cry. Then my liquid bronzer's going to get all streaky and I'm at the news desk tonight.'

Mary Jo took a step back. 'Get out! You're—'

Jules hushed her. 'Not so loud. My boss loved how I handled the Whitley scandal so he's letting me fill in at the news desk tonight as a trial run. I'll tell Tish and everyone else later, but this is her time to shine, OK?'

Mary Jo nodded her head excitedly before planting another kiss on Jules's cheek.

Meanwhile, on the other side of the room, Schuyler and Tish's embrace was interrupted by the sound of a camera clicking. The pair looked up to see Opal Schaeffer snapping away. 'This is perfect for my next book cover.'

'Opal,' Schuyler warned, 'I already told you that being a model would cause a conflict with my profession.'

'I know. I'm just using the bodies and the pose. No faces.' She turned the phone around and showed them the shots. 'See? No faces, but total warmth.'

'OK,' Schuyler capitulated, 'but—'

'I know, I'll show you the artwork when it's done, OK?'

'OK.' Schuyler took her hands by way of

greeting, then passed her to Tish, who gave her a quick hug.

'This is so exciting,' Opal declared. 'I love how you've dolled up the place.'

'Not as exciting as what I have to show you.' Tish led her to a tray of roasted tomato sandwiches. *'Morningstar Moonblush Melange.'*

'What? You named these after me?' Opal drew a hand to her chest.

'Not only that, but I made them with your homegrown tomatoes, which I roasted with thyme, salt, and a pinch of sugar overnight in a low oven before mixing with mint, olive oil, lemon, feta, and avocado. I spread that on to toast to make the sandwiches, but I have a serving of the veggies dressed with a bit of arugula, waiting in the refrigerator for you.'

'Vegetarian and gluten-free? And it's named after me. Be still my heart!'

'Let's hope not,' Schuyler quipped. 'There's been enough of that in this town to last a long time.'

Tish retrieved Opal's namesake salad from the refrigerator and then directed her to Jules for some punch. As she did so, she took note of Sheriff Reade entering the café.

'Sheriff, how are you?' she asked.

'I'm good. I was going to make my obligatory "keep the noise" down joke, as I often do at functions like these, but I was afraid you'd go door to door hunting down whoever made the complaint.'

Tish laughed. 'OK, I deserved that.'

The sheriff smiled. 'Happy to have your business up and running?'

'Happier than you can imagine.'

'Good. Then I can expect that Mr Davis and Mrs Okensholt won't be selling your food products across town any longer?'

'No, we'll be operating out of the café exclusively, except for catered events.'

'Good, because I don't think Mr Davis's Mini Cooper is quite up to the Commonwealth of Virginia's food-truck standards. I'm not one to say anything about it, but there are some with the sheriff's office who might.'

'Ah.' Tish understood the gist of Reade's words. 'Well, thank you for the heads-up, Sheriff. It won't happen again.'

'Glad to hear it. By the way, the band and I have got a gig in Ashland a few weeks from now. They're looking for a caterer and I recommended you.'

'You did? Wow, thanks. You did tell them I do literary-themed events, right?'

'I did. They may ask you to do something with song titles instead, but I figured I'd let you work that out.'

'I'm sure I can come up with something. Thanks.'

'Anything to keep you busy,' the sheriff joked. 'If not, I may soon be out of a job.'

The pair laughed and the sheriff went off to chit-chat with the rest of the crowd.

Tish grabbed a glass of punch from Jules, took a sip, and then clanged against it with a spoon. After thanking everyone for their help and for attending the event, she declared Cookin' the Books to be officially open for business, and then turned the floor over to Celestine so that she might present the cake she had designed especially for the occasion.

'Oh, I'm so nervous.' She giggled.

'Don't be, Celly,' Daryl soothed.

'Yeah, your cakes are sublime,' Jules complimented.

'OK, well, inspired by the name of this here café, and encouraged by Tish here, who told me to think outside the box, I give you . . . *Cookin' the Books*!'

Celestine pulled back the metallic cover to reveal a colorful fondant-laden stack of four books in bright primary and secondary colors, the spines of which bore titles from the genres of mystery, science fiction, romance, and western. The letters of these titles had been hand-cut from silver, gold, and black fondant in various styles of font and painstakingly applied to each book's spine. From the top book of the stack emerged a tall flame in various shades of yellow, red, and orange.

The room fell silent.

'Good Lord. It's a book burning,' Daryl gasped.

Celestine gave his arm a slap. 'No, it isn't. Look, the books are in a frying pan.'

Lo and behold, in a truly creative stroke, Celestine had placed the cake not on to a traditional platter but in a giant cast-iron skillet. 'It's cookin' the books, see?' she announced.

The crowd 'oohed' and 'aahed' and chuckled in comprehension as Celestine's literal yet highly comical interpretation was made clear.

'What do you think, Tish?' the baker asked.

Tish stole a fragment of fondant icing from the edge of one of the books and tasted it, savoring the sweet frosting while gazing around the café – *her* café – and the faces of friends, both old and new, gathered there.

'I think, Mizz Celestine' – she smiled as her eyes finally settled on Schuyler Thompson – 'that it's perfect.'